THE WRATH OF AMUN

Claudia R. Dillaire

THE WRATH OF AMUN

To Ann —
It was a pleasure to
share the World Day
of Prayer 2014 with you —
Enjoy the Journey.

Claudia

Claudia R. Dillaire

PENDRAIG Publishing
Los Angeles, CA 91040

The Wrath of Amun
By Claudia R. Dillaire
First Edition © 2011
by PENDRAIG Publishing
All rights reserved.

Edited by	Tony Mierzwicki
Cover Design & Interior Images Typeset & Layout	Jo-Ann Byers Mierzwicki
Cover Art by	Arden Ellen Nixon

PENDRAIG

PENDRAIG Publishing
Los Angeles, CA 91040
www.PendraigPublishing.com
Printed in the United States of America

ISBN: 978-1-936922-08-6

Dedication

To David,

for his insight, wisdom, encouragement, humour,
and, most importantly, friendship.

As always, life, health, and strength to you.

HISTORICAL NOTE

The use of the terms "brother" and "sister" have been used in two different contexts. In one, the terms refer to actual siblings, but in ancient Egypt, lovers often used the epithets as terms of endearment. Though it is certainly true that half-siblings of the royal families may have married, the protagonist and his lover are not blood relatives.

Another fact is that the average life span of men in ancient Egypt was 35 years and of women, 30 years. Therefore, as children were important and considered a blessing from the gods, marriage occurred much earlier than today. The usual age of marriage for girls was 12 - 15 years and for boys, 15 - 17. Though we may find this disturbing, it was a fact of life and has been reflected as such in this book.

The term "May he live, prosper, and be healthy" was used as a blessing after speaking or writing the name of the king throughout Egyptian history. As a written short cut, it was often written after the king's name as "l.p.h." and has been used as such in this book. Additionally, court proceedings were a normal occurance in ancient Egypt, however not always convened in the presence of the king. Though criminals could be sentenced to death, the pronouncement was always made through the god, since it was an abomination to kill or bring about the death of an individual, regardless of how evil that person was.

CHARACTER LIST

Temple of Amun personnel

Merti — young *shemayet* in the temple, daughter of Weni

Yuya — temple scribe

Thanuny — Second *hem netjer* in the Temple of Amun at Ramesses's III mortuary complex

Qaa — First *hem netjer* in the Temple of Amun and new Chief of the Medjay in Waset

Anedjib — *hery heb* in the Temple of Amun

Weni — *wab*-priest in the Temple of Amun; father of Merti

Harkhuf — Third *hem netjer* in the Temple of Amun

Victims

Iput — wick-maker in the marketplace

Raneb — Chief of the Medjay and First *hem netjer*; dies while investigating Iput's murder

Royal family

Ramesses III — king (*per aa*) of Egypt

Nebettawy — daughter of the king; *hemet netjer* in the Temple of Amun

Tentopet — daughter of the king

Iset — queen and great royal wife of Ramesses III; mother of Nebettawy and Tentopet

In service to the palace

Ashayt — female doctor (*swnwt*) to the royal family
Khamaat — apprentice to Ashayt
Tetisheri — Nebettawy's old wet nurse
Captain of the Medjay

In service to the Temple of Amun

Khety — goldsmith at the mortuary complex
Unas — apprentice to Khety; husband of Iput
Semti — farmer supplying the temple granaries; father of Iput
Sobekhotep — Overseer of the Temple Goldsmiths; court magistrate

Residents of Waset

Bek — wealthy nobleman and trader in the marketplace
Kiya — daughter of Bek; friend of Iput
Takhat — young widow who supports herself in the marketplace;
 lover of Unas
Sadeh — wife of Weni, mother of Merti
Aahotep — daughter of Khety
Nithotep — daughter of Khety

Foreign trader

Ghedi — Phoenician

Court magistrates

Djehuty — Vizier of Waset; lives on the East bank
Ankhtify — Lord of the Treasury
Intef — Royal Scribe
Hemon — Royal Scribe
Nebka — Royal Cupbearer
Kheperkare — nobleman and merchant
Djeserkare — Chief of the Royal Chariotry
Siptah — Doorkeeper of the Palace
Amenhirkopshef II — *wab*-priest of Mut in Karnak; son of
 Ramesses III; lives on the East bank
Usermaatre — Great Commander of the Army; son of Ramesses
 III; lives on the East bank

 Claudia R. Dillaire

Egyptian Words

Hem netjer	Servant of the god; priest
Hemet netjer	Female servant of the god; priestess
Dwat-netjer	God's Wife; title used by priestesses
Swnw	Male doctor
Swnwt	Female doctor
Swnwt per aa	Female doctor to the palace and royal family
Swnwt n per hemet nesut	Female doctor to the house of the royal wife
Wesekh	Type of collar necklace
Hery heb	Lector priest
Wab	Pure one; type of priest
Medjay	Police; often Kushite or Libyan mercenaries
Shemayet	Female musician serving the temple
Senet	board game
Mehen	board game
Deben	Unit of metal trade measure
Kidet	Unit of metal trade measure (10 kidet=1 deben)
Cubit	Unit of measure (length of a man's forearm)
Waset	City of Thebes

Men-nefer	City of Memphis
Auser	God Osiris
Auset	Goddess Isis
Het-Heru	Goddess Hathor
Menu	God Min
Nebet-Het	Goddess Nephthys
Nit	Goddess Neith
Bes Tattoo	Tattoo on upper thigh of temple dancers
Ma'at	order
Ka	soul; person's essence

Day 4 in Month 3 of the Peret Season, in Year 17 of the Reign of Ramesses III

"Merti, have you come to speak with your father?" the shadow voice wheezed from the darkness.

"My father is Weni, *wab*-priest of Amun. Who are you? Why can I not see you?" Though her tone was arrogant, the unknown voice frightened her.

"Your mother used to come here to pray for a daughter and she was rewarded for her prayers. You look so much like her. I have watched you blossom into a lovely young woman."

Merti backed up against a column in the First Court, peering into the darkness, listening for any sound that would indicate movement, but saw and heard nothing. "How do you know my mother?"

"It was I who gave her a daughter, not the man you call your father."

If Weni was not her father, than who was? Could this be the god Amun, having blessed her mother, making her daughter of the god? She was fifteen, a noblewoman, and wanted to be envied and admired. She harboured dreams of becoming a *hemet netjer*, but her father wanted her to find a suitable husband. But, she did not want a husband; there were too many handsome men in Waset to just choose one. Had the god Amun really favoured her mother? Her mind raced — the voice came from nowhere — who but the god could do that? The terrified girl fell to her knees, prostrate on the stone tiles. "What do you want of me, Father?"

"Iput, wife of Unas, comes here. What does she seek?" The voice was gentle, comforting, but insistent. "I need to know, my child, so I may help her."

"She comes to speak with the *hemet netjer*. She asked for a protection amulet. She comes here often." Merti trembled at the sound of the voice.

"When Iput comes again, I want you to listen. Find out when she will return. Place a reed at the base of the first column on the north side of the First Court. I will come to you and you will tell me what I need to know."

"But, Father, I know when she comes again. She is coming to the temple this night. I heard her speaking with the *hemet netjer* and they arranged a meeting." Merti looked up to the heavens and saw the sliver of moon almost directly above her. "She should be approaching soon."

"Go to your chambers and do not return here this night. Tell no one what I have revealed to you. If you speak of this night, you will never see the face of your true father. I will watch for you and approach you again. Now go, my daughter," the raspy voice commanded.

Merti got to her feet and, without looking any further for the voice, ran to the safety of the temple.

♀♀♀♀♀♀♀
⌠⌠⌠⌠⌠⌠⌠

Iput hurried down the narrow streets of Waset. As she tried to conceal herself in the shadow of the southern wall, passing the darkened homes of noblemen and priests, she reached up to finger the protection amulet around her neck. The *hemet netjer* had given it to her the previous day at the temple, which is where she was now going. There was less activity on this side of the temple complex, less chance for someone to follow her.

With just a sliver of moon to light the way, she could almost make out the pylon gate rising off to her left. She would be safe when she reached the First Court. The *hemet netjer* awaited her at the temple; she would know what to do because not only was she *hemet netjer nt Amun*, skilled in magic, but also the king's daughter. The princess would offer her protection, but Iput would have to tell her everything, regardless of the danger.

Iput stopped to catch her breath at the edge of the last house, knowing the First Pylon lay only a short distance ahead. With fingers trembling, she again reached for the amulet. She sensed movement, but at this late hour, no fires burned to chase away wild animals. Holding her breath now, she strained to listen. She inhaled deeply, summoned up all her courage, and spun around to see ... nothing. The street behind her was empty and quiet. She exhaled with relief.

As she turned back toward the pylon entrance, she flinched from a sharp pain in her abdomen. Instinctively, she touched her side and felt something warm, wet, sticky; she knew from the smell it was blood. Before she could scream, she felt another sharp pain in her chest, making it almost impossible to catch her breath, let alone scream. She lurched forward, hoping to reach the gate, when she felt one more sharp pain, this one in her back. Iput gasped, sank to her knees, and fell face first onto the sand.

Her attacker, hidden beside the last house, stepped out from the shadows, knelt beside her lifeless body, and turned her over. After several grisly minutes of further indignities, Iput's murderer stood up, dragged her body to the pylon gate, placed the weapon beside her, and quietly disappeared into the cloudless night.

DAY 8 IN MONTH 3

As he strolled home from the temple, Raneb was relieved this ugly business was finally about to end. Iput's body had been found four days ago and, though Raneb had fought in many campaigns, he had never witnessed such a disturbing scene. Poor Nebettawy. She was on her way to the Sacred Lake to purify herself for the day when she stumbled upon Iput's body at the pylon gate. She was still shaken by what she had seen. He did not have the heart to tell her that the injuries inflicted upon Iput were not from wild jackals, but from a very deliberate killer. How anyone could mutilate a body like that ... he thought he had seen everything.

He glanced up and saw Ghedi waiting for him in front of his residence. He had been a natural suspect; he was a foreigner, and the dagger found next to the body was similar to the one he carried, but Raneb had been able to clear him quickly. What could he want at this hour?

"Ghedi, how may I assist you?" Raneb called out to the trader.

"Raneb, I wanted to offer my thanks again for believing in me. You could have closed this case the first day, if you had thought what everyone else does. As a foreigner, I am always suspect. So I wanted to bring this to you before I set sail. I depart for Phoenicia at sunrise."

Ghedi withdrew a clay vessel from his robe. The two men, engaged in conversation, did not notice the figure concealed in the shadows across from Raneb's home.

"Come in, so I may see this gift you have brought." Raneb entered his house, lit the oil lamp next to the door, and motioned Ghedi to enter.

"I received this in trade today in the marketplace. One of my other customers thought it the perfect gift for you to show my gratitude."

Raneb took the clay vessel and looked at it. It was wine, imported from the Near East, and certainly something he could not normally afford. He lit a second oil lamp on the table, next to his scribe's palette.

"Ghedi, this is a rather extravagant gift. You could fetch quite a prize by trading this. I do not mean to sound ungrateful, but do you really want to part with such treasure?"

"You were the only one who believed me. And now that you know my secret, I am indebted to you." Ghedi bowed to the Chief of the Medjay.

"Your secret is safe with me. I do not care if you are not Phoenician, the only thing I care about is finding the truth. Will you join me in a drink?" Raneb reached for two clay drinking bowls on the side table, trying not to smudge them with his ink-stained thumb.

"I would join you, but I do not take strong drink. I shall take my leave now. May you enjoy the wine, and I shall look forward to seeing you on my next journey."

Raneb had already opened the vessel, poured some wine into one of the drinking bowls, and placed the vessel on his table. He took a drink and smiled approvingly. "It is an excellent wine. Many thanks, my friend," he reached out to stop the trader from going. When Raneb's wife and only child joined with Auser, he dedicated himself to his king and his work. He lived a simple life away from the temple and had few visitors. He drained the drinking bowl and poured himself another.

"If you wish to rest awhile here, I would enjoy the company." Raneb's speech was slightly slurred and he started to sweat a bit, even though it was a cool evening. He rubbed his temples and his eyes darted around the room. He swayed from side to side, as if already drunk. Ghedi looked puzzled, as the Medjay began to gasp and convulse. His body threw wildly exaggerated shadows around the small, simple mud-brick home. The convulsions, combined with the shadows, were a horrific sight to Ghedi. Raneb reached for the trader and grasped his

Claudia R. Dillaire

hand with the strength of ten men. His eyes were staring wildly and his face began to turn a gruesome shade of blue. Finally, his body collapsed onto the floor, smashing the clay bowl against the table, and lay still.

Ghedi, fearing he would be blamed for yet another death and suspecting now that the wine had been purposely poisoned, turned and wanted to run back to his ship. But, rather than calling attention to himself, he exited the house, walking slowly and deliberately down several narrow streets to the Eastern gateway. Once he passed through the gate and his feet touched the road to the dock, he ran to the relative safety of his ship.

The figure, who had been watching for Ghedi to depart, emerged from the shadows and entered Raneb's house. After a thorough ransacking, no new scrolls were found; maybe Raneb had not had the time to write his report to the king. Possibly he was preparing to do so, since his palette was on the table. The shadow figure stood over Raneb's body, satisfied that the truth would not be revealed, and left the house, again to quietly disappear into the enveloping embrace of the night shadows.

 THE WRATH OF AMUN

Day 9 in Month 3

Yuya, a temple scribe, called at Raneb's home. It was not like the First *hem netjer* to miss morning ritual. He looked in and saw the man, lying on his side, dead on the floor. Running several houses down, to one of the soldiers stationed in the capital city, Yuya brought him back to Raneb's house. The soldier, seeing the disorder, along with the dead man, sent the boy to notify the palace, while he stood guard at the Medjay chief's house for further instructions.

As he strode from the docks, in the direction of the Great Gate, Qaa was astonished by what he saw. When he left Waset twelve years ago, construction on the mortuary temple of Ramesses III was just beginning. From the Nile, he had seen the completed complex, safely ensconced behind the high, vividly adorned walls and pylon gates. At the entrance, giant carved marble obelisks, capstones layered in gold, glinted in the harsh relentless sunlight. Waset buzzed with activity — workmen painting the columns, scribes and priests marking the symbols for the stone cutters, the distant sound of the goldsmiths. The din from the marketplace was just audible and the smells from the stalls, as well as the temple bakery, were more exotic than he remembered. The braying of goats and sheep mingled with the clucks from the live chickens and geese, awaiting slaughter, the scents of roasting meats blended with the pungent spices, which would be laid out for sale in front of each stall. Breads and cakes, flavoured with anise, cinnamon, honey, and numerous other spices, could be savoured when the breeze shifted to the east. But all that could wait; he would have plenty of time later to explore his boyhood home.

Blue and white banners, signifying the status of this enclosure as a mortuary complex, swayed lazily in the nearly still air above the Great Gate. As he passed through the First Pylon, he could see the palace off to his left, flanked by columns brightly decorated with reeds and lotus flowers. Qaa quickened his step; he would much rather appear before the king early than be late. He had crossed half the courtyard when he saw someone approach. As the distance between them closed, he recognized the familiar kilt and *wesekh* of a *hem netjer.*

"The king wishes me to direct you to his private chambers. There has been a rather unfortunate event and he wishes to see you immediately," the priest said.

He followed the priest through the palace corridors to King Ramesses's private chambers. The only sound was the soft, crunching noise of the reed sandals, worn by both men, against the polished tile floor. Ushered into the room, they observed the seated king, deep in conversation with a Medjay, the elite guard of the palace.

"Your majesty, I have brought Qaa as you requested." The priest bowed deeply to the king.

"Leave us. We have much to discuss." The king looked troubled as the priest and Medjay both exited the private chamber. Qaa had not seen the man he once called "Father" for five years. He was no longer the warrior-king he fought so bravely alongside. Ramesses had begun to take on the guise of the Nile god, enlarged breasts, rounded belly. Egypt had been enjoying peace and prosperity these many years, and it showed upon the king. His face was weary and worn, as if he were a noble statue, too long in the sun and blowing sand. Qaa approached and bowed low, in deference to his king.

"Your majesty, I have come at your request. How may I serve you?" Qaa straightened and looked at Ramesses.

Ramesses smiled broadly. Qaa had served him well in the campaigns against the Libyans and the Sea Peoples, earning him the Flies of

Valour for his bravery, which he still wore around his neck on top of his *wesekh*. For his unwavering service he had been well compensated by being elevated to the post of Viceroy of Kush. Unlike the sons of his body, Qaa would do anything his king asked. Ramesses stood, approached Qaa, and embraced him warmly.

"Qaa, you do not have to observe formality with me in private. You are still like a son to me."

The two men walked out to the palace gardens and sat overlooking the royal pond. It was a beautiful, lush oasis in the middle of this inhospitable desert. Tranquil and restful, the blue lotus flowers floated on the surface of the pond, their scent heavily perfuming the still air. Date palms and fig trees lined the perimeter, creating a barrier from the responsibilities of kingship, providing a private respite from the pressures of governing an empire. For quite some time neither of them spoke. Qaa sensed Ramesses was burdened by whatever unfortunate event had occurred. Ramesses seemed quite content to just sit in his private gardens, breathing in the aroma of the plants that were now in full bloom. Qaa patiently waited for his king to speak.

"I had summoned you to head up the military, here in Waset, but the gods have interceded. I now need you more in another capacity. My advisors have informed me you are not only First *hem netjer* in Kush, but also fair and just in legal matters. Any good soldier may work his way up the ranks, but you have excelled in keeping the peace and seeking out evildoers. It is in this capacity that I now need your skills."

"My lord, I have always prided myself on my military accomplishments, but you know I serve you and my beloved land. I shall assume any role you feel appropriate."

"My Chief of the Medjay, who also held the post of First *hem netjer nt Amun*, was found dead this morning in his home. He had been investigating the brutal murder of a woman found at the entrance of the temple complex. We were to meet this morning regarding the investigation. I now fear the crime may go unsolved, and I am uneasy about his death." Ramesses stared directly at Qaa, his gaze never wavered from the young man's unusual blue eyes.

"Had he been ill?" Qaa understood the seriousness of the situation. Waset was the capital city of Upper Egypt and a brutal murder was not an everyday occurrence. The safety of foreign travelers to the city could have a devastating effect on trade if this were not dealt with swiftly.

"Aside from having lived a long life, he was in good health. I need to know that the murder shall not go unresolved; it has disrupted my daughter's life and she is quite shaken by it. She not only found the body, but in her capacity as *hemet netjer nt Amun*, she had counseled the young woman at the temple and was expecting her the very night of her death."

"May I see the chief's home and his body? I may be able to discern if this was an unfortunate accident or something more sinister. Do you suspect his death could be related to the murder investigation?"

"Raneb had told me he was close to solving the crime and he had been an outstanding officer for many years. If he wanted to see me, he must have had some information that was vital," Ramesses said.

"What has become of the young woman's body? Did her family have the means for a proper burial?"

"My daughter is taking care of her burial. She feels responsible for this woman's untimely death. The body is at the temple embalming tents being prepared."

"I shall examine her body myself and question the priests who handled her with Raneb. I do not know what he observed, but the priests may be able to shed some light on this matter. I shall also need to speak with your daughter at a later time, since she found the body, if that is acceptable with you?"

"I shall have Thanuny take you to Raneb's house. His body is still there. When you have assessed the scene, the priests may take his body to the temple for preparation. Return here after you have seen the woman's body. I shall summon my daughter when you are ready to question her. I trust your judgment in this matter."

"My king, I shall consult you in all matters concerning this business," Qaa stood, bowed to Ramesses, turned, and exited into the corridor where the priest was waiting to conduct him to the home of the dead Chief of the Medjay.

The home of Raneb was still being guarded by one of Ramesses's soldiers. The soldier stepped aside to let Qaa enter. The interior was cool and dark, providing respite from the morning heat. The main room was small and showed evidence that someone had been here looking for ... what? A broken drinking bowl lay on the floor, next to the body. An open wine vessel sat on the table. An imported wine, far more expensive than he surmised the chief could afford, based on the simple residence he occupied. Qaa picked up the vessel and sniffed its contents. The aroma was full and fruity, but with a hint of something unpleasant. He put it back on the table and bent down to examine Raneb.

The man was twenty or so years older than Qaa, but he looked fit. He obviously had not let the benefits of the temple go to his stomach. Numerous flies and beetles covered various parts of Raneb's corpse. His face was purple and contorted in a grimace; his eyes were staring out at nothing and had clouded over. His body showed no evidence of blows and there were no drag marks on the earthern floor, so he had not been moved. Whoever had ransacked Raneb's home had done so without disturbing the body. Although the body was warm, it was likely that he died the previous evening. He tried to move Raneb's head, but the neck was stiff, as were his limbs. He had seen this often in Kush; the man had died the night before and turned completely to stone. To make carrying him easier, he laid Raneb on his back; he noted the side of the body was dark where the blood had settled.

Qaa looked at the various papyri strewn about the simple mud-brick house, but most were sacred texts. The few that were secular in nature contained no mention of murder. On the side table, he noticed another drinking bowl with a black smudge on it. Qaa turned back to the body and noticed the thumb on his right hand was stained, but dry. He carefully examined the clay shards of the broken bowl and found a similar smudge on one of the larger pieces. He had seen all he needed to see for now; he would further examine the body at the temple this evening when the preparations were performed.

He stepped out into the bright intense sunlight, blinking to adjust his sight. He looked up and down the street at the close-set structures; any unusual noise would have been heard in the neighbouring houses. He looked down at the sand outside the house. Too many feet had passed this way; it would be impossible to tell if Raneb had more than one visitor the previous evening. He walked a short distance in the direction of the temple and then back. He looked in between the houses on the left and right, but again, too many feet had walked these paths.

He turned to Thanuny. The priest was older than he by possibly fifteen years. He was a short, fit man who looked like he kept himself well. His kilt was pleated sharply and gleaming white. He carried

himself with confidence and appeared to be the type of man who liked order. Thanuny looked to be a man upon whom he could depend to carry out his wishes.

"Thanuny, you may remove the body, but I would like to examine it further, before you start the preparations. Bring the vessel of wine back to the temple, but take care with it; it may tell me what I need to know. I have to return to my ship, and then I shall come to the temple to see the young woman's body." Qaa turned to the guard. "I do not want anyone to disturb this house. But I fear the sun may be strong today. Step inside the door and I shall see to getting someone to relieve you."

Qaa ambled toward the Eastern gateway, threading his way through the narrow streets, looking side to side and down at the sand. He found only one set of footprints leading to the gate from this area, whether it had anything to do with Raneb's death, he did not yet know. He walked down to the docks, bustling with passengers embarking on ferries for the East bank, workmen unloading wine vessels from Canaan, and watched a ship, its cargo of wheat and barley scenting the air, navigate expertly into the open water of the Nile. Motioning for the Harbour Master, he inquired of the man if any ships had departed earlier this morning. One had put out at first light, headed down the Nile, to Phoenicia, and three others had left headed to Kush. He stopped briefly at the ship on which he arrived, to change into a lighter linen kilt, and then hurried to the Temple of Amun.

Thanuny had arrived before Qaa and notified the lesser priests to direct him to the body of Iput. When he entered the preparation tent, he found Thanuny and three priests waiting for him. They had removed the linen and loose natron covering the dead woman.

"I would like to know who handled the body and assisted Raneb in his initial investigation. And, would someone tell me the name of this unfortunate woman," Qaa edged close to the table. He looked briefly at the desiccating body; his stomach lurched and he had to look away.

Thanuny spoke for the group. "Her name was Iput, daughter of Kawit, and she was a wick-maker. She was married to a temple goldsmith's apprentice, Unas, and her father is Semti, a farmer supplying the temple granaries. Raneb took the *hemet netjer* to her quarters after she found the body, and then he and I carried the body into this tent. Raneb directed Anedjib to remove all traces of blood outside the entrance. After Raneb had examined her body thoroughly, I began the preparations with Harkhuf and Weni."

One of the priests stepped forward and bowed. He was a small, thin man; Qaa estimated he and the priest were about the same age. He appeared nervous in Qaa's presence and his hands trembled. "I am Anedjib. It was my responsibility to remove any trace of blood from outside the entrance. When I completed my task, I assisted the priests by preparing jars of clay for the internal organs. I am a *hery heb* and not allowed to touch the body." He returned to stand next to his brother priests.

The second priest stepped forward, bowing low. By his clothing Qaa knew he also was a *hem netjer*, as was Thanuny. But, unlike Thanuny, he did not keep his kilt as well. He was about the same age as Thanuny, but was short and thin, as were many Egyptians. He seemed to like the status service in the temple afforded him, by wearing a great deal of adornment. "I am Harkhuf. Raneb and I removed what was left of her clothing and washed the body. I brought Raneb the unguents and oils to anoint her." He returned to his place.

It was now up to the final man, who wore the kilt of a *wab*-priest. He was short and plump, old enough to be Qaa's father. He evidently had enjoyed the luxury of the temple for many years, and now wore a weary countenance. He too bowed in deference to Qaa. "I am Weni. I prepared all the instruments for Raneb, brought in the natron for the organs, placed it on the tables with their jars, and assisted him while he packed her body with the natron packets."

"Which of you assisted when Raneb removed her organs?" Qaa needed to know.

"It was I who assisted Raneb in the removal of the organs," Thanuny replied.

"I shall wish to speak with each of you at length. You shall be my eyes as to what Raneb observed and you, Thanuny, shall be invaluable as to what Raneb may have told you. I would like to look at the body myself, and then I must return to the palace. This evening, I shall oversee the preparation of Raneb's body. I would ask that you have the linen, natron, unguents, and oils at the ready. Raneb served this temple well and deserves to have only the finest preparation. Thanuny, you knew Raneb so it is only proper that you prepare the body and I shall assist," Qaa dismissed the three lesser priests to begin their tasks. He turned to Thanuny.

"Would you assist me in turning the body so I may look at her back?"

Thanuny and Qaa turned the body so her back was facing them. Her back and buttocks showed numerous healed wounds, which had been inflicted over time. There appeared to be a healed burn mark on her left buttock as well. There was a large open wound in her lower back on the right side, which could have been the fatal wound.

"Let us lay her back down," Qaa said to Thanuny. He had seen some horrible wounds in his military campaigns, but this woman had lived a short and brutal life. She bore telltale burn marks on both wrists and ankles, like many a captive, which told him someone had restrained her against her will. The marks were not recent, and also appeared to have occurred over time, so they may not have been inflicted by her killer. Qaa further noted that the fingers on her left hand appeared to have been broken, as they had not healed properly.

Qaa now turned his attention to the front of Iput's body. There were two large wounds, probable stab wounds, one in her lower left abdomen, the other in her left chest. Again, either one of these could have been a fatal wound if delivered with enough force, but taken together, mercifully she must have died within minutes. However, it was the other wounds on her body which disturbed him more than what he had observed on her back. He prayed they had been inflicted after death.

Her throat had been slashed numerous times, making it appear she had been attacked by a wild animal. But the wounds were all of varying length and depth, which meant her killer had deliberately taken the time to inflict them. Both breasts had been slashed in a similar manner, as had been her genital area. He would ask each of the priests about any internal injuries Raneb may have observed. Qaa felt like retching; doing battle against an enemy was one thing, but brutalizing a woman ... there were no words to describe a person like that.

***

"My lord, I have examined the house of Raneb. Aside from the disarray, I saw no outward signs of injury. I directed Thanuny to remove his body to the temple for preparations. I shall observe the removal of the organs this evening. The gods may provide me with some answers at that time. I also examined the body of Iput. I now understand why your daughter was shaken by what she saw."

Claudia R. Dillaire

Ramesses, seated on his throne, said nothing. He had lost a close friend and advisor, and this unpleasant business which had so unsettled his favourite daughter still had not been solved.

"I left a soldier guarding Raneb's home. Is there a soldier or Medjay who may relieve him? The sun is high in the sky and he has been keeping watch since early morning." Qaa looked to Ramesses for some direction, but still none was forthcoming.

"I also inquired with the Harbour Master before I returned to the palace. This may not be related to the crime, but one ship departed for Phoenicia at sunrise. Could the ship be intercepted at the next port? I await your orders, my king." Again, Ramesses sat mute, struggling with his inadequacy at the current state of affairs.

"Did you not say your daughter has information about the murder?" Qaa asked, hoping to prod some response from Ramesses.

Ramesses finally looked up and considered the young man in front of him. Even though Qaa's mother was not Egyptian, he was like a son to him, more trusted than some of his own sons. He was a strapping man, towering a full head and shoulders above most people, quite capable in battle, strong as a bull, most likely able to overpower the most dangerous individuals in Waset.

"Qaa, I am appointing you Chief of the Medjay in Waset, as well as First *hem netjer* in the Temple of Amun. The soldiers and Medjay are yours to command; they shall obey you as they obey me. You may make your quarters here in the palace, or at the temple. Raneb kept quarters in the temple, which can be made available to you as well. As for a guard, I shall dispatch one to Raneb's home to keep watch until you are satisfied you need nothing further."

"I am honoured by your confidence in me, your majesty, and I shall serve you well," Qaa bowed to Ramesses. "I would prefer to stay at the temple for the present, to oversee the burial preparations, and meet with the temple administrators."

"Please, Qaa, you may still call me 'Father' when we are alone. You grew up in my home, with my sons and daughters. Your father served both my father and me well; I treated him like a member of my family and shall treat you just as well," Ramesses replied, smiling faintly. The king stood and crossed the room. "Medjay, dispatch a soldier to Raneb's home. Have a guard there at all times until dismissed by Qaa. Summon my daughter at the temple. Tell her I wish to see her in the palace gardens. And dispatch a Medjay to the ship Qaa arrived on and have his belongings brought to the temple," Ramesses commanded. The guard at the door scurried away as the king turned back to Qaa.

The two men walked out into the gardens and talked at length about past battles, the state of affairs in Kush, and the foreigners who seemed to be prevalent in Waset. Qaa inquired about the health of the royal family, and Ramesses spoke passionately about his children. Although three of his sons had joined with Auser, and his youngest daughter was plagued by evilspirits, he had many children. Aside from his son, Pentaweret, they brought him a great deal of joy; his daughter, Tentopet, was due to deliver her fifth child soon. When Qaa asked about the king's daughter, Nebettawy, he flushed deeply, unable to hide his feelings for her. Ramesses laughed heartily; his daughter still captivated Qaa, even after an absence of twelve years.

Nebettawy was escorted to the palace gardens. Her father was laughing, and quite animated with the stranger seated next to him. She had not seen her father this happy in some time; she had broken his heart when she made her choice to serve the temple, and even now when she came to the palace, she could see the sadness in his eyes.

"My beloved father, I have come at your request. How may I serve you?" Nebettawy bowed deeply in front of Ramesses.

"Our new Chief of the Medjay has arrived and is anxious to hear what you know of Iput's death."

For the first time, Nebettawy really looked at the stranger who had made her father laugh.

"Qaa?!" Her voice was barely audible. She stared intently into the blue eyes she had never forgotten, they threatened to overpower her, drown her like the Great Sea. The blood drained from her face and her knees buckled.

Instinctively, Qaa rushed forward to steady her, grabbing her by the arms. They were so warm to the touch, soft and supple, like a dancer's. Being this close to her, he could feel the heat of her body and smell her musky scent. She smelled of myrrh and cinnamon, blue lotus and rose, and it was intoxicating. He felt his desire for her rise up inside of him, uncontrollable like a wild jackal. The heat in his loins burned like a torch, the throbbing between his legs unbearable. He wanted to pounce upon her and carry her off, possess her, devour her. His head ached, his chest pounded, and his ears buzzed. He forced himself to breathe but the air, heavy with scent, clogged his lungs, like the Nile at inundation. His thoughts swam in all directions until ...

"Qaa! Release my daughter!" Ramesses's words struck him like a thunderbolt.

Ramesses met first with his daughter in his private chamber, while Qaa waited in an antechamber with a Medjay.

"Father, how could you not tell me you were bringing Qaa back to Waset?" Nebettawy was red with anger and embarrassment.

"Sit down, Daughter."

Nebettawy did as she was commanded. Ramesses looked at his daughter. She was his favourite; he denied her nothing. But he would not allow her to be insolent to him.

"Daughter, why did you choose to serve the temple?" Ramesses demanded.

"My mother's mother was *dwat-netjer* and *hemet netjer*. She taught me a great deal and I wished to be like her. When she joined Auser, it was only natural for me to assume her duties in the temple. Why do you ask me such a question?"

"You made a choice to serve the temple. Even though I offered you many suitable husbands, you refused each one. Now, this man comes back to Waset and with a look you bewitch him in such a manner."

"I was to be the wife of the First *hem netjer*. You could have given me to Raneb, but you did not. I chose to remain untouched, so you would stop offering me to men I did not want. When you were fighting the Libyans, you were ready to trade me to the Libyan prince for peace. How can you love me when you would use me like a concubine to make peace with a man so far beneath me?" Nebettawy wanted her father to hurt, the way she had been hurt when she found out his scheme.

"I knew you had affection for Qaa as a child, and he may have affection for you, but you are not a child anymore. You defied me once by not taking the Libyan and I shall not tolerate defiance from you now. As befitting your status, you must conduct yourself with restraint."

"That is the first point we agree upon, my father. I am no longer a child, and though I am only a woman, I am very much like you. I was ready to give myself to Qaa, twelve years ago, before you sent him away from me. I have learned many hard lessons from you. But I have also learned the ways of magic. And if it is Qaa who I want still, it is Qaa who I shall have." She turned to leave her father's private chamber.

"No, you shall not. As *dwat-netjer*, you came to me and told me Amun himself commanded you to become *hemet netjer*, and to remain pure, untouched by man, faithful only to the god himself." Ramesses could feel his anger at a dangerous pitch. "Did you lie to me?"

"I became *dwat-netjer* out of love for my country, my gods, and you, my father. I studied well and learned magic in the temples of Auset, Het-Heru, and Bast. I learned the sacred creation and fertility rituals of Amun and Menu. I learned dark magic from Set, Nebet-Het and Nit, and I performed the spells to protect you from harm in battle."

"You did well, Daughter, and brought *ma'at* back to our land. Do you now wish to return us to chaos by defying your father and the Great Amun?"

"I love you, my father, and I love this land. But, Qaa is the man I love. Amun commanded I become wife to the First *hem netjer*; my mother's mother foretold you it was my destiny and still you resist. So it was you who defied Amun when you did not give me to Raneb." Nebettawy raised her voice in anger. She would not allow him to keep her from Qaa.

Ramesses reached out to his daughter, to calm her, but she evaded his grasp. She wanted to hurt him some more, the way he was hurting her. She continued to rant at him.

"Out of deference to you, Raneb would not even allow me to perform the sacred rituals I am bound to perform. If you should appoint Qaa as First *hem netjer*, I must take him as my earthly husband, for it is the will of Amun. All I ask, my father, is your blessing so I may be with him. You were more than willing to give me to the Libyan, but you shall not give me to Qaa, who grew up in your house, a man you trust with your life, and call 'Son'?" Nebettawy stopped before she pushed her father too far; she choked back tears, not wanting her father to know how much she desired Qaa.

Ramesses considered all she had said. He had denied his daughter nothing, but the gods and the land came first. Before she became dwat-netjer, they had suffered much from war and famine, and now the country was filled with prosperity and peace reigned. But, could Amun want his daughter, daughter of the king and Amun himself, to become wife to a man who was not fully Egyptian?

"You shall go to Men-nefer until this unfortunate business is settled. Then, you may return to Waset and we shall consult Amun. I shall not allow you to take this man as your husband, at this time, and I shall not give you my blessing."

Nebettawy walked toward her father and stood her ground. She looked into his eyes and saw no compassion. She would do whatever was necessary to change his mind.

"I shall not go to Men-nefer; I shall return to my duties at the temple, my king, and I shall consult with Amun, for the decision is not yours to make. Should you choose not to allow me to take my husband, I shall leave your palace, the gods I love, and this land, so that I may be with Qaa. But you shall give me your blessing, for my magic is stronger than yours." She bowed in deference to him, and turned away; her heart was broken and she could no longer hold back the tears.

Ramesses grabbed her by the arm, to prevent her from leaving. He spun her around and searched her face. He saw the anger and resolve in her eyes, the tears on her cheeks. He hugged her close to his body and felt her relax, ever so slightly, in the arms of her father.

"Nebettawy, I have loved you above all my other children because you are proud, headstrong, fearless; more like a son than a daughter. You are the light of my life, my favourite child." Ramesses pushed her away to look at her. "But I need Qaa to solve the murder of your servant, and the death of my friend. I can not have his mind clouded by your bewitchments. There is much you need to consider; this is not a decision to be made lightly. Promise me you shall not join with this man during his investigation. When this incident has been resolved, then we shall see what Amun has to say on the matter. Will that please you, my daughter?"

Nebettawy wiped the tears from her cheeks. She hated being angry with her father; he was the only one to whom she could turn. She loved him deeply and only wanted to please him. "Yes, Father. I shall wait until this business is resolved."

Ramesses crossed the corridor to meet with Qaa. He knew they had been infatuated as children, but he would not tolerate this behavior. Nebettawy was sacred; Qaa was forbidden to touch her under any circumstance. Only if a union with her was blessed by the god, could he touch her. And Ramesses was not prepared to bless a union between his daughter and a man who was only half Egyptian.

He entered the room to find Qaa waiting for him, on his knees, head bowed. He dismissed the Medjay.

"My king, I await whatever punishment you deem fit for me," Qaa did not look up.

"Qaa, you may rise. I have spoken with my daughter; I shall now speak to you as I would a son of my body. I can not allow you and my daughter to act in such a manner."

Qaa stood and faced Ramesses. He could not hide his embarrassment and shame; nor could his loincloth and kilt hide his desire for the king's daughter.

"My lord, I have been in love with your daughter since the day I first saw her, but that is no excuse for my behaviour."

"My son, when you first came to my father's house, I treated you like one of my own children. But, you must know why I have reservations. Your father was an Egyptian, and served me well. I could not have asked for a better man as my friend; I named one of my sons to honour him. You were just a child, and though your mother observed our ways, she was not Egyptian."

Qaa had always been noticeably different, striking blue eyes, light skin, hair the colour of wheat, towering over the royal children. He only looked less out of place once his sidelock was shaved. The one person who never seemed to notice was Nebettawy. He had always struggled with who he was, though he had been brought up Egyptian and knew no other ways. "My king, the waters of the Nile sustain me, as they sustain all the people of Egypt. I would give my life for you and my country."

Ramesses knew that was true. "Son, I mean no disrespect. I know how you feel about this country and you saved my life, more than once, in battle. But, my daughter knows little of your mother and, as her father I have tried to protect her as best I can. I know the difficulties you endured as a child; your own children may suffer the same. And if they are the children of my daughter, then it is my concern."

"I do understand, my king, though I have never been able to love any woman as I love your daughter. I could not take an Egyptian woman, for that would be disrespectful to Nebettawy. I have lain with foreign women, but they gave me no pleasure. Nebettawy is the only woman I could ever take as my sister, my wife." Qaa could not look directly at his king, as he spoke of such intimate matters.

"I am not without feeling for your distress; my daughter has made it abundantly clear to me she feels the same for you. Until this ugly business has been resolved, I must have your promise that you and Nebettawy shall not lie with each other, or engage in the pleasures of the flesh. Then, we shall consult with Amun."

"I shall do as you command, my king," Qaa breathed a sigh of relief. He had waited twelve years for Nebettawy, he could wait a bit longer. "If I may take my leave, I would like to return to the temple to oversee the preparation of Raneb's body. I shall report to you after I have questioned the priests. Then, I shall question your daughter here at the palace, so you may be present."

"You may go, my son, just remember what I have said. My daughter is skilled in magic, and I do not envy the position in which she has placed us both."

Qaa returned to the temple to assist Thanuny and the other priests with the preparation of Raneb's body. Having served as First *hem netjer*, Raneb would receive only the best, and it was only proper that Thanuny be in charge. Anedjib stood next to the embalming table, scrolls trembling in his hands, reciting the proper words, and keeping the censer burning. After Qaa removed Raneb's kilt and loincloth, he examined the body for any signs of injury, having Thanuny assist him in turning the body. There were no fresh marks on the body, only an old healed wound on his left shoulder.

As the proper spells were spoken, Qaa reverently washed the body; Thanuny then deftly inserted an instrument into the nasal cavity, to break the nasal bone. After several minutes of movement, the body was turned to allow the brain matter to drain from the nose. The instrument was inserted a second time, through the other nostril, and the procedure was repeated. Liquid was forced into the nasal cavity to remove any further brain matter. Natron coated linen strips were finally inserted to swab out the brain cavity.

Qaa handed Thanuny the ritual obsidian blade to make the abdominal incision. The incision, no more than four inches in the lower left abdomen, would be sufficient to remove the organs. Being closest to the body, both Qaa and Thanuny noticed the smell; it was not just the smell of death and decay, but something else, the same unpleasant odour Qaa smelled earlier that day in the wine vessel. Thanuny reached into the incision and removed the first organ, handing the intestines, along with the pancreas and spleen, to Qaa, who examined the intestines and placed them in a clay bowl on a separate table, covering them with natron. The pancreas and spleen, along with the kidneys and bladder, which were removed next, were not preserved.

Next, Thanuny handed Qaa the stomach. Qaa picked up the obsidian blade and made a small incision to examine the contents. The odour was much more pronounced and the only liquid in the stomach appeared to be wine. The stomach was then placed in a bowl on the table and packed in natron. The same procedure was followed with the liver and the lungs. Weni placed the alabaster jars on the table, next to each of the organs in natron, while more spells were intoned.

Qaa again washed the body while Anedjib walked around the table with the censer, reading the spells to cleanse and chase away the harmful spirits. The table was then prepared with a bed of natron and the body laid upon planks, resting just above the natron. Thanuny and Qaa packed the body cavity with natron packets. Weni held the unguent jars while Thanuny and Qaa anointed the body, crossed the arms across the chest, covered it with natron, and finally with a sheet of linen. Thanuny dismissed the two priests to bathe. He turned to Qaa and directed him to a separate area in the temple where they could bathe, as well, but speak privately.

It was a large, mud-brick room, with a bathing area constructed in the middle of the floor, spacious enough to accommodate four priests. Along the left wall were stone benches, with pegs above, for linen robes. Two such robes had been furnished by the temple servants. The back wall contained a wooden table with oils and unguents upon it; under it was a large clay vessel of natron. There appeared to be a closet-like room on the right wall, which Thanuny explained contained indoor waste facilities for the priests of the temple. Egypt was a civilized nation — each sleeping chamber came equipped with a personal waste receptacle of clay, though many men still preferred to urinate outside, directly onto the sand — but a specific room afforded the occupant a measure of privacy. Qaa knew such luxuries existed but he had never expected to enjoy such comforts.

"*Hem netjer*, it is apparent you have formulated an opinion as to the cause of death. I directed the other priests to carry Raneb's body and I carried the wine vessel myself to the temple. Once we have cleansed ourselves, I shall conduct you to my quarters, where the vessel still remains." Thanuny understood the seriousness of what might be in the vessel, and Qaa felt he could depend on him for assistance.

Thanuny had turned his back to get the oils for cleansing. Qaa quickly undressed and eased himself into the cool clean water. The older priest removed his bloody clothing and joined Qaa in the cleansing water and handed him a bowl of natron and a jar of oil.

"You have done well. My belongings were brought to the temple today and I would like to stop at my quarters to dress." Though he considered himself Egyptian, Qaa had never been comfortable naked in the presence of others. His height and pale skin had been a source of ridicule when he was growing up; when he reached manhood and was ritually circumcised, his large phallus had then become a source of astonishment and envy. He rarely bathed with others and never left his quarters naked, as some priests did.

"You do not have to explain, *hem netjer.* Some of the priests prefer to be naked, Anedjib and Harkhuf prefer it, but I do not, though it is common in many of our temples."

When the men had finished cleansing, they wrapped themselves in the linen robes. Thanuny directed Qaa to follow him the short distance down a dim, deserted corridor to two private rooms, one on either side. "My quarters are on the left, I had your belonging put in the room on the right. It had been Raneb's quarters. I shall remove his items after you have finished your investigation. When you have dressed, I shall be awaiting you." Thanuny disappeared into his room.

Qaa entered his room and found a clean loincloth and kilt laid out on the bed, his other belongings undisturbed and still in his travel chests. He dressed quickly and crossed the corridor to speak with Thanuny.

"I believe Raneb was poisoned and the poison is in that wine vessel. Are you troubled by any wild animals at the temple?" Qaa inquired.

"We often have to chase away dogs and jackals from the Western gateway."

"Bring me two clay bowls."

Thanuny exited his quarters and returned shortly with the bowls as requested. Qaa poured half the liquid into one of the bowls and handed it to Thanuny. He poured the remaining wine into the other bowl and placed the vessel on Thanuny's table.

"Lead me to the Western gateway; we shall place these outside the entrance and wait. I need to observe the animals after they drink."

Thanuny led Qaa through the back of the deserted complex to the Western gateway. They placed the bowls in the sand several cubits from the entrance and returned to the safety of the enclosure. The two men did not have long to wait. A male jackal approached from a rocky outcropping to the north, making no sound but casting a long shadow from the light of the moon. It sniffed tentatively at one of the bowls, walked around it, and sniffed again. Looking from side to side, the jackal sniffed the bowl once more. It began to lap the wine eagerly.

While they watched, the jackal started to pant and growl. Its body shook and its legs could not propel it back to the safety of the rocks. The jackal was drooling and panting when it fell to the sand and began to convulse. The sight and sound of its agony was disturbing. With a final growl, the jackal convulsed violently and then lay still. After several minutes, Qaa went out to retrieve the clay bowls and handed them to Thanuny.

"Dispose of the liquid where it shall harm no one, but I want to examine the bowls. I may be able to discern what plant was used. I also wish to examine the vessel to see if there is any residue in the bottom."

Both men returned to the temple in silence.

DAY 10 IN MONTH 3

Qaa deferred to Thanuny to perform the morning ritual in the temple, preferring to observe, to understand the workings of this temple and the priests. When the ritual was completed, Qaa requested the priests he had met the previous day to join him in the Great Hypostyle Hall.

"Thanuny, I know you have much to do, and I would like to speak with these men first. Where may I find you?"

"I need to meet with the scribes and lesser priests, have unguents to prepare, and am expecting two new workers. I shall return here after I have met with the scribes, to see if you are in need of me at that time." Thanuny bowed and walked in the direction of the Second Court.

"Harkhuf, it was you who assisted Raneb in removing the clothing?"

"Yes, *hem netjer.*" Harkhuf bowed his head to Qaa.

"Tell me all you observed. Leave out no detail."

"There was sand on the front of her clothing, as well as the back. Her dress and loincloth had been badly slashed, where her injuries were, but there was little blood around the neck, breast, and genital wounds."

"Did you notice any other marks on the clothing?"

"There appeared to be a blackened smudge on the cloth of the right shoulder."

"I know this is a difficult question. You said you assisted Raneb in washing the body. Could you tell if she had been violated?" Qaa did not know if he wanted to hear the answer.

Harkhuf looked away, the colour having drained from his face. "I asked Raneb to examine her and he saw what I saw. It appeared her attacker had used an object to defile her."

"You have done well, Harkhuf. I shall ask no more. If you may be of further assistance, I shall speak with you at that time." Qaa considered what he had heard. Some of the crimes he had investigated in Kush had been brutal, but he had never encountered anything like this. "You may return to the temple."

As Harkhuf walked toward the terrace, Qaa turned his attention to the two remaining priests. He wished to speak with Anedjib last, so he could show him the scene.

"Weni, you assisted Raneb when he packed the body in natron. Did you also cover the organs?"

The *wab*-priest bowed to Qaa. "I did, *hem netjer*. Ask me whatever you need to know. I have a young daughter, Merti, who serves here in the temple. I want to know that this shall not happen to her."

"I appreciate your honesty. Can you tell me of any injuries you observed on her organs?"

"There was a great deal of blood in the body cavity, when Raneb made his incision. Both lungs had wounds from a knife, as did the stomach. And there were several wounds to the intestines. There may have been wounds present on other organs, but I do not know, as they were not preserved."

"Weni, I have no further questions at this time. I shall do all in my power to see that this does not happen to anyone else. You may return to the temple."

Weni bowed to Qaa and proceeded toward the terrace, from which Qaa saw Thanuny approach.

"Thanuny, Anedjib and I were about to look at the scene. Are you able to join us?"

"The scribes are at work and the lesser priests are taking care of the new workers. I shall prepare the unguents after the noon ritual."

The three men walked through the Great Hypostyle Hall, the Second Court, and the First Court. When they arrived at the First

Pylon, Qaa stopped briefly, looking through the opening to see what the *hemet netjer* might have seen that morning.

"Thanuny, show me where the body was found."

The priests walked through the gate opening to the spot where Iput's body had lain. "She was found here."

"Anedjib, did you find much blood on this spot?"

"No, *hem netjer*." He bowed in deference to Qaa. "There was a blood trail, if you shall follow me."

The three men walked in the direction of the southern wall, past the opening to the palace enclosure, to the corner of an inner wall of the temple complex. Beyond were the residences of soldiers, merchants, and priests. But the homes of the artisans were along the northern wall of the enclosure. Iput's husband was a goldsmith's apprentice and their residence would have been on the other side of the complex. Why had she chosen this route to her meeting at the temple?

"I found a great deal of blood here, *hem netjer*. It appeared she had been dragged to the pylon gate. There were marks in the sand and some blood found along the marks."

"Did you notice anything near the corner of the wall?"

"I found a protection amulet. The *hemet netjer* had prepared it for Iput and given it to her at the temple."

"Anedjib, you have done well. If I need further assistance, I shall call on you. You may return to the temple." Anedjib bowed to Qaa and walked in the direction of the pylon gate.

Qaa waited for Anedjib to enter the pylon gate before he spoke. "Thanuny, let us prepare for the noon ritual. I shall assist you with the unguents and we may speak in private. I need to know everything you observed and everything Raneb told you. I heard some disturbing information and I need you to confirm it, if it is true."

After the preparation of the unguents and the noon ritual, Thanuny and Qaa retired to their private quarters. Qaa took out a new scroll and wrote notes about his observations of the poisoned wine and what the priests had told him. When he had finished, he secured the reeds in the palette, took the scroll and palette with him, and crossed the corridor to Thanuny's room.

"Thanuny, may I speak plainly? The king has appointed me First *hem netjer*; I need to know if you had hoped to gain the position."

"I am quite content with my duties here at the temple. I often have to act on behalf of the First *hem netjer*, but without all the political intrigue that comes with the position. I do not envy you your task. I shall serve you well, just as I did Raneb. Harkhuf, Weni, and I are the only permanent full time priests here, as was Raneb. I shall notify them of your appointment. Whatever you need, *hem netjer*, I am at your service." Thanuny bowed to Qaa.

"I would prefer informality from you and hope to count you as a friend, Thanuny. I have spent much of my life in military service, never settling in one place very long. My previous appointment, Viceroy of Kush, required my dedication to protecting our southern border. I hope to settle in Waset and would enjoy the company of my fellow priests."

"You may depend on me, Qaa, if I may address you as such."

Qaa smiled for the first time in the presence of the priest. "Yes, Thanuny, you may. There is much I need to know, and you are my eyes and ears. Please sit and we may begin."

Thanuny sat on his bed and Qaa sat on the stool at the writing table. He spread the scroll on the table, set the palette next to it, prepared the inks, and consulted his notes.

"Thanuny, do you have the bowls and vessel? I think I would like to examine them first."

The priest motioned to a side table. Qaa was able to reach them from his position at the writing table. The bowls contained some sediment, but it was difficult to determine if it was from an herbal mixture or just from the wine itself. The vessel, however, was much more informative. Just looking down the neck, Qaa could see a great deal of "mush" in the bottom. He gently tapped the clay vessel on the edge of the table to crack it. With his large hand, he grasped the neck and broke it off, to expose the inside. The first item of note was the unmistakable odour of lotus flower. It was often used for pain or to quiet those suffering from evil spiritsbut in large doses it could lead to unconsciousness and death. The plant material looked like it had been filtered through cloth; there was little that was recognizable. From the smell, however, he suspected one of the ingredients could be monkshood or henbane. He placed the broken vessel on the table, scribbled some notes on the papyrus scroll, and then turned his attention to Thanuny.

"You and Raneb carried Iput into the preparation tent, after the *hemet netjer* had been settled in her quarters. Tell me what he said of his observations, as well as what you observed. No detail is unimportant."

"You should know the weapon was recovered. It was found next to the body. Raneb directed me not to wash it until he examined it. I placed the dagger on a piece of linen cloth and brought it into the preparation tent for him."

"Tell me about the dagger and, if it is still in the preparation tent, I would like to examine it as well." Qaa picked up the reed, dipped it in the ink, and took notes as he listened to Thanuny.

"It is an unusual dagger, foreign; I have seen daggers like that being traded in the marketplace. Many of them come from the Near East. Rather than describe the dagger, I shall show it to you when you have finished your questions."

"Thank you, Thanuny. Tell me what Raneb saw when he examined the body."

The older priest shifted uncomfortably on the bed. He had been troubled greatly by what he had seen.

"Take your time. I know this has been a very unsettling event. I have seen men killed in battle, but I have never seen anything as brutal as this." Qaa looked sympathetically at Thanuny. "I would not ask for such information if it were not necessary."

"I have been greatly affected by this murder; even sleep offers me no solace."

"Then tell me, Thanuny, and allow me to carry the burden of this crime."

The older priest took a deep breath and commenced his narrative, as Qaa made notes.

"Raneb examined her body thoroughly, just as you did. He also spread her legs and examined her genitals and rectum. Aside from the wounds you see, her attacker used an object on her, tearing her open in both areas."

Both men sat for some time in silence; Qaa was trying to understand how a person could do such a thing, while Thanuny continued to struggle with the horrors he had seen inflicted on Iput.

"After Weni helped Raneb pack the body cavity, Raneb dismissed the other priests and asked me to remain. He told me he was troubled by something he had seen and asked me to assist him. We removed some of the natron packets from the body and Raneb examined other organs." Thanuny's face was ashen, his voice quavered, and he looked quite ill.

"Let me get you some wine. We can speak of this later, when you are feeling up to it."

Qaa exited the room and crossed the corridor to his room. He had a vessel of Kushite wine in one of his traveling chests. He extracted it from the chest and found the two new drinking bowls on a shelf in his room. He brought the bowls and vessel to Thanuny's room, poured him a generous amount, and held the wine out to the older priest. With hands shaking, he took the bowl and drained it straight away.

"Qaa, you must not reveal what I am about to tell you. Only Raneb and I knew what he had found when he again examined that poor woman."

Qaa poured more wine into Thanuny's bowl, poured himself a bowl, and sat down again. When they had both drunk, Qaa spoke to the priest.

"Raneb was the Chief Medjay in charge of the investigation. It now falls upon my shoulders to complete his work. I need to know what he knew."

"Iput was with child when she was killed." Thanuny buried his face in his hands, trying to erase the scene from his memory.

 Claudia R. Dillaire

Day 11 in Month 3

Having assisted with the morning ritual, Qaa with two Medjay escorts headed across the Nile to the verdant fields on the East bank. They found Semti, with his wife and children, tending an emmer field; he was lowering the shaduf into the water channel while his wife and children weeded. Qaa motioned to the man he wished to speak with him privately. Off to the left of the emmer field, there was a small personal garden; the plants appeared to be barley, radishes, leeks, and onions. As a farmer in service to the temple, he also had a few goats, sheep, and geese, for his family's consumption, grazing in pens in front of the mud-brick house. Qaa could not shake the melancholy, which seemed to blanket the place. The animals had a haunted look to them, the area smelled of decay and hopelessness, and Semti's family appeared beaten, like horses ridden too long and hard. Iput's father was a small, wiry man dressed only in a loincloth, flint cutting blade with a wooden handle tucked into the waist, bare feet caked with mud; Semti barked orders to his family to keep working. He carried himself like a man who was accustomed to being obeyed.

"You are Semti, father of Iput, the woman who was murdered at the temple?"

"I am. Who are you, *hem netjer*?" Semti looked up at the imposing figure, sporting a reed switch tucked neatly into the waist of his kilt.

"I am Qaa, the new Chief of the Medjay. I have been called to Waset to look into the death of your daughter. Did you see your daughter on the evening of her death?"

"No, Medjay. I had worked all day in the fields and had another long day ahead of me." Semti bowed low before Qaa.

"Was your daughter happy in her marriage?"

"Unas was divorcing her. He came to me and asked to send her back. She was barren; what other use is there for a woman except to pleasure her husband and provide him with children. She was trouble all her life; I told him she was his wife, not my responsibility. I had no use for another mouth to feed." Semti seemed untouched by Iput's murder.

"You say she was trouble. Did you beat her as a child?" Qaa's stomach lurched, remembering the abuse he had seen on Iput's body.

"I had to. She wouldn't cook, do her chores, work in the fields. How else could I get her to do anything?" Semti looked to Qaa for sympathy, man to man.

Qaa was outraged. He tried to keep his voice measured and his anger in control. "Did you tell Unas how to make her obey?"

"Of course." Semti smiled broadly. "He needed to know how to handle her. Unas always did like the wild ones. Her mother was like that when I took her the first time. Screamed and kicked, almost bit my ear off. She still has some fight left in her, but I too know how to use a switch." He chuckled to himself.

In one swift motion, Qaa withdrew the switch from his waist, raised it above his head, and struck the farmer a sound blow across the cheek, drawing blood. Qaa fought hard against lashing out in anger, preferring combat in battle, but intentionally inflicting pain on a woman was something he would not tolerate.

"If you have lied to me, farmer, I shall return and shall not stay my hand at just one blow."

After traveling back across the Nile to the West bank, and still in the company of the two Medjay, Qaa found Unas at one of the temple metalworking tents. Wearing only a loincloth, he was sitting on a stool in front of a brazier, tongs in hand, a glowing piece of metal in the charcoals. Even from this distance, the heat was palpable and breathing

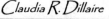

was an effort. Qaa motioned to the overseer to bring Unas to him. The overseer spoke to Unas who put down the tongs, stood, and compliantly followed the overseer's instructions.

Qaa appraised Unas, having seen the brutality on Iput's body. The man was about his own age, but at least a cubit shorter. He had powerful hands and shoulders from working the various metals, and bore numerous burns and scars, both fresh and healed. His hands had the familiar appearance of crocodile skin, brown, scaly, and toughened from the heat of the crucibles and hearths. He sported a dagger at his waist, bronze with a bone handle. He moved with the swagger of a man too self-confident; he exuded an air of importance though he was only an apprentice.

"I am Qaa, the new Chief of the Medjay. I am looking into the death of your wife. Did you know she had left your home to go to the temple the night she died?"

"I was asleep. She must have slipped out; she did that often. I suspected she had taken up with another man. I had no use for her, she was barren and I was going to divorce her."

Qaa's temper simmered just below the surface of his calm exterior. Semti had put him in a foul mood. This man's wife is brutally murdered and he speaks disrespectfully of her. He withdrew the switch and slapped his own palm with it. "Did you beat her often?" Qaa's voice had taken on the tenor of a confidante, one man to another.

"She would not submit to me. I would have to bind her hands and feet in order to mount her." Unas laughed.

Qaa could feel his anger dangerously close to exploding. Even a reed switch, in his hands, could inflict serious injury. "She may have been more receptive if you had been patient or kind with her."

Unas leaned in to speak low, so only Qaa would hear. "Chief Medjay, do you have a woman? Trust me when I say they need to be beaten regularly. How else can you make them submit?" He stepped back and continued to speak. "I now have a woman who knows her place and will do whatever I demand. Is that not the duty of a woman?" He smiled broadly.

Qaa wanted to retch. Brought up in an abusive home, married to an abusive husband, what chance did she have? Were all the men in Waset this brutal toward their women? He could not contain his anger any longer. "In the future, apprentice, when you see me, I expect you

to bow before me, showing your respect. Medjay, hold this man while I interrogate him further."

Each Medjay grabbed an arm of Unas and held him tightly. Qaa began beating Unas on the back, just as Unas had beaten his wife to submit to his needs. "How does it feel, Unas, to be powerless? Do you think she enjoyed her beatings? If you have lied to me, I shall be back. And if I hear of you beating any more women, you shall wish I had killed you." Qaa's chest heaved and sweat trickled down his back, having taken out his anger on the man who had inflicted much of the torment on Iput. He again raised the switch above his head.

"My Chief that was twenty lashes." The Medjay saw the wrath in Qaa's eyes and fell silent. His rage spent for now, he lowered the switch. Qaa straightened up, wiped the bloody switch on Unas's loincloth, and slid it into the waist of his kilt.

After taking a deep breath to bring his emotions under control, Qaa spoke smoothly and authoritatively. "Medjay, you may release him." When the Medjay released Unas's arms, he fell, in a crumpled heap at Qaa's feet. He looked down, spat on him, and turned back to the temple, followed by the Medjay.

Following the noon ritual, Qaa asked Thanuny to show him the dagger. It was still in the preparation tent where Iput lay on the embalming boards. Raneb had left it on a side table after his examination and it had not been touched since.

"As I said, it appears to be a Near East dagger. I have seen some of the traders in the marketplace selling them, and many of the Phoenicians carry them at their belts." Thanuny stood by the table, but did not wish to touch the dagger, which was still stained with blood.

Qaa looked at the dagger. It was an ivory handled dagger in the Amorite style, with gold leaf on the hilt. The ivory was beautifully carved and the figure on the hilt appeared to be a foreign deity, with inlay of lapis lazuli and onyx. The bronze blade was bloodied, but the handle of the dagger interested him more. Although there was blood on it, there was something else. He gingerly picked up the edges of the piece of linen the dagger was laying on. Upon closer examination, it appeared there was some linen fabric clinging to the inlaid gems on the handle, possibly from Iput's dress or loincloth.

"Thanuny, has anyone touched this since it was brought in?"

"To my knowledge, no, it has not. Raneb examined it after we prepared the body and no one has been in this tent since, other than the day you examined Iput's body."

Qaa put the linen back on the table. He placed his fingers at the tip of the blade and the tip of the hilt, and gently turned the dagger over, placing it back on the linen. There was something on that side of the handle, as well, though it did not look like linen fabric. Qaa leaned in to look closer and was horrified at the realization that, what was clinging to the dagger, was flesh, Iput's flesh, and most likely this was the object which was used to defile her.

"Thanuny, tell the priests not to disturb the dagger. I may need to examine it further, but this apparently is the murder weapon." Qaa folded the linen over the dagger, to preserve the evidence he had found. "I have seen all I need for now."

Qaa and Thanuny left the preparation tent, Qaa to his quarters to make notes, and Thanuny to handle temple affairs.

DAY 12 IN MONTH 3

Qaa helped Thanuny with the morning ritual, before leaving the temple. He needed a break alone after the previous day, to question some of the traders in the marketplace about the wine vessel and Iput. And he wanted some time to think over what he already knew, what pieces of the puzzle were still missing, and how to fit them all together. He went to his quarters and retrieved a large piece of linen, to cover his head and shoulders, protecting him from the unrelenting sun. He then stopped by the military barracks to inquire where he could get the leather belt and chest sash he needed to wear, as befitting his appointment as Chief. The Medjay directed him to a leather worker at the far end of the marketplace, where all the Medjay went for their equipment.

Qaa located the leather worker and was outfitted properly in no time. The worker also included the leather switch to carry in his belt. The man refused payment, but Qaa insisted; the kidet of silver he gave the worker could feed him and his family for several months, and it was well worth it. Qaa wandered through the marketplace, looking at the goods being offered. Brilliantly coloured fabrics from Phoenicia, resins and spices from Punt, gold and gemstones from Kush, exotic foods and animals from Babylon and Mittani, there was no end to the variety of goods. The sounds and smells transported him back to when he was a child, growing up here in Waset. But, the marketplace now was much larger than he remembered, and the goods were of far superior quality.

Qaa noted many of the merchants dealt in finished goods, lamps, furniture, clothing and the like. Only a few dealt in wines. After inquiring with two traders displaying vessels of imported wine, both mentioned that Bek would be the person to speak with. He was directed to a large tent near the end of the houses along the southern wall.

"Are you Bek, merchant in imported wines and fine goods?" Qaa inquired of the man in the brightly coloured, striped foreign robe, who was partially hidden beneath a table of goods.

"I am. Who inquires?" The merchant straightened up. He was tall for an Egyptian, but not quite as tall as Qaa. He looked to be about ten years his senior, and, even under the robe, Qaa could see he was a strong, muscular man. He also wore the traditional loincloth and kilt of an Egyptian nobleman, as well as sporting an elaborately decorated, foreign dagger at his waist. When the merchant saw the leather belt and sash, coupled with the kilt and *wesekh* collar of a *hem netjer*, he bowed in respect.

"I am Qaa, the new Chief of the Medjay. I am investigating the murder of Iput, but I am desirous of some information about a vessel of imported wine."

"Have you located the vessel which was stolen from me?"

"If I bring you the vessel, can you identify it?"

"I mark all my goods with the date I receive them and my special mark. On the second day of this month, I took the vessel in trade from a Canaanite I do a large business with. The vessel went missing three days later, when my daughter was alone here at the tent." Bek motioned to the young woman who was at the far end of the tent.

"Was that before or after Iput's death?"

"It was one day after her death."

"Have any other items disappeared recently that you had on display?"

"A Near East dagger, a rather fine bronze weapon, similar to the one I wear, which I received from a Phoenician trader I know well. It disappeared a few days before Iput was killed." The merchant's voice dropped slightly, and he seemed genuinely sad.

"Did you know Iput? Could you tell me about her? I would like to know what kind of person she was." Qaa knew a stranger would be more apt to tell the truth, than her husband or father.

"Do you have some time, Medjay? We can walk around the marketplace and I can tell you all I know of Iput."

"I have as much time as you can spare."

"Kiya, can you watch the tent while I speak with the Chief Medjay?" Bek motioned his daughter to come forward.

"Yes, Father. I shall make sure nothing disappears today." The young woman was lovely, about the same age as Iput. Thin, willowy, with the figure of a dancer, she moved with grace, but did not seem to realise how beautiful she was. Qaa could not help but stare at her. The two men had walked a safe distance when Bek spoke.

"Are you married, Medjay?"

"No, merchant, I am not." Qaa flushed visibly, as he thought of Nebettawy.

"You seem familiar to me, but I understand you are new to Waset. Nothing is secret here in the marketplace."

"I grew up in Waset, but have been in military service to the king the past twelve years, most recently in Kush." The men passed a trader selling fabric and threads. Next to him was an herbalist, selling potions and cures.

"Qaa, I know that name. Was your father Pentaweret, diplomat to the Lands to the West and Chief of the King's Chariotry?"

Qaa was puzzled. His father had been Chief of the Chariotry, but a diplomat, and the Lands to the West, why that was just a myth. "My father was Pentaweret, in service to both Sethnakht and Ramesses."

"I was young, but I knew your father. He and my father both served at the palace. You were the tall child, very serious, very quiet. Your father would be quite proud of you."

"Many thanks. I would like to speak with you again about my father. There are many things I do not know about him and many things I have forgotten. It would bring me great pleasure." Qaa had finally found a connection to his past, a past that was sketchy at best. "At present, I need to know what you can tell me about Iput and any recent thefts." A trader, sizing up the Medjay chief as a foreigner and an easy target, was trying to attract Qaa with silver and gold jewelry. With a fingering of his switch and a withering glance, Qaa stopped the man in his tracks.

"Iput was an outstanding wick-maker. I employed her to supply me with wicks for the lamps I export to the Near East. She wove a tight

wick, like no other, which was important to my Phoenician trader. He deals with some wealthy clients in Babylon, Punt, and Mycenae. She had become friendly with my daughter, which is how I met her."

"Did you know she had a husband?" If Iput was pregnant at the time of her death, it was only natural to assume the child was Unas's.

"I knew her husband was a pig; he beat her mercilessly. And he had taken up with another woman." Bek was red with anger.

"Pray continue. I would like to know all I can about her."

"She was well-liked by the merchants. We have heard the *hemet netjer* is providing for her burial preparations. The merchants would be more than willing to aid with the cost, she was quite special to us, and to me personally." Bek acknowledged one of the merchants selling local wine.

"What do you mean, merchant?"

"When I noticed the marks on her wrists, I asked her about her marriage. She told me how brutally Unas treated her; he already had a new woman, Takhat, a widow with three children. She supports herself by selling bead jewelry in the marketplace. She would leave her children with her sister and go to Unas's house at night. Unas would make Iput sleep on the floor, while he took Takhat to his bed."

Qaa was dumbfounded. It was not a difficult legal procedure to get a divorce in Waset, why would Unas humiliate his wife like that? Bek continued with his tale.

"I told Iput to leave his house; I would gladly welcome her in my home. At the very least, she would be safe and not have to witness her husband taking another woman. She moved into our house in the month of Epipi, in the season of Shemu last year."

"She had been living away from her husband for nine months?" A young woman was trying to attract Qaa's attention with her live chickens, geese, and goats; Qaa waved her off.

"Yes, Medjay. She had filed for divorce because she was barren, and Unas wanted children. Takhat has children and is willing to have more."

"Merchant, this is very important. Had she changed recently? Did she seem troubled or afraid?" Qaa now had another puzzle to solve. If Iput was not living with her husband, who had fathered her child? And why had Unas lied to him? Qaa was thankful he had not brought guards with him. He would need them when he again questioned the husband tomorrow.

 Claudia R. Dillaire

"She often went to the temple at night. Sometimes I would accompany her, though she preferred to go alone. One night in Paopi, I heard her crying after she came home from the temple. I asked her about it the following morning, but she said I must have been mistaken. After that, she always seemed sad."

Paopi, five months ago. What had happened that night and why had she not told someone? Or had she told Nebettawy? He needed to speak with her today.

"I never pressed her for answers, but the longer she lived in my home, the more I found myself attracted to her. She was so delicate, so fragile. She had suffered so much and deserved better. I told her that if she wanted, I would be happy to take her as my wife, when she divorced Unas. That seemed to please her. I told her she was welcome in my bed, but she never came to me, and I would not force myself on her. I am not that type of man, though I have been without a woman for many years now."

"What can you tell me of the days before her death?"

"She had been ill for several days, but refused to stay home. She was working in my tent, with Kiya, when Unas and Takhat came by to heckle her. She and Takhat exchanged angry words. Unas was berating her for being a worthless woman and Takhat was acting like a whore, touching Unas and kissing him."

"You saw this for yourself!?"

"My daughter was with Iput. I was trading with the Canaanite; it was the day I received the wine vessel. It was also the day the dagger went missing. Do you think Unas or Takhat had something to do with Iput's death?" The colour drained from the merchant's face. "If I thought Unas killed her, I would gladly strangle him with my bare hands." Bek was furious now. They had made the circuit around the southern marketplace and were almost at Bek's tent.

"I do not yet know who is responsible, but, since you cared so much for her, I shall be sure to let you know when I solve the case. You have been an immense help to me; I shall not forget your assistance. And I shall tell the *hemet netjer* of the merchants' generous offer. She will appreciate your kindness. May I call on you again?"

Bek bowed to the Medjay. "I look forward to meeting with you again. I hope the next time the conversation shall be more festive."

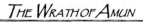

THE WRATH OF AMUN

Qaa, in turn, bowed to the merchant and his daughter. "You have been a great help and I know how to reward a kindness." He turned and headed to the temple, to record his notes of the conversation.

Qaa left the temple after performing the noon ritual with Thanuny and walked the short distance to the palace. He wished to speak with Ramesses before he questioned Nebettawy. He found the king in his private quarters, reading a message brought from Men-nefer.

"Father, I have instructed the Medjay to dispatch soldiers to the next port on the Nile. The day of Raneb's death, three of our traders put out from Waset to Punt, but one vessel set out at first light to Phoenicia. I would like to question the Phoenician captain and passengers. The dagger used to kill Iput is from the Near East and was traded in the marketplace by a Phoenician trader."

"Do you think this Phoenician killed Iput and Raneb?"

"At this point, I have more questions than answers. I have heard much that troubles me and I now need to speak with your daughter. The questions I have for her are quite disturbing, but I must know what Iput told her."

"I shall summon her and remain while you speak with her."

"Father, she may speak more plainly if you are not present. But, I shall not be alone with her. I have asked the Captain of the Medjay to meet me here."

"Qaa, do you fear the magic of my daughter?" Ramesses looked quite amused with Qaa's dilemma.

"I do not fear her magic, but I shall be more at ease in the presence of others."

"That is wise, my son." Ramesses crossed to the entrance of his quarters. "Medjay, summon my daughter at the temple and tell her the Chief of the Medjay has some questions for her."

Ramesses and Qaa sat and discussed some of the particulars of Iput's death. The Captain of the Medjay joined them, while they awaited Nebettawy. A servant brought in fruit, cheese, sliced meat, wine, beer, and bread for them to refresh themselves, and exited without a word. The men had opened a third vessel of wine when Nebettawy arrived. She had dressed carefully, hoping to be alone with Qaa. A sheer linen full length tunic clung to her body, like a second skin, and the outer full length tunic, although nearly transparent, had lovely gold and silver embroidery covering her breasts. She wore an anklet of bells and a belt of gold and silver, cinched tight around her slim waist, which also chimed as she moved. Though her expression never changed, it was obvious she was displeased Qaa was not alone. She bowed low in respect to her father.

"Daughter, how lovely you look today. Qaa has some questions for you about Iput. I have matters to attend to, so I shall take my leave. Qaa, I expect you to keep me apprised of your investigation."

Qaa bowed to Ramesses. "Your majesty, I shall meet with you after I have made further inquiries."

Ramesses kissed his daughter on the forehead before he exited the room and the Captain of the Medjay moved to stand at the doorway. Qaa turned to look at Nebettawy, praying he would be able to elicit the answers he so desperately needed. He also prayed he could withstand the power of her spell over him.

"Nebettawy, I shall try not to upset you, but I have heard some rather disturbing information about Iput. I need to know why she was seeing you, what she may have told you in confidence, and why she was coming to see you the evening of her death."

Nebettawy sat in her father's chair and Qaa offered her a bowl of wine. She took the bowl and brushed her hand against his. Her touch was like a feather, so soft, so gentle. He could not let her cloud his mind, but she always had the ability to enthrall him.

"Qaa, why do you not send the Medjay away so we may speak in private?" Nebettawy's eyes pierced him to his very soul.

"I can not do that. I made a promise to your father and the sooner I finish my investigation, the sooner I may be released from that promise." Qaa could play her game, though not quite as well.

"If I assist you in your investigation, will you then allow yourself to be alone with me?"

"Yes, Sister, I welcome the day when we may be alone. So, I beg you, help me, Nebettawy." His voice had taken on the tenor of pleading; by the gods how he ached for her. Qaa could feel himself slipping under her spell. He turned away from her so as not to look into her eyes.

"Then, my brother, I shall assist you. Ask whatever you need."

Qaa turned back to face Nebettawy. "What did Iput tell you of her father?"

"She told me her father used to beat her as a child. She did not travel to the East bank often, so she would not have to see him."

"What did she say of her husband?"

Nebettawy was uncomfortable discussing the intimate details of Iput's marriage with Qaa. But, if she did not tell him what she knew ... She had waited twelve years to lie with him, and she could wait no longer. She blushed deeply as she looked at Qaa, thinking of him as her lover, taking her in his strong arms.

"Sister, are you feeling ill? You are quite flushed." Qaa poured her more wine.

Nebettawy took a sip and that seemed to calm her. "Iput's husband was a brutal man, who took up with another woman."

"Did Iput ever tell you what Unas did to her?"

"I would rather not say, but, she did tell me many confidences about her marriage." Nebettawy looked away, the memories of Iput's stunning admissions still disturbed her.

"I understand, and I shall not press you for further details, unless it becomes necessary. Do you know the woman he has taken up with?"

"Her name is Takhat. She is a widow with three children. Her husband was a stone cutter in the tombs, who was crushed to death in an accident. She supports herself selling necklaces in the marketplace."

Nebettawy had confirmed some of the information he had heard. Unfortunately, the questions he now had to ask were rather delicate.

"Sister, I must ask, did Iput tell you she was divorcing Unas?"

"Yes, she did so at my urging. Unas wanted children and Iput was barren. She would have been better off without him. I told her she could find work at the temple."

"Nebettawy, this is very important. Did she tell you if she was still living with Unas?"

Again, Nebettawy blushed. Iput had told her about Takhat coming to their house. "Iput said she had left Unas and had moved into the house of Bek, the merchant, and his daughter."

"When did she move?" Qaa held his breath.

"I do not remember the month, but it was the season of Shemu last year."

"Did something happen to Iput in Paopi? Did she mention anything to you?"

Nebettawy gasped. How could he know what Iput had told her in confidence? "Yes, but Qaa, how did you know?"

"Bek told me she came home from the temple one evening crying. When he questioned her, she told him he must have been mistaken. I need to know what happened, for it may be the reason she was killed."

"Qaa, I do not know if I can repeat what she said." Nebettawy trembled, her hands shook, and she reached for the drinking bowl. After draining the wine, she held it out for Qaa to again fill.

"Sister, I am sorry to have to ask. I have spoken with Unas and he has lied to me. I need to know if he killed her, or if someone else had reason to kill her."

"I offered to go with her to speak with Raneb, but she was too ashamed. She begged me to never speak of the matter. The night of her death she was coming to see me at the temple to tell me everything."

"What do you mean 'everything'?"

"I do not know, for those were her words. She was troubled by many things, but I know only what she told me."

"Nebettawy, what happened in Paopi?"

Nebettawy's face had turned the colour of sun-bleached linen. She bowed her head and began to cry softly. "Iput was attacked on her way to Bek's residence, after leaving the temple. She did not see who attacked her, but she said she knew who he was."

"What was the nature of the attack? I know this is difficult, but it is vital." Qaa wanted to reach out to Nebettawy and hold her, but he risked the wrath of Amun and her father. "Do you want to continue at a later time? I could have the Medjay summon one of your sisters to sit with you until you are feeling better."

"No, I wish to finish this now and never speak of it again. I have been troubled with dreams since she told me of the attack. If I reveal what I know, I may find solace in sleep." Nebettawy composed herself. She sat for a few minutes and took another sip of wine. After a deep breath, she continued to speak. "A man grabbed her from behind, took her violently, and ... abused her with an object."

Without warning, Nebettawy bolted from the room. The Captain of the Medjay started after her, but Qaa stopped him.

"Medjay, summon the king for me."

The Medjay captain exited the room, while Qaa pieced together the information he had. Iput knew who had attacked her five months ago, and she must surely have known she was pregnant. Was that what she was going to reveal to Nebettawy the night of her death? If her attacker knew she was going to the temple, could Nebettawy be in danger as well? Qaa looked up to see Nebettawy leaning against the doorway, pale, shaking, tears staining her face. Her father was right behind her, with the Medjay captain.

"Father, would you please help Nebettawy to her seat. She is feeling ill."

"I found her retching in the antechamber. Qaa, how could you upset my daughter like this?" Ramesses was crimson with anger.

"When I have finished questioning her, I shall answer for my actions. Nebettawy, if you feel you are up to a few more questions, I shall be brief and have you escorted back to the temple."

Nebettawy was again seated. "Father, I shall be fine. You may leave us, so we may continue."

"I shall be right outside in the corridor. Qaa, I hope I have not misplaced my trust in you." Ramesses turned and stormed out of the room.

Qaa could not help himself. He had upset Nebettawy and wanted to comfort her. He reached out and put his hand over hers, squeezing it gently, before Ramesses could see this breach of protocol.

"Nebettawy, my apologies I had to ask you these questions. But I just have two more. Did Iput ever tell you who the man was?"

"No, she did not." Nebettawy could barely speak, she was trembling and clearly distraught.

"Was Iput ill at the time of her death?"

"She said she had been feeling ill for several days, but ..."

"But, what? What did she tell you?"

"She said she would tell me everything at the temple that evening. She said she could prove everything she was going to tell me. But, she never made it to the temple."

"Let me get someone to escort you back to your quarters."

"Many thanks, but I would like to lie down here at the palace before I return to the temple." Nebettawy struggled to her feet, but her legs did not want to support her. She sat down again.

"My king, would you join us?" Qaa knew Ramesses would attend to his daughter. He could collect his thoughts before he had to explain himself to the king.

Ramesses strode into the room and went to his daughter.

"Father, may I stay here until sunset? I would like to lie down." Nebettawy was pallid and shaking. Ramesses put his arms around his daughter and helped her to her feet.

"Qaa, let me attend to my daughter. I shall return presently and I expect an acceptable explanation for your behaviour."

After settling Nebettawy, Ramesses returned to his private quarters. The king was seething with anger; no one treated his daughter in such a manner.

Qaa, taking liberties, put up his hand to silence the king. "Your majesty, before you speak, I feel it is my duty to inform you that your daughter's life may be in danger. The person who killed Iput may think your daughter knows who he is and why he killed Iput."

"What did you ask my daughter?"

"I asked her to confirm the information I learned from Bek, the merchant. She did so, and gave me further information that Iput had told her in confidence."

Ramesses crumpled onto a chair and poured himself a bowl of wine, offering Qaa the wine vessel. Qaa filled his bowl and he sat, facing the king. After taking a drink, Qaa revealed to the king his suspicions.

"Iput was raped going home from the temple in Paopi. I believe her attacker threatened her into silence, but Iput had had enough of living in fear and was about to tell Nebettawy. I suspect Iput was killed to prevent her from telling anyone the truth. And, if her attacker thinks Iput revealed the information to Nebettawy, he may make an attempt on her life."

Ramesses was incredulous. No one would dare touch the princess. "I can have Medjay with her at all times, but I know my daughter. She is proud and feigns bravery; she shall refuse."

"I would prefer you speak with her about the matter. She may listen to you; I have upset her greatly, though that was not my intention. I ask you, Father, for your forgiveness. I pray I do not have to ask her anything further about this incident."

"Qaa, I would ask you to not bring up this matter with my daughter. If you wish to question her about it further, it shall be in my presence."

"I understand, my lord."

"Do you know who committed this crime?"

"Each piece of information leads me to a new puzzle. I know Unas is lying, but I do not think he attacked his wife. Whoever raped Iput in Paopi felt it was worth killing her to keep her quiet."

"What could be accomplished by killing that poor woman?"

Qaa wrestled with what he knew; Iput's pregnancy may have been worth killing for. "Father, I have learned many disturbing facts from your daughter and the priests who assisted Raneb. But there are things your daughter does not know, and it is best she be protected from them. When I am able, I shall reveal what I know. For now, you must trust me."

 Claudia R. Dillaire

DAY 13 IN MONTH 3

Qaa departed the temple after the morning ritual, stopping by the military barracks for two Medjay. The men headed for the goldsmith tents at the far end of the mortuary complex. Qaa did not see the overseer and, ignoring the oppressive heat, strode to Unas, who was sitting in front of a brazier. Upon seeing the Medjay Chief, Unas dropped the tongs and attempted to flee. Qaa, his long legs easily closing the distance between them, knocked Unas to the ground and held him in place with his reed-sandaled foot until the Medjay caught up. Pulling the apprentice to a standing position, Qaa handed him to the Medjay.

"Unas, did I not tell you if you lied to me I would return?" Qaa struck the man a sharp blow to the abdomen.

"Me-djay." Unas tried to fill his lungs with air.

"Tell me about Takhat. And if you lie to me, again, it shall be your last lie."

Qaa motioned for the Medjay to release Unas. He waited for the apprentice to catch his breath.

"Medjay." Unas bowed low to Qaa, preferring not to get another beating like the last one. "I ... I told you, I have another woman now." The terror showed clearly on Unas's face and Qaa wanted to make him even more uncomfortable.

"How long has she been coming to your bed?"

"I ... I did not want anyone to know Iput had left me." Unas began to squirm like a water fowl caught in a trap.

Qaa was in no mood for more lies. Unas had been flaunting his new woman in the marketplace, yet he claimed he did not want anyone to know. All he seemed capable of doing was lying.

"If you do not tell me the truth, now, you shall beg me for death. Speak, apprentice."

"Iput had to be beaten to submit to me. I wanted a woman who would not fight my desires. When I found one, I took her to my home, and told Iput to leave. She had no where to go, so she chose to stay, until she found another man to take her in." Unas cowered, expecting to be struck.

"When did she leave your home?"

"Last year, in the season of Shemu."

"You have been lying with Takhat since last year. Had you lain with Iput since she left your house?"

"No, Medjay. I was glad to see her go."

Qaa looked at the Medjay and nodded his head slightly. The two men grabbed Unas by the arms and held him tightly. Qaa withdrew his leather switch from his belt and struck Unas a sound blow across the left cheek, drawing blood. He wiped the switch on Unas's loincloth, before securing it in his belt.

"Unas, I do not wish to return. Do you have any information about Iput's death?"

"No, Medjay."

"I pray, for your sake, you have told me the truth. If you have concealed any fact, I shall not be as merciful the next time. Medjay, you may release him."

Qaa sent the Medjay back to the barracks, while he leisurely strolled down the avenue of the Festival Calendars on his way to the palace. The time alone, in the warming rays of Ra, gave him time to consider all he knew so far.

"My lord, if I may speak with you?"

Ramesses was playing *senet* in an antechamber with his daughter, Tentopet, who was great with child. She smiled when she saw Qaa. They were the same age and she had been smitten with him when he first came to live in their home, but he only had eyes for her sister, Nebettawy.

"Daughter, excuse me. And I shall know if you cheat." Ramesses stood, kissed his daughter on the forehead, and escorted Qaa across the corridor to his private quarters.

"I have an unusual request, Father. I need to gain some information from a young widow, Takhat. She supports herself in the marketplace. I have questioned her lover, Unas, and do not feel she would be forthcoming with me. May I ask Nebettawy to speak with her?"

"How do you think my daughter can help?" Ramesses was concerned for her safety.

"I would like to take Nebettawy for a walk around the marketplace and temple complex. There is much I would like to see and I could not ask for a better guide. I shall be with her at all times. When she questions the young woman, I can move a discreet distance away to give them privacy to speak."

"This is highly unusual, but I appreciate the seriousness of this crime. You came to ask my permission and I have no objections."

Qaa bowed to Ramesses. "Many thanks, Father. I promise I shall keep her safe."

"Who shall protect you from my daughter?" Ramesses's eyes twinkled with their shared knowledge of his daughter's magical abilities.

Qaa sauntered the short distance from the palace to the temple residences. He strode the corridor to Nebettawy's quarters with anticipation. When he reached her doorway and looked in, she was sitting at her writing table, which was covered with her magical objects and ingredients.

She was the only person in the temple to prepare all the amulets requested of her and the temple priests. She oversaw the design of each one — the material to be used, the inscriptions, and its intended purpose. On this day, there must have been twenty or more in front of her, made of clay, faience, and precious metals.

She carefully handled each one, anointing it with the appropriate oil or unguent and reciting sacred spells to infuse it with magic. She worked quickly, but not carelessly. She was intently focused upon her work and did not appear to notice Qaa in the doorway.

Her hair was splayed on her shoulders, resembling a shawl coloured of lapis lazuli and onyx. He had never seen her in public without her hair pinned back. Her sheer, loose fitting robe, made of the finest royal linen, puddled at her feet. He imagined this was how she looked when she arose each morning. Seeing her like this was like seeing her naked, free of constraint, natural, vulnerable. He could not bear to look at her, she was so captivating. He loved her so much it was painful.

She stood and slowly turned, her eyes fixed upon his, as she let the robe slip from her shoulders. The nearly transparent tunic she wore under it clung to her body like morning dew. She smiled as she walked toward him, slowly, deliberately, with the grace of a gazelle. The heat began in his loins and started to spread up into his abdomen and out into his thighs.

"Do you still desire me, Qaa?" She stood directly in front of him, legs apart, their bodies almost touching.

"I have, always. But I gave your father my word I would not lie with you." He could feel himself slipping under her spell yet again.

"It is our destiny to be husband and wife. But, I can still pleasure you without joining with you, my brother."

She reached out, took his left hand, and placed it on her breast. His entire body shook with desire. She slowly slid his hand down her chest, her abdomen, to bring it to rest on the hot, moist flesh between her legs.

"Sister, we can not do this." Qaa could barely breathe, nor could he stop himself or her.

Qaa's body was trembling so badly, he placed his right hand on the doorway to keep his knees from buckling. Still holding his hand, she reached out to him with her free hand and ran her fingers down his bare chest. Her touch, like a feather, made his loins throb and the friction from his loincloth made the feelings even more intense.

Her hand slid down the outside of his loincloth and rubbed his erection, deftly massaging him, stimulating him through the coarse linen. He was panting like a jackal in heat and his legs felt like water. His rational mind ceased fighting and he surrendered to the sensations around him.

Her lids were heavy with desire, her pomegranate lips opened slightly as she gasped in delight. Her breathing quickened and her thighs, like the jaws of a crocodile, held his hand fast, as she ground against the moist linen between her legs. He could feel her hot, wet flesh and the sweet aroma of her musky passion pushed him beyond reason. Her body began

to shudder and her hand sped up its pace to relieve his torment. As Qaa swallowed his anguished cry of pleasure, mixed with shame, his seed drenched the inside of his loincloth. She leaned in and kissed him gently on the lips, then his entire world went black.

She had to work fast. She had not been expecting Qaa and if anyone found out he was in her quarters while she was not dressed, they would both face punishment. Her clothes had been laid out by her attendant earlier that morning. Nebettawy stripped off her tunic and tossed it aside. She snatched a piece of linen off her writing table and wiped the wetness from between her legs. She placed the linen in a clay vessel, pulled on her loincloth, and slid her fresh tunic over her head. Expertly, she twisted her hair up, around, and held it tightly at the nape of her neck, as she secured it with two gold and lapis hair pins. She then slipped her pleated linen wrap over her shoulders, cinched it at the waist, and smoothed it over her hips.

Now she could turn her attention to Qaa. He was far too heavy for her to lift, but she could have the priests move him, now that she was dressed. She took another piece of linen from her table and knelt down beside Qaa. She reached her hand inside his loincloth to moisten the fabric with his seed. She stood up, put the linen in the same vessel with her cloth, and hid the vessel in her magical cabinet.

"Thanuny, priests, come, I need your assistance." Nebettawy again knelt beside Qaa.

Thanuny came running down the corridor, to find Nebettawy tending to Qaa. She was fanning him and mopping his brow with the hem of her dress.

"He must have been overcome by the heat. He came to speak with me and just collapsed in the doorway. Place him on my bed. I shall get water and a vessel of wine."

As Thanuny and two of the lesser priests struggled to move Qaa, Nebettawy sprinted down the corridor to the provisions room in the temple. She grabbed a vessel of wine, a vessel of water, and a large bowl. Before returning, she made a detour to Qaa's quarters. There she found him a clean loincloth, which she concealed beneath her wrap. Now she could return to her quarters and attend to Qaa.

Thanuny and the two priests had managed to get Qaa onto Nebettawy's bed. The men were panting and sweating from their labourious task. Nebettawy placed the vessels and bowl on her dressing table, poured water in the bowl, and soaked a linen cloth in it. She wrung it out, placed it on his forehead, and knelt beside him.

"Many thanks, Thanuny. I shall attend to him. If I have any further need, I shall call for you."

The priests exited Nebettawy's quarters. She stood, took a drinking bowl from her shelf, and poured some wine into it. She took the linen cloth from Qaa's head, cooled it in the water, and replaced it. He was beginning to stir. She brought the drinking bowl to him and raised his head to drink. He opened his eyes and saw the concern on her face.

"Sister, why ... ?"

"I can think of nothing but you. I can not control my desires."

"Nebettawy, we risk the wrath of the gods and your father. And in the temple; Nebettawy, how could you do that to me, to us?"

"I love you, Qaa. And I know you love me. I had to touch you, feel your touch, to quell the passion which consumes me." Nebettawy had tears in her eyes. "You do not know how I suffer, each time I see you. I want you, my brother, and I am not ashamed of what I have done."

Qaa tried to rise but his head swam. He put his head on her headrest and took her hand.

"We must be careful. We can not touch each other here in the temple. If word got back to your father, we would never be allowed to join together."

"The only reason my father withholds his blessing is because your mother was not Egyptian. And yet, my father surrounds himself with advisors, Syrians, Canaanites, Sherdens, who are full-blooded foreigners. Do they really have the interests of my father and Egypt in their hearts, as you do?" Nebettawy's cheeks were flushed with anger.

She took the cloth from his head and cooled it again in the water. As she placed it on his forehead, he reached up and grabbed her arm. He looked into her eyes, pulled her close, and kissed her palm. She reached for the drinking bowl. Qaa was able to prop himself up on one elbow and drained the wine. He held out the bowl for her to fill. After a second drink, he felt well enough to sit.

"I was coming to ask you to accompany me to the marketplace when you ambushed me. I asked your father if you could help me with my investigation."

Claudia R. Dillaire

"Me? How may I help? I am a *hemet netjer*, not a Medjay."

"You know these people far better than I. And Takhat may speak more plainly with you than she would with me. I have questioned Unas twice and still he lies to me." Qaa's head was still buzzing, but he was regaining his senses.

"I know Takhat from the temple. She has consulted with me on a number of occasions. I shall get whatever information you need."

"I shall need to stop at my quarters before we leave for the marketplace." Qaa started to rise from the bed.

"I took the liberty to stop by your quarters. You may dress here." She removed the loincloth from under her wrap and handed it to him.

Qaa was thunderstruck. He could not undress in front of her, and certainly not in the temple. What they had done was bad enough.

"Are you still shy in front of me, Qaa? You were as a child. You are to be my husband, it is our destiny, and yet you continue to fight it. There is no shame in showing yourself to me."

"I am different, Nebettawy. You are the only one who did not seem to notice. But, still I am uncomfortable naked in the presence of others." Qaa's face had turned as red as the desert sand.

"Accept my apologies, my brother. I shall turn away and you may dress." Nebettawy turned her back to Qaa.

He stripped off his kilt and undid his loincloth. He dried himself and dropped the loincloth on the floor. He quickly pulled on the clean coarse linen and tied it around his waist. He shook the sand from his kilt before putting it back on. He reached out and touched Nebettawy on the shoulder. He turned her around to face him. She had been crying.

"Nebettawy, you have always treated me as an Egyptian. You witnessed the torment I endured as a child because I was different from you and your brothers and sisters. Coming back to Waset has reawakened many of those memories, making me feel just as I did as a child, wanting to hide myself from you."

"Qaa, when I look at you, all I see is the man I love. To me, you are as Egyptian as I. My hope is that one day I shall no longer see that torment in your eyes." Nebettawy bit her lower lip to stop it from quivering.

"That is my hope, as well. And, that may be one reason why I love you so." Qaa put his arms around her and stroked her back.

 The Wrath of Amun

They left the temple residences by the eastern exit. Passing the housing for the lesser priests, who rotated in monthly, they wandered through the temple gardens. The trees blocked much of the unrelenting sun, creating a cool, restful sanctuary. Fruit trees were in bloom, vegetables were close to harvest, and flowers and herbs were in abundance. Beyond the garden, temple workers were tending the beehives, extracting precious honey, to be used in food, wine, and medicinal preparations.

"The marketplace shall be crowded at this time of day. Let us rest here for a moment and you can tell me what I need to know." Nebettawy led Qaa to a stone bench underneath a grape arbour.

"How well do you know Takhat? Will she be forthcoming with you?"

"I have counseled her on several occasions, during her marriage and since the death of her husband. I have never felt she was being anything but truthful with me."

"You knew she had taken up with Unas?" Qaa looked at her intently.

"Yes, I knew. I do not know why women find him so appealing. I sense that he is not trustworthy and he makes me uncomfortable."

"You know Unas?" Qaa was interested in what she knew about him.

"I know some of the temple workers well, some I know only by face. Until Iput came to me, I only knew him by face, but I already disliked him. He did not act properly for a man of his lowly status."

"I am well aware of his nature. He failed to bow before me, but he shall not make that mistake again. I fear he may have threatened Takhat, or told her what to say to me. She may speak more plainly with you."

"I shall do whatever you ask, my brother. What do you wish to know from Takhat?" Nebettawy reached over and took Qaa's hand.

"Nebettawy, you may be in danger. I have consulted with your father and have assured him I shall be close by. If you sense anything, I shall be with Bek, the merchant. I shall not allow any harm to come to you." Qaa's face was deadly serious. He raised her hand to his lips and kissed her palm.

"Qaa, I know these people. Who would want to harm me?"

"Sister, Iput's secret was worth killing for, which puts you in danger. If you do not wish to assist any further, I shall not press you."

Claudia R. Dillaire

"I am not afraid, and I shall not be intimidated. Tell me what you need, and I shall get your answers." Nebettawy's demeanour was cool and confident.

"Confirm for me how long Takhat has been lying with Unas and where they were the evening of Iput's death. If she is willing, ask her what she and Iput fought about in the marketplace. And, finally, find out why she wishes to remain with him and if he beats her. I know this is much to ask of you, but the sooner I have answers, the sooner I may solve this puzzle."

They passed behind the palace and came to the end of the inner wall. Qaa could not bring himself to tell Nebettawy this was where Iput had been attacked. From here, if they turned left, they would approach the First Pylon. Rather, they turned right, beside several residences which faced the southern wall. The marketplace was just a short walk, but the sounds and smells filled the air, giving Waset a festive atmosphere. The noise from the shouts of the vendors made it difficult to speak to one another. Qaa gently guided Nebettawy along the streets of the marketplace. She was greeted warmly by many of the sellers; it was apparent she was loved by her people. Many wished to give her goods, but she gently refused, telling them they could fetch a good price, rather than donating to the temple. She stopped briefly at an herbalist's tent to give the woman a list of items she would need and requested the woman bring them to her at the temple in the next few days. The woman bowed her acceptance.

"If you wish to refresh yourself, any one of these vendors shall gladly give you whatever you desire."

"Let us find Bek. Then we can seek out refreshment." Qaa did not want Nebettawy out in the open any longer than necessary, though he did not suspect anyone would make an attempt on her in this crowd.

They continued through the southern marketplace, drinking in the aroma of cooking meat, fresh fruits, vegetables, herbs, spices, and live animals. It was like a city within a city, with its own rhythm, its own voice, its own code of conduct. Vendors squabbled with each other over a fair exchange, while others hawked at passersby. Qaa had missed leisurely walks through the marketplace; he had wandered these same streets as a child, with his mother. Now, he walked, head held high, with the woman he loved at his side. Clearly, he was the most fortunate, and the most euphoric, man in Waset.

"Merchant, how is trade today?" Qaa greeted Bek as he and Nebettawy approached his tent.

"Medjay, it is good to see you again." Bek bowed in deference to Qaa and the *hemet netjer.*

"I was looking for a guide to show me the marketplace, and the *hemet netjer* offered, since she wished to see the herbalist. Would you join us for some wine?" Qaa hoped to lure Bek away from his tent for a short time.

"Since nothing went missing, I think my daughter is quite capable of taking care of the tent in my absence. Kiya, I shall return shortly." Bek called to his daughter, who complied with her father's wishes. "*Hemet netjer,* it is always a pleasure to see you. Is your father well?"

"Yes, Bek, he is well. I shall give him your regards when I see him this evening. Qaa, I see the stall I wish to stop at. Why do you and Bek not go on ahead and partake in some wine?" Nebettawy had spied Takhat's stall and she was alone.

"Medjay, there is a fine wine merchant I trade with. Let me get us a vessel of wine and we can converse."

Nebettawy walked away from the men and began to engage Takhat in conversation. Bek was negotiating with the wine trader, when Qaa turned and offered to meet the trader's price. Bek was astonished to see Qaa hand the man a kidet of silver.

"Medjay, he has not seen that much wealth in years. He may not wish to trade with me any longer if he can fetch that kind of price from you."

"Merchant, I need your assistance." Though Qaa was speaking to Bek, his eyes never left Nebettawy. He could not hear her, but he could see Takhat was unhappy.

"What do you need?"

"I need your impression of Unas and Takhat. What kind of woman is she?"

"Why do you not ask the *hemet netjer?*" Bek could see the concern on Qaa's face.

"Merchant, she is taking a great risk by speaking to Takhat. I need to know if Takhat might harm her, or if Unas is capable of it." Qaa's face flushed at the mention of Nebettawy.

"My apologies, Medjay. Takhat is lonely and a widow. She is quite a caring mother and I do not think her capable of harming anyone. Unas is a pig and I think he delights in hurting women. But, I do not think he is man enough to harm the *hemet netjer.*"

"Many thanks. Let us have a drink. I must keep watch on the *hemet netjer,* but we can still enjoy ourselves."

Bek opened the wine vessel and offered it to Qaa. He took a sip and handed it back to Bek. For a local wine, it was quite fine and refreshing. Bek took a sip and handed it back to Qaa.

"Medjay, I heard something from one of the wine dealers. It may not be important, but Takhat traded an expensive vessel of wine with Ghedi, the Phoenician, the day before he departed Waset. I wondered how she could afford such wine, unless it was the one stolen from me."

"You do not have to observe formality with me, Bek." Qaa was watching Nebettawy and Takhat. Takhat was shaking her head, not wishing to speak any longer. Nebettawy reached out and touched Takhat on the arm and continued to talk to her. "Have you seen anyone with Takhat recently?"

"I have only seen her with Unas. Often they look happy, but I have seen her look frightened of him."

Nebettawy had turned away from Takhat and walked back to rejoin Qaa and Bek. Qaa took a sip from the wine vessel and held it out to Nebettawy. She took a quick sip and handed it to Bek. She looked troubled by what she had learned from Takhat.

"My bro ... , *hem netjer,* I have much to tell you." The look which passed between Nebettawy and Qaa was not lost on Bek, and he smiled knowingly at them both.

"Bek, have you ever seen Unas in the marketplace with anyone else? Does he have a friend who might know him well?"

"I do not know him well enough to answer that. You should inquire with the Overseer of the Temple Goldsmiths. If anyone would know, he would."

The three of them continued their walk through the marketplace, sharing the wine vessel, until they arrived back at Bek's tent. He bid Qaa and Nebettawy farewell.

"Many thanks, Bek, you have been a great help. May I call upon you again?"

"Yes, Qaa, you may."

Qaa, still in possession of the wine vessel, let Nebettawy guide him back to the temple complex and the grape arbour. When they were settled on the bench, Qaa handed Nebettawy the wine vessel, which she eagerly accepted.

"What did you learn from Takhat?"

"She and Unas have been meeting for over a year, but he took her into his home about nine months ago. She was lying with him the night of Iput's death."

Qaa took the wine vessel, which she had offered him. He took a drink and set the vessel on the bench. Their stories matched, but Unas could have told her what to say.

"I asked her about her fight with Iput. She did not wish to talk to me about it. But I pressed her and she said she was angry that Iput had not yet obtained a divorce from Unas. Takhat told Iput if she did not obtain it soon, Unas would request one, on the grounds that she was barren."

"Nebettawy, you have done well. I did not wish to include you in this investigation. I shall do my best to not involve you any further." Qaa took her hand and squeezed it gently.

"Qaa, I have more to tell you. Takhat has a pressing reason for wanting Unas to be free to marry her. She is pregnant with his child." Nebettawy's lower lip trembled. "And, I noticed, Takhat had fresh bruises on her arms, as if someone had held her and shook her. When I asked if Unas had hurt her, she refused to answer me." She rested her head on his shoulder and started to cry. "Qaa, I do not wish to see her end up as Iput did."

DAY 14 IN MONTH 3

Before leaving the temple on further investigation, Qaa assisted Thanuny with the morning ritual. Today he would speak with the Overseer of the Temple Goldsmiths to find out the kind of man Unas really was. He left the residences and walked to the northern edge of the temple enclosure. The tents were set up outside the inner wall and enclosed by mud-brick walls, near the Western gateway. The smiths were hard at work and the overseer was walking around the tents to make sure no one was idle. When he saw Qaa, he immediately bowed and walked quickly to find out how he could be of service.

"Overseer, I have some general questions about the apprentice, Unas. I am new to Waset and would like to know if he is a good worker. Have you ever had any trouble with him? Does he socialise with any of the other workers?"

The overseer relaxed noticeably. "Unas works as long as someone watches him. I do not have trouble with him, though I suspect he would prefer to be the one giving orders." His breath was laboured and he wheezed as he spoke, like many of the smiths and stone cutters.

The man had evidently been a smith at one time, bearing many of the usual scars and burns. He apparently had served the temple for many years to have attained the position of overseer. Qaa did not know if it was because he had been skilled enough to work his way into the position or if he had been elevated to the position as a result of an injury suffered on the job. The man had a jagged scar across his left cheek, which ran down his left shoulder, ending at the stump of what had been his left arm.

"Is Unas friendly with any of his fellow workmen?"

"He keeps to himself, but has developed a friendship with Khety. They have been seen taking their meal break together."

"How long has Unas worked at the temple?"

"He started out as a fire tender, when his father was still alive. He was ten or so at the time. He did not become an apprentice until a few years ago. So he has been with the temple fifteen years or more."

"Who did he first apprentice with?"

"He first worked under his father. He has been apprenticed to Khety for two years now."

"Many thanks, overseer. I appreciate you answering my questions. I have seen some of the items your men produce for the temple and they are quite remarkable." Qaa meant that sincerely.

"Thank you, *hem netjer*. I have served the temple all my life and am here at your service." He bowed in deference to Qaa.

"I would like to speak with Khety. I shall not take much of his time."

"*Hem netjer*, we serve the temple. You may speak with him as long as it takes."

The overseer led Qaa to a tent near the end of the mud-brick wall, with one man inside. The overseer bowed and took his leave. Khety was a short, solid man, old enough to be Qaa's father. Dressed only in a loincloth, he was sitting in front of a stone anvil, which rested atop a wooden anvil block. The chasing hammer stone lay on the ground next to him as he applied the smoothing hammer stone to a gold ritual bowl. His hands were large and powerful and bore the unmistakable signs of a smith. He had a persistent cough, probably from breathing in the smoke and dust from his many years of service, and his left eye was permanently closed from an old injury. Qaa noted the goldsmith wore a dagger, bronze with bone handle, at his waist.

"Are you Khety?"

The goldsmith looked up at the imposing figure of the *hem netjer*, also wearing the belt and sash of a Medjay. He put down his hammer stone, stood, and bowed low to Qaa.

"I am Khety. How may I serve you, *hem netjer.*" The goldsmith hissed his words.

"I am Qaa, the new Chief of the Medjay. I have come to Waset to look into the death of Iput, wife of Unas. I understand he is your apprentice."

"He is. I knew his father and have taken to him as I would a son."

"Did you know his wife?"

"I did not know her well, *hem netjer.* I did know Unas was unhappy she had not provided him with a child." The goldsmith coughed loudly and spat. He wheezed with each breath.

"Do you know the new woman he has taken up with?"

"Takhat, the widow. She is a lovely young woman. She will provide Unas with many children, as she should."

"Takhat was seen in the marketplace trading an expensive vessel of wine. Could she and Unas afford such an item?"

"*Hem netjer*, Unas is fortunate to get his ration of bread and beer. Takhat comes from a family of farmers on the East bank. Whoever said she had a vessel of wine must have been mistaken."

"Many thanks, Khety. I appreciate you speaking plainly with me. I shall not forget your assistance." Qaa turned and headed toward the marketplace to speak with Bek. Khety, with eyes narrowed, watched Qaa depart, then hurried to speak with Unas.

Qaa found Bek at his tent in the marketplace.

"If you continue to come to my tent, Qaa, I shall try to sell you something other than information." The trader was amused by Qaa's quizzical look. "How may I assist you today?"

"I have just come from the temple goldsmiths. Khety tells me you must have been mistaken about Takhat and the vessel of wine."

"Khety said that. I do not believe you. I trade with him often and he knows I am a man of my word." The merchant flushed with anger.

"I did not tell him who gave me the information. Tell me more about Khety."

"He has five daughters, some still at home. He supplements his income from the temple by fashioning replica ritual cups and statues which he trades with me. I usually trade them with a Phoenician trader, Ghedi, for his wealthy clients in the Near East." Bek had calmed down slightly.

"Bek, I purposely did not tell Khety how I knew. I wanted to ask him about Unas and Takhat. The information you gave me is reliable?"

"I would stake my life on it."

"Have you ever seen Khety with Unas and Takhat in the marketplace?"

The merchant thought for a moment. "Until recently, I never saw Khety with anyone. But I have seen him twice with Unas and Takhat."

"Tell me what you saw."

"The first time, Khety was pushing his finger into Unas's chest. I could not hear them, but they were arguing. Khety stormed off and Unas grabbed Takhat and dragged her from the marketplace. The second time, Khety had Takhat by the hair. He touched her roughly and let her go. Unas looked frightened that time."

"When was this, in relation to Iput's murder?" Qaa wondered if they had conspired to kill Iput, but to what end.

"The first incident occurred about a week before Iput's death. The second incident was the day after her death. I remember because I thought it strange that Unas was in the marketplace when his wife had just been found murdered."

"Bek, do you have any of the goods Khety has traded with you?"

"I think I still have one item." Bek went to the back of his tent. He returned shortly with a ritual cup.

Qaa took the cup from Bek. The craftsmanship was outstanding, and Qaa knew immediately this was no replica. It was far too heavy to have been made of copper or bronze with a gold coating.

"Bek, I would like to make you an offer on this."

The merchant laughed. "My friend, I was not serious about trying to sell to you. It is not worth much, but it fetches Ghedi and me a respectable price in the Near East."

"I would still like to make you an offer." Qaa reached into his belt and withdrew a kidet of silver. "Would this be sufficient?"

"Qaa, do you know how rare silver is here in Waset?"

"I do. But, I do not believe in taking anything without proper payment. Take the silver, Bek. You do not know how much this purchase pleases me."

The merchant shook his head. "I can not thank you enough. I may be a nobleman, but even I do not have silver in any quantity."

"Bek, I never forget a kindness. You have given me much information and I hope to spend some time with you to learn about my father. You have more than earned that kidet of silver, my friend." Qaa bowed to the merchant and took the ritual cup with him to the temple.

After the noon ritual, Qaa requested Thanuny join him in his quarters. The two men walked the corridor in silence and Qaa offered Thanuny the chair at the writing table. Qaa opened one of his travel chests and retrieved the ritual cup he had purchased in the marketplace that morning. He kept the item concealed behind him while he spoke.

"Thanuny, I wish to thank you for assisting the *hemet netjer* yesterday. This investigation and the Egyptian sun drain me of strength." Qaa tried to hide his embarrassment.

"You need to offer me no explanation. I saw nothing improper."

"Can you tell me if Raneb was working on any cases of thefts here at the temple at the time of his death?"

"Yes. In fact, several ritual items had gone missing. Raneb first suspected the staff, but the thefts have occurred during all the rotations of temple personnel. Raneb questioned Harkhuf and Weni and did not feel either one was involved."

Qaa brought the cup from behind his back. "Is this one of the items?"

"It is, Qaa. Where did you find it?" Thanuny was astonished. The cup had been missing for months.

"I purchased it in the marketplace this morning."

"What merchant would trade in stolen goods?"

"The merchant did not know it was stolen. He was told it was a replica, only coated in gold. From what the merchant told me, he has received other items. Do you remember what has gone missing?"

"I can do better. Raneb made an inventory of the items. He kept the scroll here in his quarters. It would be my pleasure to assist you in locating it." Thanuny stood and walked toward the shelf in the corner of the room.

"That shall not be necessary at this time. I wish to speak with one more person regarding the information I have. After the evening ritual, you may assist me in locating the scroll."

"May I ask if you have a suspect?"

"I do. And he works for the temple, though he is not a priest or scribe. I want to know how he manages to get into the temple without anyone seeing him. He may have someone assisting him or bringing the stolen items to him."

"The only persons in the temple after sunset are the *hemet netjer*, her attendant, Merti, and myself. Raneb often went to his residence and Harkhuf and Weni both have wives and homes separate from the temple. On occasion, Anedjib stays to assist me when I need him."

"Merti? Is she Weni's daughter?" Qaa remembered Weni said his daughter worked in the temple.

"Yes, you are correct. She started staying in the temple some time ago."

"Though you are not suspect, Thanuny, why do you prefer to remain in the temple? Do you not have a family?" Qaa wanted to know as much about the men he would be serving with.

"My wife joined Auser two years ago. Both my sons, aged 15 and 19, are scribes, here in the temple. They are old enough to no longer need their father. We share a meal several times a week, but I make my home here."

"You do not have to offer me an answer, but you are still a young man. Do you wish to take another wife?"

"I have lived 41 years. I took my wife when I was 17 and never thought of another woman. My sons have told me I should take another wife, but I have no desire for one." Thanuny bowed his head. It was apparent to Qaa that this was still painful to the priest.

"I am sorry, Thanuny." Qaa put his hand on the priest's shoulder. "I shall inquire no further."

"If I may, Qaa, why have you not married?" Thanuny looked directly into the younger man's blue eyes. "I know you have been in military service to the king, but you are beyond the traditional age of marriage."

Qaa blushed a deep crimson. "I have no answer."

"It is obvious to me how you feel about the *hemet netjer*, and how she feels about you. I saw the concern and devotion in her eyes. I speak from experience. If you wish to take her as your wife, do so while you are still young."

"It is not that easy, Thanuny."

"Qaa, I know you struggle with who you are. If you truly think of yourself as Egyptian, then you shall take the *hemet netjer* as your wife, regardless of the obstacles." Thanuny now put his hand on Qaa's shoulder to comfort him.

Qaa travelled the avenue of the Festival Calendars to the palace. He wanted to speak with Nebettawy about her impressions of Khety, the temple goldsmith. He still had more questions than answers, but the pieces were beginning to make sense. He strode down the corridor to the antechamber, where he found Ramesses with Nebettawy. She was quite animated as she was beating him soundly at a game of mehen.

"My lord, may I speak with you and your daughter?" Qaa bowed to the king.

"Qaa, you are always welcome in my home. You can save me from my daughter. I do not know how she does it, but she wins every time." Ramesses looked relaxed and happy for the first time since Qaa's arrival.

"*Hem netjer*, how is your investigation progressing?" Nebettawy smiled and looked deeply into his eyes. He felt himself drowning; she could bewitch him with a look, a word. He averted his eyes and looked at Ramesses.

"I have learned a great deal over the past few days. The investigation has taken many turns, but I hope to have a suspect before you, my king, very soon."

"Excellent. I knew I could depend upon you, my son. What is it you need to know from my daughter? You do not intend to upset her again, do you?" Ramesses's face turned serious.

"No, my father, I have no intention of upsetting her. I just need to ask her what she knows of the temple goldsmith, Khety." Qaa turned to Nebettawy. "*Hemet netjer*, can you tell me what kind of man he is, what is your impression of him?"

"Khety? I do not recall the name. What does he look like?"

"He is a short, solid man. I would estimate his age to be at least 50. His left eye is permanently closed from an injury. Do you know of whom I speak?"

"I do, now. I did not know his name. He has worked at the temple as far back as I remember. I do not believe he has ever spoken to me." Nebettawy knew very well who he was, but not by name. "Why do you ask about him?"

"I would like to know what kind of man he is. What are your impressions of him?"

"Qaa, is this really important?" Ramesses did not understand how this could have any bearing on the case at hand.

"Father, I assure you, this is quite important. I was with your daughter in the marketplace yesterday. It is apparent the people of Waset think highly of her. And she has the ability to see things in people that you and I do not. So, I must ask again, what is your impression of Khety?"

Nebettawy shifted nervously. "He always bows to me, though has never spoken to me. But, he makes me uncomfortable. I do not like the way he looks at me. I have seen him look at other women at the temple in the same manner. And he seems to have an unusual interest in Merti. I do not know what more I can tell you."

"Nebettawy, this is important. Do you trust the man?"

"I have no evidence, but no, I do not trust him. He shows the proper deference, but I sense he is really not a respectful man. Many of the women who serve the temple seem frightened of him." Nebettawy reached out and took her father's hand, as if for protection.

"Raneb may have suspected Khety of another crime. Thanuny and I have many scrolls to study this evening, which may shed more light on this case. Until I have proof of any crime, I want to know where Khety is. And, as long as he does not suspect I am investigating him, he may provide me with just the proof I need."

"Qaa, you shall keep me informed." The concern showed on Ramesses's face.

"I shall return here, as soon as I have the proof." Qaa bowed to Ramesses and Nebettawy and exited the antechamber, to return to the temple residences.

Qaa was working on his notes of the past few days before he was to meet with Thanuny. Was Khety robbing the temple? Was someone helping him? Could it have been Iput, or had she caught him in the act? And if not Iput, then who? Who had attacked Iput and killed her? Was Raneb killed because he had found out too much? What was Khety's interest in Merti? Could all these incidents be related? He still had more questions, when he looked up from his work to see Nebettawy in the doorway of his quarters.

"Nebettawy, you should not be here. I await the arrival of Thanuny. If he finds you here ..."

"I told Thanuny you did not need him this evening. Qaa, I had to see you in private. I need to be with you."

Qaa could feel his desire for her rising, unbearable, uncontrollable. He could think of nothing but making love to her, possessing her, making her his own. The throbbing between his legs was insistent. But, she was sacred and she had never been with a man; he could not take her by force, not like the foreign women he had taken out of sheer desperation. He had given her father his word he would not join with her. He had to hold firm and not give in to their uncontrolled desires.

"I am willing to risk the wrath of the gods to be with you. Only you can quench the fire that burns within me." Her eyes sparkled like polished onyx and her face was flush with passion.

"You can not be here with me. I do not have the willpower to overcome my desire for you. Do you not know why I have never taken a wife? You are the only woman I could take as my sister, lover, wife."

"If you mean what you say, then come with me, my brother. I know a place where we shall not be found," Nebettawy motioned to him. Her eyes, her body, her scent beckoned to him; his resolve was forgotten. As if enchanted, he stood up from his table and hurried out to the corridor.

It was difficult for Qaa to keep up with her, the fire in his loins made each step agony, but he could think of nothing but her; her kiss upon his lips, her arms around his neck, her legs entwined with his. She was leading him away from the temple complex, into what appeared to be the Red Land. She quickly turned back toward the temple; there, they found a small pool of water enclosed on all sides by palms and reeds.

"I come here often to be alone. The priests have never found me, so I know we shall be safe," Nebettawy's voice came to him from behind a palm. When she stepped out, she was completely naked. By the gods, she was more beautiful than he had imagined. She dove into the pool of water and called seductively to him, "Come and bathe with me, my brother."

Qaa could stand it no longer. He reached inside his loincloth, and after a few quick strokes, relieved himself. Now he would be able to take his time with Nebettawy. He could be gentle and patient with her;

he did not want to hurt her, she was too delicate for him to be forceful. He removed the loincloth and dove in to join her.

She swam over to him and put her arms around his neck. She kissed him square on the mouth with a passion he was not expecting. She wanted him as much as he wanted her; she had already demonstrated her desire for him. She tasted sweet, like pomegranate wine mixed with honey.

"Sister, are you sure of what you are doing? You know what could happen to us both, if anyone finds out that we have made love, especially on the temple grounds."

"But, my brother, this is not the temple grounds. The enclosure begins on the other side of these palms. As for my father, I told him I want his blessing so I may be with you. He has never denied me, and it is the will of Amun."

She was even more beautiful in the moonlight. Her hair shone like silver, her skin glowed and made her appear translucent, like a shimmering vision in the desert. She swam away from him and he followed quickly. She led him to a place in the pond where it was shallow. He reached out and took hold of her arm and pulled her close. She looked up into his eyes with such desire; he knew he had found the only woman he could make love with. But, he could not lie to her. She needed to know she was not the first woman he had been with.

"Nebettawy, I must tell you I have lain with other women. I have only taken foreign women, out of necessity, but they brought me no satisfaction," Qaa said, avoiding her gaze.

She laughed lightly. "Qaa, your needs are stronger than mine. My father and my father's father had many wives and concubines; it has always been our way. Men have desires that must be quenched. I have no quarrel with what you have done in the past."

"I promise to be gentle; I shall try not to hurt you, but you have never known a man." Qaa could feel his passion returning. He reached under the water and placed his hand between her thighs. She moved against his hand and moaned slightly. Even in the cool water, her flesh was hot and slick with desire. She closed her eyes and moved her hips, tentatively at first, then with more urgency. He gently inserted one finger inside her, which made her sigh deeply. As he probed her with his finger, she moaned again. He inserted a second finger.

"I need you, Qaa. Join with me." She was beginning to pant, her breath coming in short, quick bursts.

He bent his head forward and suckled one of her firm breasts. She moaned more loudly and steadily. He inserted a third finger and pushed them in as far as he was able. While he made love to her with his hand, she reached for him. Her touch inflamed him, excited him, propelling him beyond reason; he knew he had to have her, now.

"I want to feel your seed inside me, Brother." Nebettawy, gasping for breath, moaned in his ear.

He could no longer restrain himself. He pulled her close and slowly entered her. She cried out as her virginity was torn away, but continued moving her hips up and down, undulating against his hardness. She began to quicken the pace, her body shaking. He could feel her reaching the heights of ecstasy. He pushed in to her deeper and deeper with each stroke, until he had reached his own brink of pleasure. As he plunged in as deeply as he could, his seed exploded inside her.

They held each other for some time at the edge of the pond, the water lapping against their bodies, trying to cool the passion they felt for one another. Qaa extricated himself from Nebettawy and got out of the pond. He laid both their loincloths on the ground at the edge of the pond and beckoned her to join him. She came to him, dripping wet, the water glistening like polished metal on her naked body. He had never seen a woman so perfect — long athletic legs, round hips, a waist he could encircle with his two hands, small taut breasts, slender neck. She was Auset and Het-Heru come to life.

She lay on her loincloth and Qaa wrapped his arms around her, to warm her from the cool water and the evening breeze. "My sister, I have wanted you all my life. It brings me no satisfaction to hide our love, but out of necessity we must join in secrecy. No woman has ever brought me such pleasure."

"Qaa, you told me you have made progress and I know you shall soon solve the riddle of this horrible crime. Then we shall not have to hide. But, I too have waited twelve years and could wait no longer to have you, to feel you inside me."

With tears in his eyes, Qaa gently took Nebettawy's hand in his. "I too shall risk the wrath of the gods and the punishment of your father. With Nut above and Geb below as witness, I take you as my wife. You are my life and breath, you have captured my heart and soul, and I can love no other but you."

"Qaa, I gladly take you as my husband. I could never give myself to any man but you. I love you more than life itself. May the gods, and my father, bless this union." Nebettawy leaned in and gently kissed his lips.

By the side of the pond, Qaa finally made love to Nebettawy, as his wife, slowly, deliberately, drinking in every moment of pleasure. He explored every inch of her, kissed her, tasted her. She was just as eager to explore her husband, touch him, caress him, taste him.

The moon had not yet reached its highest point in the night sky when they dove into the pond to bathe. Qaa knew they should be returning to the temple soon, before either was missed. Nebettawy swam to him, dove under the water, and began to kiss and stroke his thighs. As she surfaced, he pulled her to him and kissed her deeply. She was like drinking wine mixed with lotus flower, a drug and he could not get enough of her. He turned her around and entered her as wild jackals mate. Her breasts were in his hands, the nipples hard. He pressed them gently between his fingers and Nebettawy whimpered in delight.

She reached below the water and fondled his inner thighs, the heavy sack between his legs, and the flesh between her legs as well. She kept pushing against him, bringing him deeper and deeper inside. She shuddered in pleasure as he once more felt his seed building up inside him. He plunged into her, over and over, holding back as long as he could to enjoy each exquisite thrust. As a cry escaped his lips, he pushed himself into her as deeply as he could and again filled her with his seed.

♀♀♀♀♀♀♀

"Why do you ask about the *hemet netjer*?" Merti was frightened by the questions the shadow voice was asking her.

"Daughter, she is in great danger. This man, Qaa, puts her in danger. You do not wish to see any harm befall her, do you?" The voice wheezed from the darkness of the columns in the First Court.

"No. The *hemet netjer* has always treated me well." Merti loved Nebettawy like a sister.

"Then, you will help me. Stand by the pylon gate. When you see her approach, tell me. Do not let anyone see you."

Merti went and stood by the pylon gate, hiding in the shadows of the great columns. She saw the *hery heb*, Anedjib, come into the court.

Claudia R. Dillaire

He must have heard her speaking with her father. She kept very still until he headed back toward the temple residences, then she returned to the column where the voice came from.

"She approaches, my father."

Nebettawy entered the temple enclosure from the Western gate and hurried down the darkened streets of Waset, along the northern wall, to the Sacred Lake. At this hour, there were no fires burning, but the moon offered her more than enough light. She often walked the temple enclosure at night, preferring the solitude to the noise and bustle of the marketplace. As she walked around the Sacred Lake, which she did most evenings, she saw a figure at the pylon gate. The moon lit him sufficiently and she could see it was Anedjib. She was thankful Qaa persuaded her to return alone by the northern wall. As soon as this ugly business was settled, she did not care who saw them together.

Qaa entered the temple enclosure a few moments after Nebettawy, also by the Western gate, but took the route past the embalming tents, which led to the nobles' and priests' residences. This would have been the route Iput took to the temple the night of her death. The houses were dark and quiet; any unusual noise should have been heard. The southern wall, with the moon high in the sky, did not lend itself to concealment. If someone followed her, there were few places to hide. The killer could have concealed himself between the residences, but he would have taken the chance on being seen as she passed. But, if he had been waiting for her beside the last house, he would have had to approach from the northern wall ... or the temple itself.

"Merti, you must tell no one of this night." The shadow reached out and grabbed her by the throat. "You will blame Unas for all that has happened, for if you do not, you may suffer the same fate as Iput."

"I shall do as you say." Merti was so terrified her legs could hardly support her.

"Now, go to the safety of the temple. Do not look back. Do not disappoint your father." The shadow released her and she ran toward the entrance of the Second Court. But, rather than seek safety, she hid behind one of the last columns. She wanted to see her father.

Nebettawy passed through the pylon gate and felt a hand grab her arm. The sharp, cold hardness at her throat was unmistakable — it was the point of a knife scrapping against her flesh.

"Princess," the voice wheezed. "If you do not forget what Iput told you, you will regret it."

Nebettawy said nothing. She tried to free her arm, but the grip was firm. She touched the skin of his hand; it was rough, scaly, like a crocodile. His voice was low, but insistent. He took the knife from her throat and wrapped his arm around her neck, making it difficult for her to breathe. Releasing his grip on her arm, he then ran his free hand over her breasts and down her body.

"You are very beautiful, yet have never been with a man, have you, Princess? Allow me to show you what it is like to have a real man."

He forced his knee between her legs. She tried to squirm free, but he was too strong for her, and lack of breath was making her weak. He took the knife, turned it around, and shoved the hilt into her. Pain and horror coursed through her body, causing her to cry out.

Merti, seeing what was happening to the *hemet netjer*, rushed to her aid.

The shadow figure, dressed completely in black, withdrew the knife handle. As Merti reached out to the *hemet netjer*, the shadow slashed her across the hand.

"I warned you. Now you will be sorry, as well." The figure, his face in shadows, ran through the pylon gate, toward the north wall of the enclosure.

Qaa was just rounding the corner of the last house, when he heard someone cry out. He was about to give chase when he heard Merti.

"*Hem netjer*, help me." Merti cried out, diverting Qaa's attention from the fleeing figure. "The *hemet netjer* has been injured."

Claudia R. Dillaire

Qaa still ran after the suspect, but by the time he reached the corner of the inner enclosure, the street was empty. He hurried to Nebettawy, just as Anedjib arrived. Nebettawy was lying on the sand, curled up in obvious pain, struggling for breath. Disregarding the consequences, he took her in his arms and held her, while Anedjib ran to awaken the other priests.

"Qaa, take me to my quarters and summon the *swnwt per aa*." Nebettawy whispered, still unable to catch her breath.

As Thanuny and two lesser priests arrived on the scene, Qaa picked her up. She put her arms around his neck and laid her head against his shoulder. Feeling safe, she started to cry from the shock and the pain.

"Attend to the *shemayet*. I shall speak with her shortly. Anedjib, summon the *swnwt per aa*. Have her come to the *hemet netjer's* quarters. Thanuny, come with me." Qaa barked orders to the priests.

Thanuny followed Qaa to Nebettawy's quarters. As Qaa settled her on her bed, both men saw the blood on the front of her dress. She curled up in a ball and rocked back and forth, still crying softly.

"Nebettawy, can you tell me what happened?" Qaa gently placed his hand on her shoulder.

She looked at Thanuny and shook her head.

"Thanuny, wake the Captain of the Medjay and have him bring his best men. I want to bring Nebettawy to the palace after she has been seen by the *swnwt*. The king needs to be notified of the incident."

When Thanuny had exited the room, Qaa sat next to Nebettawy on the bed. She leaned against him and he put his arms around her, she was shaking so badly.

"Can you tell me, Sister?" Qaa gently prodded.

"A man grabbed me at the pylon gate. He put a knife to my throat. He said and did disgusting things to me."

"Nebettawy, you are bleeding. Did he stab you or cut you with his knife?" Qaa did not know how seriously she might be injured.

"No." She buried her face in her hands. Her entire body shook and she could barely get the words out. "He defiled me with the hilt of his knife."

Qaa held her close until the *swnwt* arrived. This man, bold enough to attack Nebettawy at the temple entrance, walked the streets of Waset. And, it was Qaa's fault that he had allowed this to happen.

 THE WRATH OF AMUN

"Let me examine the *hemet netjer*. You may return when I have finished." Ashayt sat next to Nebettawy on her bed and started to ask her questions about the attack.

"*Swnwt*, may I first speak with you in the corridor?" Qaa and Ashayt exited the *hemet netjer's* room. "I do not wish to ask her, but I need her dress to examine for evidence. I shall wait here for it."

Ashayt entered Nebettawy's room, returning shortly with her dress. Qaa requested the first of the arriving Medjay to accompany him. As Qaa walked to his quarters he met Thanuny, with Merti. He grabbed the young woman by the arm and dragged her down the corridor with him. Leaving Merti with Thanuny and the Medjay and after depositing Nebettawy's dress on his writing table, he came out into the corridor.

"Medjay, no one is to enter this room until I return." The guard bowed low to Qaa in response. Now, he turned his attention to the young woman. Qaa had never struck a woman, but what had happened this evening was unforgivable.

"Speak, Merti. Who was the man who attacked the *hemet netjer*?" He loomed over the small girl.

"He threatened me to silence." Merti trembled in front of the *hem netjer*. She knew she would have to lie, knowing what the punishment could be, for the voice had told her it was the *hem netjer* who was dangerous. Qaa reached out and, with one hand, put it around her throat and picked her up off the ground.

"Know, *shemayet*, I can break your neck with this one hand. You shall tell me, or you shall tell your king. And I may be more merciful than he." Qaa would get an answer from her, whatever he had to do.

"It was Unas, the goldsmith apprentice."

"*Swnwt*, you must never speak of what I have revealed to you this evening." Nebettawy was terrified for the first time in her life. "If my father were to find out, both Qaa and I would be punished."

"I understand, Princess. Unless you release me from this confidence, I shall not reveal your secret. Now, I must examine you." Ashayt had Nebettawy lie back on the bed. "I shall be as gentle as I can."

The *swnwt* noted that Nebettawy was still bleeding, most probably from the attack, rather than from having joined with Qaa. She felt inside Nebettawy and found an open wound, likely from the hilt of the knife. She took her long tongs and coated a piece of linen in honey and herbs. Ashayt gently inserted it into Nebettawy and swabbed her womb, to guard against infection setting in to the wound. Nebettawy flinched and choked back tears, as the pain spread through her abdomen. Ashayt prepared a large linen ball, treated with the same honey/herb mixture, and inserted it into the womb.

"Princess, I want you to leave the linen in place until I return tomorrow morning. I shall examine you and pronounce further treatment."

"Many thanks, *swnwt*." She reached out and squeezed Ashayt's hand. "Qaa wants to take me to the palace for my safety." Nebettawy rose and pulled on a clean loose fitting linen tunic.

"I think that is wise. I shall make that my first call after sunrise." Ashayt heard voices in the corridor. She walked to the doorway and saw Qaa and Thanuny, with Merti in tow, in the corridor speaking with the Medjay captain. Anedjib joined them almost immediately.

"Medjay, I want the temple secured for the evening. Dispatch your men to locate Unas, the temple goldsmith apprentice. And, I need an escort to the palace for the *hemet netjer*."

"Will two men be sufficient for you?"

"I believe I can handle this young woman. Two Medjay shall be adequate. Thanuny, while I am at the palace, could you check the temple to see if anything is missing?"

"Qaa, I shall have a full accounting when you return."

DAY 15 IN MONTH 3

"Father, I am more shaken than hurt. The *swnwt* has pronounced me well and said the pain shall subside." Sitting in the comfort of the palace reception chamber, Nebettawy winced though she felt safe in her father's arms, just as she had as a child.

"But, still you bleed, my daughter. Why were you not in the safety of the temple?" Ramesses's face was red with anger, but his words were filled with concern for Nebettawy. Someone had attacked his own daughter at the First Pylon.

"I often walk to the Sacred Lake at night. The water is cool and I can be alone. I shall not be frightened into hiding in the temple." Though her words were confident, she still shivered in Ramesses's embrace.

"Qaa, were you with my daughter at the Sacred Lake?" Ramesses wanted to believe his daughter, but his temper was at a fever pitch.

"My lord, I was not at the Sacred Lake. I was walking near the south wall, looking to see where the killer would have had a clear view of Iput, yet be able to conceal himself from view." The words were difficult for Qaa to speak. What he said was true, even though it felt like a lie, as he had not been near the lake.

"Daughter, were you alone at the Sacred Lake?" Ramesses loved his daughter, but knew she did not always do as he commanded. His voice was gentle but insistent. Before she could reply, Anedjib interrupted.

"If I may speak, my king?" Trembling, he bowed before Ramesses. "It was I who heard the muffled voices coming from the First Court. I walked to the pylon gate but saw no one in the court. It was then I saw the *hemet netjer* coming from the Sacred Lake. She was alone, my lord. I had reached the Second Court when I heard voices again and the *hemet netjer* cry out. I saw Merti with blood on her hand. I ran to alert the other priests, then hurried to your daughter."

Qaa continued the story. "I was coming from the nobles' houses behind the palace wall when I heard her cry out. I started to give chase when Merti called out to me. After Nebettawy was settled, I questioned her in Thanuny's presence. Medjay have been dispatched to bring the man responsible to the palace." Qaa looked at Ramesses holding Nebettawy, aching himself to hold her, comfort her.

"Your majesty, when I was in the First Court I did see Qaa giving chase from the direction of the nobles' residences." Anedjib confirmed Qaa's story.

Ramesses's anger at his daughter and Qaa had subsided, but he wanted the perpetrator caught and dealt with severely. No one touched his daughter; as *hemet netjer*, she was sacred. This attack was tantamount to defiling the temple itself. "Bring Merti forward so I may question her."

Merti, who had been sitting quietly in a corner of the reception chamber, was brought forward by Medjay. Delicate and reed-like, she was stunning and used her looks seductively; she was too anxious to please a man, any man, but Ramesses was one man she could not charm. She shook in the presence of her king, the living god. If her lie was uncovered, she could be put to death.

"Who attacked my daughter?" Ramesses's voice boomed throughout the chamber. "Speak and I might spare you punishment!" The king was in no mood to trifle with this young temple *shemayet*.

Merti could barely speak. The words quavered from her lips. "He forced me to help him. He promised to marry me then took up with another woman. He took me against my will and said if I told anyone, he would kill me." She fell to her knees in front of Ramesses, her legs unable to support her.

Ramesses exploded in anger, "Do not test my patience. I want his name, now!" He flew up from his seat, almost knocking Nebettawy to

Claudia R. Dillaire

the floor. Those assembled in the reception chamber recoiled from the king's outburst.

"He is Unas, a goldsmith apprentice at the temple," Merti croaked out in a whisper.

"Take her from my sight and hold her at the military barracks until I decide what the appropriate punishment shall be. " Two Medjay lifted her roughly from the floor and carried her away as she wailed for forgiveness. Ramesses turned back to his daughter. "I want Medjay with you at all times. I could not bear to lose you, my daughter." Nebettawy, for the first time in her life, saw tears in the eyes of her father.

"You may rest easy. I shall do as you wish, Father. I would like to remain here with you and Qaa until they find Unas. Though he kept his face from me, I shall never forget his voice, or the words he spoke to me. I wish to see what kind of man would risk his life by touching me in such a foul manner."

"Anedjib, you may return to the temple. You shall be well rewarded for saving my daughter. Qaa, summon a Medjay to accompany my daughter to the palace gardens so we may speak in private." Anedjib left the chamber for the temple and Qaa exited behind him, returning shortly with a harem Medjay.

Ramesses kissed his daughter on the forehead and sent her with the Medjay, with this warning, "Do not let her out of your sight. Your only duty is the protection of my daughter." The Medjay bowed to the king and guided Nebettawy, wincing with pain, into the gardens.

"Qaa, you spoke with the *swnwt per aa*? My daughter did not tell me of her injuries. If you know, do not spare me the truth." Concern etched the king's face.

"You may wish to sit, Father. From what I have gathered, Unas held a knife to your daughter's throat to keep her quiet. He told her she should forget whatever Iput had told her." Qaa dropped his gaze from the seated Ramesses, unable to look him in the eyes, to finish the indignity which had been inflicted upon her. He inhaled deeply and spoke in a measured tone. "Apparently, Unas forced her legs open, took the knife from her throat, and inserted the hilt forcefully into her. When she cried out, he withdrew the hilt, released his grip, and ran into the darkness." When Qaa finished, he had to swallow hard to keep from being ill, remembering the similar injuries inflicted upon Iput.

He now looked directly at Ramesses, tears clouding both men's eyes. The words Qaa had spoken hung heavy in the air, engulfing the king, threatening to smother the brave and noble ruler.

"Qaa, my son, you must tell no one what you have revealed to me. My trust in you has not been misplaced, I asked for the truth and you did not waiver, though I know this is difficult for you as well. I see the love in your eyes when you look at my daughter. You may go to her, my son. Dismiss the Medjay and keep her safe until Unas is brought to me."

Qaa bowed to Ramesses, but, rather than exit the chamber, he crossed to the king. "My father, I should not have let this happen. I questioned Unas. He is a liar as well as a disgusting pig of a man, but I do not believe he has the stomach to have killed Iput. I may not deserve your trust, if I am proved wrong." He had no words to comfort his king.

Ramesses, sensing Qaa's distress, stood and held out his arms. The men embraced, sharing the pain both felt, one struggling with the concern of a devoted father, the other, the inability to protect the woman he loved.

"Medjay, you may return to your duties. I shall stay with her until Unas is found." Qaa could not bring himself to look at Nebettawy. He had failed her miserably. He alone was responsible for her attack. How could she ever forgive him?

"Qaa, come and hold me. I need to feel your arms around me now more than ever."

He rushed to her and fell to his knees in front of her. He dropped his head into her lap and wept. He was inconsolable. She stroked his head and back, gently, tenderly, as a mother would comfort a scared child. "My brother, do not punish yourself with guilt. You could not have prevented this. You are my husband, but you can not protect me at all times. Look at me, Qaa."

He raised his head and looked deeply into her eyes. There was no blame, only compassion, in her dark, shining eyes. She pulled his face toward hers and kissed him lightly on the lips. "I love you, my brother, my husband, and shall until the day I join with Auser. Nothing shall ever change how I feel."

Qaa stood up, pulled her to her feet, and put his arms around her. She melted into him, feeling safe, finally able to relax and let go of the chill that had crept into her bones since the attack. Without warning, the pain and her emotions overtaking her, she could hold back no longer and wept uncontrollably. Qaa wept along with her.

Ramesses, though unable to hear what they said, watched them through the trees. Qaa loved his daughter in a way that Ramesses could not. And it was obvious his daughter was devoted to Qaa. They were willing to risk the wrath of the gods and their king for their love. He would have to concede; he could not fight them both.

"Have refreshments brought to my daughter and Qaa in the gardens. I shall meet them there presently," the king ordered of a kitchen servant.

Ramesses went to his private chamber and retrieved a vessel of wine the *swnwt* had given him. She had prepared it for him after a fall from his chariot. The wine was steeped with mandrake to lessen pain and quiet the nerves. He would mix some in Nebettawy's wine, to calm her. He exited his chamber and walked the corridor to the palace gardens. The servant was spreading out the refreshments, fruit, cheese, bread, wine. With a wave of his hand, Ramesses dismissed the servant. Nebettawy was now seated next to Qaa on a stone bench, head on his shoulder, nuzzled into his neck.

"My lord." Qaa stood quickly.

"Qaa, please sit. These are extraordinary circumstances. You may hold my daughter, and keep her safe."

"Many thanks, my lord." Qaa sat down again next to Nebettawy and put his arms around her to keep her warm from the chill and dew of the night.

"Daughter, the swnwt prepared this for me. This may make you feel better." Ramesses poured a small amount of the steeped wine into a drinking bowl and then diluted it well with pomegranate wine. He handed her the drinking bowl, which she sipped.

"Qaa, you must be cold." Nebettawy was snuggled against his bare chest, and only now realized he was still clothed in just a loincloth and light linen kilt.

"My son, let me get you one of my heavy linen robes." Ramesses departed for his private chamber.

"Brother, your body warms me, but still I am chilled to the bone." Nebettawy trembled, but she had calmed down a bit, possibly from the steeped wine.

"You do not have to confront this man, when he is found. Your father and I shall interrogate him and get to the bottom of this." Qaa stroked her hair and back.

"No, Qaa, I must do this. I shall not be afraid. All I need to hear is his voice and I shall know if he is the man who touched me."

"I shall keep you in the shadows, so he shall not see you. If he is the man, tell your father and we shall have him taken to the military barracks to await punishment."

"All I ask, my brother, is to have him speak the word 'Princess', for that is how he referred to me. I shall know when I hear him speak that word." Nebettawy shivered at the thought of hearing his voice.

"My daughter, I shall sit with you while Qaa interrogates him." Ramesses had returned with the robe, threw it over Qaa's shoulders, and pulled it around him and Nebettawy. Ramesses poured wine for himself and Qaa; the three of them sat in relative silence, waiting for news from the Medjay. The wine and the atrocity had taken a toll on Nebettawy. She rested her head against Qaa's shoulder and drifted off to sleep. Qaa continued to stroke her hair and back, to comfort her, to protect her.

"My king, the Medjay have returned with Unas." The Captain of the Medjay spoke urgently, but softly, so as not to wake Nebettawy.

"Hold him in the antechamber. We shall summon you when we are prepared to interrogate him." Ramesses looked at his daughter, unwilling to wake her. Even in the moonlight, he could see the marks around her neck where her attacker had held her, cutting off her breath. "Where did you find Unas?"

"He was on the East bank. He and Takhat were taking part in festivities with her family. A feast had been prepared in their honour, celebrating Unas taking Takhat as his wife."

"Did he say anything to you?"

"He does not know why he has been brought in for questioning. He travelled across the Nile before sunset. I confirmed this with Takhat's family and the ferry captain. He has not left the festivities."

"Many thanks, Medjay. Give us a few moments." Ramesses dismissed the Medjay Captain.

"If Unas has been in celebration since sunset, then it is Merti who is lying to us." Qaa was red with anger; he should not have been merciful, he should have struck her. "Why would she want to throw suspicion upon him, if he is not involved?"

"Could they be working in concert with another person?" Ramesses, furious that one of his subjects had lied to him, would make his punishment swift.

"If Merti is willing to lie to both of us, she shall not reveal further information. However, Unas may prove useful. He may be able to shed some light upon why she would lie and who she is protecting. Shall I wake her, my father?" Qaa looked lovingly at the sleeping Nebettawy.

"If Unas is not her attacker, what can be gained from waking her? She has been through a terrible ordeal this night. Let her sleep. I shall tell the Medjay to take Unas to the military barracks. We may interrogate him at our pleasure."

Nebettawy bolted upright, eyes staring wildly, her body rigid. She looked at her father and then at Qaa. Her mind was clouded from the wine and sleep. Qaa held her close and kissed her forehead.

"Sister, you are safe." Qaa felt her start to relax in his arms.

"Have you found Unas?" Nebettawy began to tremble again.

"My daughter, he has been found. But we do not think he is the man who attacked you."

"Father, bring him to me. I want to hear his voice. Then, I shall be sure."

"Are you feeling well enough?" Ramesses did not want to upset her further.

"Yes, Father, I need to hear his voice."

"Qaa, stay with my daughter. I shall have the Medjay bring Unas." Ramesses left the gardens to find the Medjay Captain.

Nebettawy, finally alone again with Qaa, took his hand in hers. She turned his palm to her and kissed it gently. He, in turn, did the same.

"You do not have to do this, Sister." Qaa had not protected her; guilt gnawed at him each time she looked into his eyes.

"Qaa, I love you. But I need to know if he is the man. You do not have to blame yourself. I am as much to blame, by luring you out of the temple this night. I wanted you so desperately I paid no heed to the consequences." She spoke as if she had read his thoughts. She leaned in and kissed him gently, tenderly on the lips. "I do not blame you, my husband."

"Nebettawy, I ..." Qaa stopped when he heard her father approach with the Medjay and Unas.

"Qaa, have him speak as I requested of you." Nebettawy whispered.

Qaa helped her to her feet and guided her to a stone bench in the far corner of the palace gardens, where she would be out of sight. As he settled her on the bench, she squeezed his hand and smiled at him. He turned and met Ramesses and the Medjay.

"Unas, a woman has made a serious accusation against you. She is a daughter of the king. Whom do you think we shall believe, you or the princess?" Qaa was baiting him to speak.

"A princess makes an accusation? But, I have done nothing." Unas, terrified to the point he might wet himself, fell to his knees in front of Qaa.

"He is not the man." The voice came from the shadows at the far end of the gardens.

Unas looked up to see Nebettawy. He gasped at her appearance. She had bruises on both sides of her throat, a scratch on the front of her neck, and finger marks on her left arm. She walked toward him slowly, unsteady on her feet.

"His voice is most certainly not the voice I heard this evening."

"Medjay, take him to the military barracks. Hold him until the king sets his punishment." Qaa barked to the Medjay Captain. But before he was taken away, Qaa reached out and grabbed the bone handled dagger, which was sticking out from the waist of Unas's loincloth.

"Punishment? But I have done nothing." Unas wailed like a trapped animal. Horrified, not knowing of what he was accused he lost control of his bladder, as he was carried away by the Medjay.

Nebettawy was settled in the palace to rest. The *swnwt* came in and examined her after sunrise. The wound was not draining properly and the *swnwt* had to reopen it, causing Nebettawy additional pain. She replaced the coated linen ball with a fresh one, and coated the wound itself with honey and herbs. Her prescription was rest for the remainder of the day, and told the king and Qaa to do the same. She would return the following day to check on her patient.

Qaa returned to the temple after sunrise, with a Medjay to relieve the one guarding his evidence. He dismissed the Medjay who had been on alert since the attack and instructed his replacement to let no one into his quarters until he arose. He dropped the dagger he had taken from Unas on his writing table, to examine later. Too tired to even undress, he fell into bed, and into a deep sleep. But his sleep was not restful. His dreams were populated with Nebettawy, beckoning to him, calling to him, but always out of reach. He then dreamed he saw Nebettawy at the Sacred Lake, alone. When he approached her, she was covered with blood, pointing at him, accusing him.

Qaa awoke after the noon ritual. He was disgusted with himself. Military men do not sleep the day away and he had much to do. He sat on the side of his bed and looked at the evidence on his table. He was not yet ready to touch the items; he needed to cleanse himself. He stripped out of his clothes and walked the corridor to the private bath. He instructed the Medjay to remain outside his quarters, guarding the evidence, until he returned. After a thorough cleansing, his head had cleared a bit and he felt renewed. He returned to his quarters, pulled on a fresh loincloth and kilt, and dismissed the Medjay.

He turned his attention to the dagger; it was unremarkable, bronze blade, bone handle. He had seen many such daggers carried by men in Waset. He examined the handle carefully, looking for any trace of fabric or blood. The dagger did not appear to have been used in Nebettawy's attack. Next, he picked up Nebettawy's dress. He could smell her perfume, the musk of her desire from last evening, and the smell of smoke. There was a black smudge on the shoulder and traces of soot on the back of the dress. Whoever had held her must have been covered in soot. He spread the dress on the table to look closer, and found fine shavings of copper and gold. Her attacker had to be a goldsmith or apprentice, so Unas was still suspect, or he may have had help.

He turned the dress over to examine the front. There was soot near the neckline, where her attacker had put his arm around her neck. He could see clear finger impressions where he had touched Nebettawy's breasts, and the soot travelled down to the blood stain. The fabric, under the blood stain, was torn, from the hilt of the knife. He looked again at the dagger; if this were the weapon, there would still be some trace of blood or fabric. This could not be the weapon, but he would hold on to it for now.

He was startled out of his investigation by voices in the corridor.

"Thanuny? Is that you?" Qaa called out, looking toward the doorway. Almost immediately, the older priest appeared.

"Qaa, how is the *hemet netjer*?"

"She is resting at the palace. The *swnwt* shall continue to treat her against infection. Thanuny, did you find anything missing last evening?"

Thanuny entered Qaa's quarters. Qaa stood so Thanuny could sit at the table, but when he saw the bloody dress, he backed away.

"When Raneb noticed the thefts, he instructed me to move the ritual items. Only Raneb, Harkhuf, and I knew the location. Whoever came to steal did not know that; I found what looks like black dust on the shelves where we kept the ritual items."

"Could it be soot?" Qaa was beginning to see a pattern to these crimes.

"It could be soot. Is that important?"

"There is soot on the *hemet netjer's* dress. Whoever attacked her had come to rob the temple."

"So it was Unas?"

"I have more than enough evidence to clear him, but I think he knows more than he is telling me. He did not attack the *hemet netjer*, of that I am certain."

"Then who?" Thanuny was perplexed.

"I am going to question Unas and, if the gods are willing, he shall provide me with the answers I need. Thanuny, I want to put these items in the preparation tent. No one shall look there, so they shall not be disturbed." Qaa handed the dagger to Thanuny, who breathed a sigh of relief. Qaa then gently folded Nebettawy's dress and the two men went to secure the items.

"Medjay, you may leave us." Qaa dismissed the guards watching Unas at the military barracks. He pulled up a chair and sat, facing the apprentice, who was nervous and pacing.

"Medjay." Unas bowed to Qaa. "Can you tell me what will happen to me?" Unas was no longer so sure of himself; he was scared.

"Unas, do you know Merti, the young *shemayet* at the temple?"

All the colour drained from Unas's face. What was she accusing him of?

"Did you not hear the question?" Qaa could see Unas was uncomfortable.

"Medjay, she presented herself to me. I did not take her against her will. If she says I did, she is lying." Unas trembled. A man of lower status, taking a priest's daughter; he could be severely punished.

"She says you refused to marry her. Is this true?"

"She is a little whore. She has joined with most of the temple staff, scribes and lesser priests, bakery workers, and goldsmiths, even some of the Medjay. I have seen it with my own eyes."

"What have you seen, Unas?"

"She meets men behind the sanctuary. She lifts up her dress to show her Bes tattoo and does not wear a loincloth. Then she presents her naked buttocks to any man, so they can take her like an animal."

"She does this on temple property?" Qaa was appalled by what he was hearing. But, coming from Unas, he would need to confirm the story.

"I have to pass behind the sanctuary to deliver the ritual items. That is how she cornered me the first time. When I began refusing her advances, she told Iput. When I took up with Takhat, I told her what I had done with Merti. Merti would go to the marketplace and tell Takhat we were still meeting, even when it was not true."

"If she was meeting so many men, why would she go to Takhat and tell her something that was untrue?"

"When I met Takhat, I swore off other women. Merti tried everything, even going to the overseer, but I would not go near her. I do not think anyone has ever rejected her advances."

"Do you know the names of any other men she has been with?" Qaa would be discreet, but he could not take Unas at his word.

"One of the men is the Second *hem netjer's* youngest son. I have also seen her with the scribe, Yuya." Unas dropped his voice. "Medjay, one of the men guarding me, I have seen him enjoying her on more than one occasion." Unas shrank, expecting to be struck, but no blow was forthcoming.

"Merti is lying to protect someone. She accuses you of attacking the *hemet netjer* and I am fairly certain you did not. If she is willing to accuse you, I need to know why. Who would she sacrifice so much for?"

"Medjay, I do not know. I only enjoyed her twice. I know what I did was improper, but she is very persuasive. I am a man and I have needs. When a woman touches you, as she did, it is hard to resist. I make no excuse for my actions; I could not control myself."

"Unas, I need to have you remain here. Do not speak of this to anyone, even Takhat. When my investigation is complete, you shall have to face punishment for what you have done. Having contact with a woman on the grounds of the temple is a serious offense. But if your story is true, I shall do my best to intercede with the king."

The goldsmith apprentice fell to his knees in front of Qaa. "Many thanks, Medjay. I do not deserve your assistance, but it is greatly appreciated. I only want to start a life with Takhat and the child she carries."

"Merti, I have spoken with Yuya. He has told me all about you and the temple sanctuary."

She looked at Qaa in disbelief. Yuya would not speak against her, not if he wanted to enjoy her again.

"He is not the only one, Merti. Tell me what I need to know, and the king may spare you." Qaa wanted to see her reaction, and it was telling. Her face changed from contempt to doubt to terror, all in a matter of moments.

"I know nothing, *hem netjer*, and I refuse to speak to you." Her words were strong and clear, but she trembled, knowing she had already sealed her fate.

Qaa returned to the temple to make notes of his interrogation of Unas. He would speak with Yuya, but preferred not to drag Thanuny's son into this mess. He would tell Thanuny only if it became necessary.

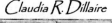

DAY 16 IN MONTH 3

After having spent the previous day resting, Nebettawy was anxious to return to the temple and her duties there. The *swnwt* examined her, replaced the coated linen ball to guard against infection, and pronounced Nebettawy could return to her tasks, but if she felt ill, to rest and summon her immediately. Nebettawy cleansed herself, put on a fresh linen tunic, and applied makeup and perfume to prepare for her day. Her abdomen still ached, and her limbs felt heavy, but if she moved around, she hoped the aches and pains would subside.

She exited her chamber in the palace and hurried through rooms before her father awoke. He would want her to stay and rest, and he wanted a Medjay with her. She did not like being sick, nor did she like being fussed over. As she reached the main reception chamber, she saw Qaa, coming to meet with her father, she surmised.

"Should you be up, Sister?" Qaa rushed to her side and slipped his arm around her waist.

"I am well. I did, however, enjoy having you take care of me the other evening. I felt so safe in your arms."

"May I accompany you?" Qaa and Nebettawy walked through the entrance of the palace into the First Court.

"I have visits to make today. The *swnwt* told me if I felt ill, to rest. I shall make my first visit and if I tire, I shall return to the temple to prepare potions and unguents. Are you here to see my father?"

"I came to see you. Takhat is coming to visit Unas at the military barracks today. I do not wish to ask, but you could assist me by speaking with her." Qaa felt guilty making her interrogate Takhat, but Nebettawy had the ability to obtain information he could not.

"If I am feeling well, I shall question her. What do you need to know?"

"Takhat was seen trading an expensive vessel of wine in the marketplace, shortly after Iput's death. I have been told she traded it to a Phoenician. I want to know how she came into possession of the wine. Bek had a vessel stolen from him and Raneb was poisoned with an expensive wine." Only he and Thanuny knew this, but he knew he could trust Nebettawy with this confidence.

Nebettawy was horrified. "Raneb was poisoned?" She had stopped dead in her tracks.

"Yes, my sister, he was. I think he was poisoned because he knew who killed Iput. Question her at the military barracks, and do not allow yourself to be alone with her. If she is involved and feels trapped, she may try to harm you."

"I am not afraid of Takhat. But, I shall do as you ask, my brother."

"I would like to have a Medjay accompany you, for your protection, and in case you feel unwell."

"Escort me to the military barracks and I shall accept your Medjay guard." She smiled at his concern for her welfare.

Qaa left Nebettawy with a Medjay before he headed back to the temple. He needed to consult his notes. He would take all the information he had so far and see where it was leading, and to whom. Ramesses wanted to see him after the noon ritual, so he had a lot to accomplish.

"Merti, talk to me." Nebettawy pleaded with the young girl she thought of like a sister.

"I can tell you nothing, *hemet netjer.*"

"My father shall punish you severely for speaking against Unas. Why would you do such a thing?"

"He is a pig, a man of his lowly status, and I, the daughter of a priest. He took me behind the sanctuary, forced me to have relations with him, on temple property, now he takes up with another woman. He shall pay for what he has done."

"Merti, he did not attack me at the pylon gate, but you know who did. Tell me, and I shall intercede with my father on your behalf."

"It was Unas. I shall say no more, *hemet netjer*." Merti turned away from Nebettawy and wept.

Frustrated, Nebettawy and her Medjay escort walked along the south wall of the temple enclosure, to the home of Weni and Sadeh. Merti was protecting someone, out of fear, out of obligation, out of what? Possibly, she had spoken to her mother. Nebettawy remembered Sadeh used to come to the temple often, before she became pregnant with Merti. After the birth of her daughter, Sadeh seemed to fade, as if the life had gone out of her. She stopped outside the house.

"Medjay, please remain here. If I need you, I shall call for you."

Nebettawy entered the residence and found Sadeh weaving in a corner of the main room, tears staining her face. She had once been quite a beauty; small, lithe, with the body of a dancer. Though just past forty, the years weighed heavily upon her, showing in her drawn, pinched face and her sad, frightened eyes. After giving Weni four sons, she had finally been blessed with the daughter she desperately wanted, Merti, but the price of her wish was more than she could bear and it had aged her considerably.

"Sadeh, I need your help."

Sadeh trembled and looked sad. "You have come to speak to me about Merti."

"She refuses to speak to me. I wish to intercede on her behalf, but she is protecting someone. If she does not reveal what she knows, I can not help her."

Sadeh looked at Nebettawy and saw the bruises on her neck and the finger marks on her arm.

"*Hemet netjer*, how were you injured?"

"I was attacked at the First Pylon, by a man who kept his face from me. It is this man who Merti is protecting."

The older woman lost all colour. Her hands were shaking so badly she knocked over the loom. Nebettawy helped her right the loom, then took her hands and held them to keep them from shaking. She sat next to the trembling woman, hoping to discover what Sadeh was hiding and why.

"Sadeh, if you know anything, please tell me." Nebettawy searched the woman's eyes and saw a knowing look that made her uncomfortable.

"*Hemet netjer*, what I am about to tell you, you must not reveal to anyone. Weni is not Merti's father."

"I do not understand." Nebettawy flushed and suddenly the room felt too warm.

"I used to go to the temple to pray to Amun to bless me with a daughter. One evening, after leaving the temple, a man grabbed me from behind. I never saw his face."

Nebettawy was shocked. "Please, tell me what happened."

"The man said he had heard my prayers and he could give me the daughter I so wanted. He covered my mouth with his hand and told me not to cry out. I felt the point of a knife in my back, so I said nothing."

"Did you recognise his voice?" Nebettawy thought back to her own attack and the wheezing voice she heard. Her head was pounding and she was beginning to feel weak from the heat.

"No, but I shall never forget that voice, raspy, wheezing. He took me from behind, like an animal. When he was finished, he defiled me further with an object, I do not know what it was." Sadeh had begun to cry, letting go of the secret she had protected for almost sixteen years. Nebettawy reached up and put her hand on the woman's shoulder.

"The man who attacked me had the same voice."

Sadeh looked up at her in anguish. "I was too ashamed to tell anyone. I could not even tell my husband."

"I shall not reveal your secret to him, but I must tell the Chief of the Medjay."

"No, *hemet netjer*, you must not. I could not face the consequences."

"Sadeh, you have done nothing wrong. This man forced himself on you and he must be stopped. But, only you and I know his voice, so we may both be in danger."

"Now, I do not understand."

"If he feels trapped, he may try to silence one or both of us. Would you like me to have a Medjay stationed at your house?"

"I have kept his secret for sixteen years, I do not have anything to fear."

"Can you think of anyone Merti would protect? Does she know Weni is not her father?"

"How could she, I myself do not know who he is."

"Many thanks, Sadeh, for speaking plainly with me." Nebettawy tried to stand, but pain and weakness in her legs forced her to remain seated. She felt sick at the stomach, as the room started to tilt. "Would you call the Medjay for me? I think I would like to go back to the temple and lie down."

The Medjay guided Nebettawy slowly back to the temple. Each step was difficult, waves of pain and heat searing through her legs and abdomen. She would lie down and rest. Thanuny could summon the *swnwt* to attend her. She dismissed the guard and barely made it to her quarters, before her legs gave out. She sat for some time on the floor, before she had enough strength to pull herself onto her bed.

She had a small table which had a clay vessel of water and a clay bowl on it. She poured water into the bowl, and, using her hands, dipped them in the cool water and patted her face. She was sweating and felt so tired. But, she had not yet spoken to Takhat, and Qaa was depending upon her. She heard voices in the corridor and called out to the priests. Thanuny looked in on her.

"Thanuny, I am not feeling well. Could you summon the *swnwt* and ask her to come?"

"Hemet netjer, should I summon your father or Qaa, as well?"

"No, Thanuny. I need to speak with the widow Takhat. Is anyone available who could go to the marketplace?"

"You should rest, you can speak with her tomorrow."

"Please, Thanuny, it is important to Qaa I speak with her."

"I shall summon the *swnwt* and will send one of the scribes to the marketplace. May I bring you some wine?" Thanuny did his best to hide his concern. Nebettawy was flushed at the cheeks, but the rest of her face was ashen. Her eyes were glassy and she seemed to have trouble focusing on him.

"Many thanks, Thanuny. I would like some wine. And another vessel of cool water, please."

Thanuny went about his errands. He had one of the kitchen servants bring her wine and water, he dispatched a scribe to the marketplace, and he went in search of the *swnwt*. On his return, he planned to stop at the palace to summon the king and Qaa.

Nebettawy got up from the bed, crossed the room, and found a piece of linen cloth on her shelf. She took it back to the bed, dipped it in the water, placed it on her forehead, and reclined until the *swnwt* or Takhat arrived. Almost immediately, she dozed off, tossing and turning, unaware of the infection coursing through her body.

"You are Takhat?" the scribe inquired of the woman selling bead necklaces.

"I am, who inquires?"

"I have been dispatched by the temple. The *hemet netjer* needs to speak with you."

"Tell the *hemet netjer* I will come to the temple before sunset."

"No, Mistress. I have been instructed to pack up your wares and bring you back to the temple, now." The scribe began to pick up the necklaces and other jewelry Takhat had on display.

Thanuny stopped at the Harem to inquire about the *swnwt per aa*. She was out visiting nobles' wives, who comprised some of her practice. He headed for the south wall of the enclosure, where the houses of the noblemen were located, hoping to catch her in the streets. After asking a few passersby, he was directed to the house of one of the merchants. He looked in and saw the *swnwt* and the merchant's wife; the *swnwt* was preparing an herbal for the woman.

"Excuse me, but I have been looking for you, *swnwt*. The *hemet netjer* is ill and requested I bring you back to the temple."

"*Hem netjer*, I shall be finished here shortly. I shall go to the temple straight away."

"Many thanks, *swnwt*. I must go to the palace and alert the king." Thanuny departed, not looking forward to the news he must now deliver.

 Claudia R. Dillaire

The scribe led Takhat through the temple residences to the *hemet netjer's* quarters. He deposited her wares inside the room and exited immediately. Nebettawy looked up to see Takhat, hands on her hips, angry and confused. Takhat carried herself well for a sturdy young woman. As a widow, she was eager to find a new husband for herself and a father for her children; unfortunately she found Unas, and would do anything to please him. She was short and proud, not afraid to do a day's work, but too easily controlled by men.

"Takhat, accept my apologies for taking you from the marketplace. I know Unas is being held for questioning, but you may be able to help him, if you shall speak to me." Nebettawy's breathing was laboured and she had trouble focusing her attention.

"Unas is innocent. I do not know how I can help him. The Chief of the Medjay thinks he is guilty, so Unas will be punished no matter what I say."

"The Chief of the Medjay is a fair and honest man. Takhat, speak to me. Tell me what you know, and I shall speak to him and my father."

"Truly, *hemet netjer*? I love Unas, I am carrying his child. How can I help him?" Takhat's eyes were filled with tears.

"You traded an expensive vessel of wine in the marketplace with a Phoenician. Where did you get it?" Nebettawy could barely hold herself up in a sitting position. Her body felt like it was on fire, her head was full of bees.

"Where would I get an expensive vessel of wine?"

"I am feeling unwell, so do not test my patience, Takhat. How did you come into possession of the wine?"

"Unas asked me to get him a vessel of wine. I took it from Bek's tent when his daughter was busy with a customer. I gave it to Unas and a few days later he told me to trade it with the Phoenician."

Nebettawy could make no sense of what Takhat said. She bathed her face with the cool linen cloth and took a sip of wine. It was hard for her to breathe, but she needed to know more.

"Takhat, what did Unas do with the wine?"

"I never saw the vessel again, until he gave it to me to trade in the marketplace."

"Did he give it to someone?" Nebettawy wondered if Unas was working with Merti. But, who attacked her? It had to be a man, a very strong man.

"*Hemet netjer*, I do not know. I have told you everything. Unas did nothing wrong. You must help him."

Nebettawy tried to stand, but her legs gave way. She crumpled to the floor, barely breathing. Takhat screamed, alerting the priests that something was wrong.

"Your majesty, your daughter is quite ill. She did not want me to trouble you, but I felt I must." Thanuny bowed deeply to Ramesses, seated in an antechamber, with Qaa and two Medjay guards.

Ramesses bolted from his chair. "Qaa, let us go to the temple."

Ramesses, followed by Qaa, Thanuny, and the two Medjay, all but sprinted to the temple residences. There they found Takhat crying, and Harkhuf kneeling next to the *hemet netjer*. Paying no heed to the consequences, Qaa bent down, picked up Nebettawy, and carried her to her bed. He placed her down gently and felt her forehead; it was hot to the touch. He saw the bowl of water and immediately began to bathe her forehead.

"Thanuny, call the *swnwt*." Qaa barked.

"I have already summoned her. She shall be here presently."

"Thanuny, you have done well." Ramesses waved away the Medjay. "Harkhuf, many thanks for attending to my daughter."

Harkhuf bowed to the king and exited the room. Takhat, seizing the opportunity, grabbed her wares and quietly slipped out of the room along with him.

"Qaa, how is she?" Ramesses's voice was grave.

"My lord, she burns with fever." Qaa, trying to keep his composure, spoke in a measured tone. Inside, he was terrified. If she had developed an infection, and it was coursing through her body, there could be little the *swnwt* could do. Nebettawy had been through a terrible ordeal, she might not be strong enough to fight the infection.

"I shall sit with her until the *swnwt* arrives. Qaa, go back to the palace, retrieve the scrolls we were reviewing, and make sense of this case. I want to know who did this to my daughter." Ramesses spoke with no emotion, the shock of the situation evident on his face. Thanuny exited the room with Qaa, followed by the two Medjay.

Claudia R. Dillaire

"Thanuny, can you handle the temple duties for me?" Qaa was paler than usual.

"Qaa, do what you must. The temple is on edge from this business. Devote your time and energy to finding this fiend."

Qaa dismissed the Medjay and went back to the palace to retrieve his scrolls. He would study them in his quarters, so he could be close to Nebettawy, and he could check on her until the *swnwt* arrived.

Ramesses sat beside his daughter, bathing her limbs in cool water, trying in vain to quell her fever. He watched as his daughter tossed and turned on her bed, crying out for help, crying out for Qaa. The oil lamps had been lit hours ago. What was delaying the *swnwt*? Did she not know how ill Nebettawy was? He was frantic with worry, Nebettawy was precious to him. He began entreating his father, Amun, to spare his daughter. A kitchen worker brought in a fresh bowl of water and exited immediately. Ramesses began to bathe his daughter again, trying to cool her forehead. She moaned and cried in obvious pain, trying to focus her eyes, calling out for Qaa. He tried to make her drink some lotus flower steeped wine, but she did not seem to be able to swallow it.

Day 17 in Month 3

"Qaa, come quickly!" Ramesses could not control his daughter and he was terrified.

Qaa ran down the corridor from his quarters. Nebettawy, feverish and delirious, was writhing on the bed, tearing her dress off. She was screaming in pain and would not let her father touch her.

"Nebettawy, it is Qaa. I am here."

"Help me, Qaa. I can not stand the pain."

Nebettawy had managed to tear off her dress and threw it on the floor. She started to claw at her loincloth. Qaa was afraid she would injure herself or reopen the wound. As she undid the loincloth, Qaa could see fluids seeping from between her legs, onto the coarse linen.

"Father, I must touch her or she shall die before the *swnwt* arrives." Qaa, a military man, was panicked by what he saw; this was Nebettawy, the woman he loved, not a soldier in battle.

Ramesses seemed to grow small and frail before Qaa's eyes. "Do what you must, my son."

Qaa reached inside Nebettawy and felt something blocking the entrance to her womb. Blood and pus oozed around his fingers, as she writhed in pain on the bed.

"Qaa, make me well. My womb aches to give you sons."

"Father, hold her fast, so I shall not cause her further injury."

Ramesses drew himself up and did as instructed. Qaa gently maneuvered his finger around the obstruction and pulled it out. As he did, Nebettawy cried out in anguish and the blood and pus began to flow freely. Qaa dropped a large clot, as well as the linen ball, onto the loincloth and reached for Nebettawy's dress, which lay discarded on the floor beside the bed. He tore it quickly into strips he soaked in the bowl of lotus flower and wine. Gently he inserted one of the strips to cleanse the wound. Again, Nebettawy screamed in pain.

As soon as he removed one strip of cloth, he reached for another, applying a bit more pressure to the wound each time to slow down the bleeding. When he removed the fifth strip, there was little blood. He stood up and went to Nebettawy's dressing table, looking through the jars of oils and unguents. He found the one he wanted, containing honey, and took it to the bedside. He knelt, tore one more strip of cloth, and covered it with the honey. Hands trembling, he gently inserted it into Nebettawy and hoped she would live until the *swnwt* arrived.

Nebettawy had stopped thrashing and was now lying, drenched in sweat and blood and pus, her breathing more regular, but still moaning ever so slightly. Qaa began to recite spells from memory, spells for protection, spells for healing, spells to guard against evil spirits. Ramesses let go of his daughter, dropped to his knees beside Qaa, and again beseeched Amun to spare his daughter, and take his life instead.

The *swnwt per aa*, Ashayt, finally arrived, with her apprentice in tow, and surveyed the scene. She was also *swnwt n per hemet nesut* and had earned her titles by being discreet, as well as being an outstanding herbalist and magician. Short and sturdy, she exuded an air of confidence and authority, and had a hard, commanding voice, though she could easily comfort as well. Her apprentice *swnwt*, Khamaat, a young thin woman of twenty or so, was frightened of her, and the *swnwt per aa* liked that just fine; she would learn the proper way to be a good *swnwt*.

Nebettawy lay on the bed, naked and exposed. She was a modest young woman and would be mortified that Qaa and her father had seen her like this. The blood and fluids puddled on her loincloth concerned her greatly. She examined Nebettawy quickly and complimented Qaa on the work he had done.

"*Hem netjer*, have you thought of adding *swnw* to your many titles?"

"I only did what I had to do. In Kush, a *swnw* is not easy to find; I have been called upon many times to ease suffering. But I do not wish to be a *swnw*." Qaa found it difficult to stand.

Ashayt inquired as to the treatment Qaa performed. He told of the clot and how he had treated the bleeding and infection.

"Thank you for thinking so quickly. Go, cleanse yourself. I shall attend to her now." She turned her attention to Ramesses. "Your majesty, I offer my apologies for being delayed. I have been attending your daughter, the princess Tentopet, in the Birth House. It is not yet her time and she is having a difficult birth. Her mother is with her. Does the queen know about Nebettawy?"

"No, she does not. I shall stay here until I know the condition of my daughter. My great royal wife would be better suited to be with Tentopet," Ramesses looked like a beaten man.

"My king, I know you have witnessed much this night. Let us now attend to her in private. You may remain in the corridor should I have need for you."

Qaa barely had the strength to trudge the corridor to the private bath he and Thanuny shared. He entered the bath and started toward the entrance of the closet-like area. He was thankful this night for the luxury of the indoor waste facility. It contained a wooden chair with a hole in the seat and a large earthen vessel beneath it. As the smell of Nebettawy's blood and pus, mixed with his sweat and fear, overwhelmed him, he ran into the closet, fell to his knees, and vomited into the hole. When he was finally able, he leaned his head against the cool, mud-brick wall, his body trembling, his limbs leaden and aching.

He forced himself to his feet, stripped off his noxious kilt and loincloth, and dropped them on the tile floor. He walked to the bath, and lowered himself into the cool, clean water. Alone, finally able to let go, he wept silently. Amun was punishing Nebettawy for her sin of joining with him. He should not have allowed his desires to control him, but he felt powerless against her charms.

As he cleansed himself, he begged Amun to spare her. He was the one at fault, he could not resist her, he was the one who should be punished. He prayed and recited spells and incantations he remembered from his childhood, the ones he heard his father speak.

As if from the grave, he could hear the words his mother recited, time and again, in the last month of her life. They were to her gods, in her language, a language he almost never heard her speak. After more than twenty years, he could still see her face, the pale, delicate skin, her eyes, a blue-green, like the Great Sea, and her lovely hair, the colour of burning wheat, flashing golden and copper in the sun.

"My son, you have grown into a fine, caring man. I could not have done better. Recite the words with me, and I shall do all in my power to save your wife. My magic is still strong and lives within you as well, so I am always with you."

Qaa, as if in a dream, began to flawlessly recite with his mother, words he did not understand, in a language that was foreign to him. The words were an incantation to bring a loved one from the brink of death back to the living. Three times they repeated the incantation and when the final word was spoken, Qaa was again alone, the vision of his mother just a memory.

Then, he heard the scream.

Qaa bolted from the bath and ran down the corridor to his quarters. Seizing a clean loincloth, he quickly pulled one corner between his legs and wrapped the other two corners over his hips. He was still securing it as he sprinted for the doorway.

In the corridor, he almost collided with Thanuny, who was awakened by the scream. The two men ran the length of the corridor to the *hemet netjer's* quarters. Ramesses paced at the doorway, and appeared agitated.

"Qaa, summon the Medjay!"

"My lord, what has happened? Is it Nebettawy?"

"She still lingers. The *swnwt* apprentice claims to have seen someone looking in my daughter's window." Ramesses fumed with anger.

"My lord, Thanuny and I shall alert the Medjay. Until we return, I want no one to leave the temple."

"*Hem netjer*, I must return to the Birth House." Ashayt stopped Qaa before he could leave.

"*Swnwt*, you shall remain here. I can not allow you to leave the temple without an escort. When the Medjay arrive, they shall escort you to the Birth House. Continue to attend Nebettawy; we shall return presently."

Qaa strode through the temple, Thanuny barely keeping stride with him. When they reached their quarters, each entered his own room to don a kilt. Qaa then opened his large travel chest and withdrew two swords, a dagger, and a *khopesh*. Thanuny was standing in the doorway when Qaa looked up from his task.

"I need your help. We shall wake the Medjay. Hurry, we have no time to waste. My friend, are you skilled with a sword?"

"I have not used one in many years." Thanuny looked less than pleased with the weapons. He was a scribe by profession, not a military man like Qaa.

Qaa handed him a sword, as he slid the dagger into the waist of his kilt. He grabbed the other sword and the *khopesh* and brushed past Thanuny. The men raced down the corridor to Ramesses.

"My king, sword or *khopesh*?"

"Sword."

Qaa tossed the sword to Ramesses, who expertly caught the handle.

After waking the Medjay, Qaa and Thanuny hurried back to the temple residences in silence. They entered the mud-brick building and headed quickly to the *hemet netjer's* room.

"My lord, Medjay have been summoned."

Within minutes the Captain of the Medjay arrived with twenty men. The captain bowed to Qaa and Ramesses.

"I have brought my finest men. We await your orders."

"I want Medjay guarding the palace and pylon gates and dispatch soldiers to guard the exterior of the temple complex, when they arrive. Two Medjay shall be stationed in this corridor outside the *hemet netjer's* quarters, with two more outside her window at all times. I want two Medjay protecting the king and I shall need two more as escorts between the temple and the palace. Place the remaining Medjay where they shall be most effective." Qaa spoke with the authority of a career military man.

"And, Captain, I want two Medjay with Qaa." Ramesses raised his hand to stop Qaa's objection. "There shall be no discussion on the matter."

"Captain, no one is to enter or leave the temple without approval." Qaa turned to his friend. "Thanuny, I need the names of the temple staff who prepare the libations for ritual. They shall be allowed to enter."

"I shall awaken the lesser priests. They are more familiar with the staff and can assist the Medjay." Thanuny bowed to Ramesses, turned, and headed down the corridor to make arrangements.

"Captain, the *swnwt* needs an escort to the Birth House. I shall leave her in your capable hands."

"I have treated the wound with honey and additional herbs, hoping to draw out the infection. Khamaat shall remain with her. At first light, I shall have Tetisheri, Nebettawy's old wet nurse sent to relieve her and she can attend to the princess until I return." Ashayt bowed to Ramesses and followed the Medjay captain.

With the Medjay guards at their posts outside Nebettawy's room and window and reassured she was protected, the two men could leave Nebettawy with the apprentice *swnwt*. Qaa and Ramesses were escorted to Qaa's quarters to speak privately. Qaa directed Ramesses to a seat at the writing table and he sat on his bed. Ramesses laid the sword Qaa had given him on the table.

"Father, at first light, Thanuny and I shall retrieve the scrolls at Raneb's home. We shall read through all he kept there, as well as the numerous scrolls here in his quarters. I pray I find notes on this case, something I may have overlooked." Qaa looked like a man who had been in combat for days.

"My son, neither of us has slept well in days. Rest and then look at the scrolls with fresh eyes." Ramesses appeared worn and defeated.

"Let me have a room prepared for you in the temple. I can not rest until Nebettawy is out of danger and restored to health." Qaa stood and began to pace the room.

"Qaa, you shall be of no use to her without rest. My son, I must command you, before you fall ill as well, rest now." Ramesses reached out and stopped Qaa from pacing.

"I feel so helpless. Nebettawy, my sister, lies wasting away before my eyes. I can not protect her, I can not ease her suffering. A murderer walks free in Waset and I have been powerless to stop him."

"I have placed my trust in you. You shall find the answers." Ramesses stood and placed his hand on Qaa's shoulder, to comfort him.

"Excuse me, your majesty, Qaa." Thanuny was standing at the entrance to Qaa's quarters. "The lesser priests shall be stationed at each entrance with Medjay."

Claudia R. Dillaire

"Thanuny, you have done well. Have Harkhuf perform the morning ritual. I want you and Qaa to rest. Is there a room where I may lie down? I want to be close to my daughter until the danger has passed."

"Your majesty, I shall prepare the room myself and return for you. I shall send a message to Harkhuf and tell him only what he needs to know. Qaa, do you have any orders for me as well?" He handed the sword back to Qaa.

"No, Thanuny. When you are done, please return. The king and I shall remain here. Thank you my friend."

Qaa and Ramesses sat together in silence until Thanuny returned. The room next to Nebettawy had been prepared for Ramesses and the two Medjay escorted him to his temporary quarters in the temple. Thanuny fell to sleep almost immediately after returning to his quarters. But sleep was difficult to come for the king, worried about his daughter, and disturbed by how Qaa had touched her. In his quarters, Qaa tossed and turned, the sight of Nebettawy's blood staining his dreams, half expecting to be banished to a desert outpost when this ugly business was resolved.

 THE WRATH OF AMUN

Day 18 in Month 3

amesses awoke before sunrise. He had slept little and was anxious to check on his daughter. He looked into her room, to find Khamaat bathing her limbs with cool water. Nebettawy was quiet, for the moment, but so pale, so fragile. Rather than disturb the *swnwt*, Ramesses went back to his temporary quarters in the temple to cleanse himself before he returned to the palace to attend to pressing matters. He would see Qaa before he left, and would leave orders to be summoned if his daughter's condition changed.

Qaa woke as sunlight began to filter into his room. He pulled himself out of bed, barely able to stand; exhaustion and uncertainty held him and no amount of sleep would revive him until Nebettawy was well. He stumbled down the corridor to the private bath and cleansed before returning to his quarters to dress. Thanuny would be awake and he would need his help today. The sooner he had a suspect, the sooner he could devote his energies to Nebettawy. He pulled on a clean loincloth and fresh kilt, before looking in on Thanuny. The older priest was not in his room, but his clothes were laid out on the bed. He walked to the private bath and called in to him.

"Thanuny, I shall await you in my quarters."

"I shall meet you presently."

Qaa went back to his room and began to take scrolls from the shelves on the wall. He and Thanuny could sort through them; the only ones of importance right now were about any crimes in Waset. Qaa looked at one of the scrolls and noted that Raneb kept detailed notes of cases he had investigated. Just cursory examination right now; he could read through them while he sat with Nebettawy.

"Qaa, I am at your service for the day. How may I assist?"

Qaa jumped at the sound of the older priest's voice. He was on edge and had begun to question his own abilities.

"Thanuny, let us go to Raneb's residence. I noticed many of the scrolls were religious in nature and do not want them handled by anyone but priests. We shall bring all the scrolls here and sort through them. Some of them should be brought to the House of Life for the scribes to copy."

"Qaa, if I may inquire, how is the *hemet netjer*?"

"I wish to stop at her room before we leave the temple." Qaa swallowed the lump that was in his throat and blinked to hide the tears.

"If you wish to unburden yourself, Qaa, it may help to talk to someone." Thanuny placed his hand on the young man's shoulder.

"Thank you, my friend. Let us see if there has been any change."

The two priests, followed by Medjay guards, walked through the temple corridors to the *hemet netjer's* quarters. Ramesses was just entering the room, so Qaa and Thanuny followed him inside. Khamaat was trying to get Nebettawy to drink some wine, but Nebettawy swatted her away. Qaa took the drinking bowl from the *swnwt* and knelt by the bed.

"Sister, it is Qaa. You are very ill and you must drink." His voice was quiet and soothing. Knowing the consequesnces for touching her, he still reached under her shoulders to raise her head. He put the bowl to her lips and got her to drink a small amount of wine.

"Qaa, I am so tired. Will you stay with me?" Nebettawy whispered, her breath laboured and her eyes unable to focus on him. She tried to grasp his hand but did not have the strength.

"Sister, I must find the man who did this to you. Your father shall sit with you now. I shall return later and sit with you, if that is your desire?" Qaa laid her back on the bed and gently stroked her hair.

Claudia R. Dillaire

"Yes, my brother. Come and sit with me." She laid her head on his hand and dozed off almost immediately. He gently slid his hand from under her head, so as not to wake her. He stood and handed the drinking bowl back to the *swnwt*.

"Many thanks, *hem netjer*. She will not drink for me." The *swnwt* began to bathe Nebettawy's face and forehead with cool water.

"*Swnwt*, put a drop or two of the *hemet netjer's* perfume in the water. I think it would mean a great deal to her, and the scent shall please her." Qaa crossed to Nebettawy's dressing table, picked up the vessel of perfume, and handed it to her.

"My king, Thanuny and I are going to Raneb's residence to retrieve his scrolls." Qaa bowed to Ramesses, as did Thanuny.

"Qaa, I must go to the palace for a short time. I shall walk with you. *Swnwt*, dispatch a Medjay immediately, if there is any change. I shall return presently."

The three men, along with Medjay escorts, walked the corridors of the temple in silence until they exited onto the avenue of the Festival Calendars.

"Father, has there been any change in her condition?"

"No, Qaa. She burns with fever and will not eat. If she does not improve ...," the king's voice trailed off, unable to bring himself to say what he was thinking.

"When Thanuny and I return to the temple, I shall try to get her to eat." Qaa could feel the terror growing inside him. Like Ramesses, he did not want to think of what could happen to Nebettawy.

"Many thanks, my son." Ramesses embraced Qaa and quickly turned away, head bowed, striding toward the palace, Medjay guards on either side of him.

Qaa, with his Medjay escorts, and Thanuny headed for the Second Court, to exit the mortuary complex.

A soldier stood guard at Raneb's residence. The Medjay remained outside while Qaa and Thanuny entered the cool, dark, mud-brick house. It had been nine days since Qaa had first entered the house, but nothing had been touched. He and Thanuny worked quickly, collecting up the scattered scrolls, and putting them on the table in the middle of the room. Thanuny and Qaa then climbed the stairs to the second story of the house. Raneb's bedroom was sparsely furnished, but he kept a chest at the foot of the bed. Thanuny opened it and found blank papyri, additional palettes and inks, and more scrolls. A thorough search of the room revealed more scrolls in a small chest in the closet where Raneb kept his ritual clothing.

Thanuny carried the small chest, followed by Qaa with the large chest, down the stairs to the main room. After searching the main room once more, no additional scrolls turned up. The scrolls on the table were packed into the two chests, filling them to the brims.

"Thanuny, Raneb was your friend. I shall leave a guard on the house. It is only proper that you and the other priests remove his personal effects. Take all the time you need. This has been difficult for all of you."

"Many thanks, Qaa. You have shown great deference for a man you did not know; I appreciate your sensitivity and understanding in this horrible business." Thanuny held back his emotions. When Thanuny's wife joined Auser, Raneb had helped him through many difficult days. "I shall have the priests come today."

"Let us return to the temple. We have quite a task ahead of us." Qaa bent to pick up the large chest, but Thanuny stopped him.

"Qaa, it is obvious to me how hard this situation with the *hemet netjer* is for you. If you do not deal with the feelings you have, it shall affect your health, as well." Thanuny pulled out a chair and motioned Qaa to sit; he refused and continued to stand.

"Thanuny, I was raised a soldier. I pride myself on being in control. But this, I can not control. All I can do is attend to the *hemet netjer* when she needs me." Qaa's shoulders drooped from the weight of his burden. "I must stay strong for her. When I am ready, I shall seek out your guidance."

"I saw the love in your eyes for her, when you were with her this morning. She responds to you because she knows the depth of your love. Being a soldier does not make you any less compassionate, nor does it make it hurt less, when the one you love is gravely ill."

"I fear if I give in to what I am feeling, I shall be unable to perform my service to the king. He has placed his confidence in me, to solve this case. It has taken many turns and I need to have a clear head to sort out what I have learned. I can not allow my feelings to distract me. The attack on Nebettawy would not have happened if I had not been distracted in the first place." Qaa tried hard to choke back his guilt and he certainly could not confess his transgressions.

"Qaa, whatever you have or have not done, I am sure it was with the best of intentions."

Qaa wanted to tell Thanuny why Nebettawy was not in the temple the night of the attack, how his desires had clouded his judgement, and now she was paying the price for his lack of self-control. He did not care what happened to him, what punishment the king would impose, but he could not allow her to be punished. She was blameless; he should have been able to resist her.

"Many thanks, my friend, but no one can help me. What is done is done and I have to live with the consequences." Tears clouded his eyes, but he managed to fight them back. "Let us return to the temple. We have much work to do." Qaa bent and picked up the large chest.

Qaa and Thanuny put the two chests in Qaa's quarters. The two men performed the noon ritual, before starting the task of reading and sorting scrolls. Thanuny went ahead to Qaa's room, while Qaa stopped to check on Nebettawy. Tetisheri had relieved the *swnwt* and had taken over the vigil by Nebettawy's bed. She patiently bathed her fevered forehead and limbs, talking to her, singing to her, as she had when Nebettawy was an infant. The wet nurse told him Nebettawy still had not eaten. Qaa instructed her to dispatch a Medjay to his quarters when Nebettawy woke. He would try to get her to eat.

Qaa returned to his quarters. Thanuny had started on the small chest, putting religious scrolls on Qaa's bed and putting non-religious texts on the table. Qaa started on the large chest, taking his time to look at each document carefully, since he was not as familiar with Raneb's script. When Thanuny finished with the chest, he started Raneb's personal scrolls, still resting on a shelf in the room. The task was time consuming, but both men hoped the outcome would merit results in this case.

"Excuse me, Thanuny, would you like me to perform the evening ritual?"

Qaa and Thanuny, so absorbed in their work, looked up to see Harkhuf standing in the doorway.

"Is it that hour already?" Thanuny inquired.

"Yes. I do not wish to take you from your work."

"Thanuny, if you wish to perform the ritual, you may. I would like to check on the *hemet netjer* and we both need to refresh ourselves." Qaa tried to straighten up, but he was stiff from sitting.

Thanuny, as well, needed to move; his legs felt numb and his head pounded.

"Qaa, I shall return after the evening ritual." Thanuny and Harkhuf exited the room. Thanuny went to cleanse himself and Harkhuf went to prepare the incense.

Qaa walked gingerly through the corridors to Nebettawy's quarters. Ramesses had returned earlier in the day and was sitting next to his daughter's bed, holding her hand, stroking her hair. He looked up and saw Qaa at the doorway, motioning him to enter. Qaa came close to Nebettawy's bed, listening to her breathing, which rattled in her chest.

"Father, has she eaten?" Qaa whispered to the king.

"No, she refuses." Ramesses was pale as linen and fear had begun to creep across his face.

"Let me go to the kitchen and bring us some refreshment. I have not eaten all day and I have much to do this evening."

"I sent Tetisheri to rest. The *swnwt* is due after sunset. Can you stay and try to get Nebettawy to eat? Do not fear punishment, my son. I just want her to recover." Ramesses voice was desperate.

Qaa put his hand on the king's shoulder. "Do not worry, Father. She shall eat for me. I shall return presently."

Qaa returned with fruit, cheese, sliced meat, bread, honey cakes, beer, and wine for himself and the king. They ate in silence, waiting for the *swnwt*. When she arrived with her apprentice, she asked them to wait in the corridor while she examined Nebettawy. They could hear Nebettawy, begging the *swnwt* not to touch her, crying out in pain. When they were allowed to enter, Nebettawy was curled up on the bed, crying. Qaa went to her and took her hand.

"Sister, I know you are in pain. I need you to drink some wine. It shall help ease the pain."

A weak smile curled her lips as Nebettawy looked at Qaa. He lifted her up and motioned for the drinking bowl of wine. He put it to her lips and got her to drink. He laid her on the bed and leaned in to speak to her.

"Nebettawy, you shall not get better if you do not eat. I can not live without you. Will you eat for me?" Qaa stroked her hair and cheek.

"I shall eat, Brother, if you feed me." Each word was an effort for her to speak.

"I went to the temple bakery and stole your favourite. Will you share it with me?" Qaa picked up her hand and kissed the palm.

"Yes, I shall." Nebettawy closed her eyes.

"Father, please give me a honey cake." Qaa stretched out his hand to Ramesses, who gave him one of the cakes. Qaa broke the honey cake into small pieces. He took a small piece and put it next to her lips. "Sister, you must eat for me." His voice was gentle, patient. "Open your eyes."

Nebettawy looked at Qaa and smiled. She compliantly opened her mouth for the piece of honey cake. Qaa slid his hand under her shoulders and raised her up while he placed the piece of cake in her mouth. She chewed contentedly; it was the first food she had eaten in days. After she swallowed, Qaa reached for the drinking vessel and had her sip the wine, then laid her down.

"Will you eat a bit of fruit for me, Sister?"

"I do not want any more." She was tired and wanted to sleep.

"Sister, do you not want to get better? I need you, Nebettawy. So, you must eat for me." Qaa was insistent, but his voice remained quiet and soothing. He stretched out his hand and Ramesses handed him a small slice of apricot. Qaa again slid his hand under her and raised her up. He managed to get her to eat the piece of apricot, before letting her drift off to sleep. He gently kissed her forehead and stroked her cheek, before he stood up.

"Many thanks, my son." Ramesses put his hand on Qaa's shoulder. "No one can get her to eat or drink."

"*Hem netjer*, she needs to eat more. She is very weak and if she does not build up her strength, she may not be able to fight the infection. Can you come back in a few hours? I shall have Khamaat wake her for you." Ashayt, not one to show emotion, was concerned about her patient.

"Have me summoned at any time. I have much work to attend to and shall be awake well into the night."

Ramesses went back to sitting next to Nebettawy and the *swnwt* apprentice took up her post near the bed, as well, to bathe her forehead. Qaa escorted the *swnwt* to the door, where Thanuny awaited him. Out in the corridor, Ashayt felt more comfortable to speak.

"*Hem netjer*, I do not wish to upset the king any more than he already is, but you know her situation is extremely grave. You must get her to eat. I am doing all I can, but still she gets weaker."

"I shall do all I can, *swnwt*. I can not bear to see her like this, suffering, in pain. I shall make her fight." Qaa bowed his head, not wanting the *swnwt* to see the tears he could no longer hold back. Thanuny put his hand on Qaa's shoulder.

"Qaa, why do you not go to your quarters and lie down? I shall wake you after you have had some rest and we shall continue our work."

"Many thanks, my friend, but I shall be able to work. I need to freshen up. I shall meet you in my quarters. And, many thanks, *swnwt*." Qaa turned quickly and strode down the corridor.

Qaa continued his work on the large chest and Thanuny resumed sorting the scrolls from the shelves. When Qaa finally came to the last of the scrolls in the large chest, he took all the religious texts from his bed and placed them in the large chest. Thanuny handed him a dozen more scrolls for the chest, put two on the table, and looked around the room. It appeared they had finally gathered up all the scrolls; now the work really began.

Qaa moved the chest to the wall near the doorway. He would have the priests bring it to the House of Life tomorrow. He looked at the pile of papyri on the table. He estimated there were close to thirty scrolls. While he had been looking through them, some appeared to deal with individual crimes here in Waset, others detailed the day to day activities at the temple and mortuary complex. The earliest date he had found was the first year in the reign of Ramesses III, which was probably when Raneb was appointed Chief of the Medjay, and Ramesses was now in his seventeenth year.

"Thanuny, was Raneb appointed by our current king?"

"Yes, he was. The king was grateful for Raneb's service and elevated him from Captain to Chief, shortly after he took the throne."

"Let's arrange the scrolls by year. I would like to start with the most recent ones." Qaa would read them all; he had seen a mention of a similar assault several years previous and wanted to read that one more thoroughly.

Once the scrolls were sorted by year, the task did not seem nearly as overpowering. Qaa picked up the most recent, but there was no mention of Iput's murder. Working his way back, he found mention of the thefts at the temple, and a complete listing of the items missing.

"My friend, this is the scroll of the missing temple items. Would you read it through and make any changes?" Qaa handed the papyrus to Thanuny.

"This is not correct." Thanuny looked puzzled. "Two of these items are here in the temple."

"Could you bring them here? I would like to examine them."

Thanuny stood and exited the room. Qaa leafed through two more recent scrolls, but still no mention of the murder. When Qaa examined Raneb's body, his right thumb was black, indicating he had recently written some type of document. The scrolls covered the current year, but stopped in the middle of the previous month. There had to be another scroll, somewhere in this room. Raneb had been coming back from the temple, so he may have left the scroll here, unless his killer had taken it with him.

Frustrated, Qaa removed his personal effects from the closet and started searching the room again. He covered every possible place a scroll could be hidden. Finding nothing, he turned his attention to Raneb's personal effects, which were still on the dressing table and stone bench. Qaa picked up each jar and vessel. Some contained unguents and oils. One vessel held wine. A small decorative container held makeup and bronze shaving blades. He picked up a large vessel, expecting it to have more weight to it. He tried to open it, but it had been sealed closed with beeswax. He took out his dagger, scored the beeswax, and removed the top. Inside, rolled and tied closed, was a papyrus scroll. Qaa shook it out of the vessel, took it to the table, and carefully removed the tie. He spread it on the table and smiled. This was what he had been looking for. It was dated the eighth day of this month, the same day Raneb died.

"Qaa, I was only gone a short time. What has happened here?" Thanuny, shaking his head, stood in the doorway.

Qaa looked confused, until he ran his eyes over the room. Clay vessels, unguent jars, clothing, reed sandals, and jewelry lay strewn around the room.

"Thanuny, my apologies. The scrolls stopped the middle of the last month. I knew there had to be another scroll. I shall straighten out Raneb's items." Qaa bent and picked up two of the unguent jars.

Thanuny placed the two ritual items, previously listed as missing, on the table and helped Qaa pick up the vessels and clothing. When they had all the items on one shelf, Thanuny directed Qaa to the ritual items. Qaa picked up a small offering bowl, which was too light in weight to be gold. He put it back on the table and turned his attention to the figurine. It was a small statue a patron had paid for as an offering to Amun. The craftsmanship was impeccable, but again, it was far too light to be gold.

"Were these misplaced? Why did Raneb list them as missing?"

"The small offering bowl disappeared several months ago. One of the goldsmiths brought it to the temple and said he found it at the Western gate when he arrived for work one morning. I do not know the circumstances regarding the statue."

"My friend, this is most important. Do you know who the goldsmith was?"

"The Overseer of the Temple Goldsmiths brought it in, but one of his men found it. Raneb questioned him, so I do not know who the man was who found it."

"These two items are replicas. I suspect the real items have already been sold." Qaa handed the items back to Thanuny.

"I shall put these in the preparation tent. Replacements shall have to be made." Thanuny was not pleased they had been using an inferior offering bowl in the temple.

"Do the goldsmiths mark their work?" Qaa could determine who had made the items from his mark.

"What do you suspect?"

"Whoever created these was fairly sure no one would notice the difference. He would have to be an experienced craftsman."

"Would you like me to have the overseer awakened? I can have him brought to the temple."

"No, Thanuny. I shall speak with him tomorrow. I have found the scroll Raneb prepared on Iput's murder. He had it hidden here in his quarters. Once I have read it, I may have all the information I need."

"My chief, the *hemet netjer* is awake and calling for you. The *swnwt* asked me to summon you." It was one of the Medjay who was guarding Nebettawy's room.

"Many thanks, Medjay. Tell the *swnwt* I shall be there presently. Thanuny, leave the two replicas. I shall bring them with me tomorrow when I question the overseer. I must attend to Nebettawy now."

"May I do anything to help?" Thanuny looked at his friend with concern. Qaa was tired, drawn, and on edge.

"Yes, have the kitchen send in a tray of refreshments. I need to get the *hemet netjer* to eat. Make sure there is a jar of honey on the tray."

After Thanuny exited, Qaa went to one of his travel chests. He lifted clothing out, onto the bed, and rummaged around, until he

found what he was searching for. It was a small, wooden box, intricately carved, obviously having belonged to a woman. He opened the box, checked the contents, and put it under his arm.

"Nebettawy, it is Qaa. Will you eat for me?" Qaa gently lifted her head. Her flesh was glistening and hot to the touch; her fever was worse, showing no signs of abating. Ramesses sat next to the bed, holding his daughter's hand and stroking her cheek.

"Qaa?" Her eyes wandered over his face, unable to focus.

"*Swnwt*, give me the honey." Qaa opened the ornate box and dipped his finger into the powder inside. He tapped his finger against the side of the box, he only needed a pinch of the powder for her, she was so thin and frail. He then took the same finger and slid it into the honey. Ramesses reached out to stop him but he placed his finger on Nebettawy's lips; she opened her mouth and weakly accepted the honey.

"*Hem netjer*, what have you given her?" Khamaat was afraid the *swnwt per aa* would chide her severely for letting him administer something to her patient.

"It is powdered willow bark. My mother used to give it to me when I was feverish."

Nebettawy had sucked the honey off Qaa's finger and appeared to have dozed off. Qaa lifted her head again and tried to rouse her.

"Sister, I need you to eat. You shall not get well, and I shall not let you leave me. I need you to fight for me." His voice was calm, insistent, but tinged with desperation. Ramesses watched how Qaa treated his daughter, his concern, his compassion with her. She opened her eyes and tried to smile at him. The *swnwt* handed Qaa a small piece of fig which he put in Nebettawy's mouth. She chewed and swallowed, but did not seem to care. Qaa kept her awake long enough to feed her a small piece of cheese and to take a sip of mandrake steeped wine. He laid her back on the bed and, risking the king's displeasure, kissed her on the forehead.

He read the notes Raneb made on the murder of Iput. Apparently, thefts had been a common occurance at the temple for the past few years. Raneb outlined how he had questioned the temple staff, priests who rotated

in, kitchen and bakery workers, as well as the permanent staff. The thefts did not fit a pattern and Raneb could find no temple worker who could be involved. In the second month of the Akhet season, in the seventeenth year of the king, a small offering bowl and statue went missing. The second month was Paopi, the same time Iput was raped. Had she seen something that evening coming back from the temple or was it just an unfortunate coincidence? In the second month of the Peret season, the Overseer of the Temple Goldsmiths came to Raneb with the two missing items.

He stated to Raneb that Khety had found them at the Western gate of the mortuary complex, near the goldsmith tents. It looked as if someone had tried to hide them there, they were covered with sand, but he had kicked the statue with his foot, which had unearthed it. Raneb's notes contained his questioning of both the overseer and Khety, but no charges had been brought against either man. Raneb, however, after examining the items, knew they were replicas and suspected Khety of more than just "finding" the missing goods. If Iput knew about the stolen items, could she have forced Khety to return them? How? Had she threatened him with exposure in the thefts? Or, had he raped her to keep her quiet? And, now that she was pregnant, was she threatening to reveal all to Raneb or Nebettawy?

Raneb knew all the merchants in Waset and spoke with Bek regarding the items. When Bek told him he had been trading with Khety for several years, Raneb had the proof he needed. Raneb asked Bek to look at the two items. Khety had brought him similar pieces months ago, which he had traded with the Phoenician. Raneb asked Bek to cease trading with Khety for the present, but did not reveal the items were stolen. Putting the pressure on Khety, threatening his criminal income, would force his hand. Bek reported to Raneb the theft of a rather expensive Near East dagger, which he had received in trade with the Phoenician. When Kiya had been questioned, Raneb was disappointed. Khety had not been in the marketplace that day.

The following day, Raneb began his investigation into Iput's murder. The missing dagger was found with the body. He immediately questioned the Phoenician trader, Ghedi, but his ship had just arrived that morning. He was only staying a day or two before returning to Phoenicia, but he wanted to see Bek and had a number of items he knew he could trade in Waset for a better price than bringing them to Near East ports. Raneb told him he was free to leave Waset when his business was concluded. Raneb spoke once more with Bek before his death. Bek had a vessel of wine go missing; he had asked his daughter, Kiya, about it. She said she had been distracted by Unas, when the

vessel went missing. She had seen him arguing with a man shortly before the theft. And her description matched Khety, right down to his closed left eye.

With all the evidence, the two replica items, the apparent marketplace thefts, and his trades with Bek, Raneb confronted Khety on the eighth day of the third month — the day Raneb was poisoned. Qaa now suspected Khety had killed Raneb, but he still did not know who had killed Iput.

Qaa turned his attention to a scroll that had caught his attention earlier; a case Raneb had investigated about an assault in the twelfth year of the king's reign. The woman, a widow, had been attacked from behind. Her attacker choked her until she was weak and threatened her with a knife. The woman refused to elaborate on her injuries to Raneb. She remembered the man smelled of smoke, his hands were very strong. Qaa quickly looked through scrolls following the attack, for any further mention. The widow apparently travelled to Men-nefer some months after the attack. When she returned to Waset, she was seen by the *swnwt per aa*; a Medjay had found her wandering the streets in the middle of the night, covered in blood. According to Raneb's notes, she had attempted to take her own life. She succeeded several weeks later.

Qaa was intrigued. He started with the first scroll, looking for any mention of other assaults. After briefly looking at each one, he had separated out three more scrolls. The first one, in the second year of the king's reign, was only speculation on Raneb's part. The report was sketchy, and concerned the wife of an unnamed priest, possibly attacked coming from the temple. A merchant reported he had heard a woman scream the previous evening. When he looked out his door, he saw a woman hurrying into the priest's residence. The woman flatly denied being attacked, so Raneb did not look into it any further.

The second attack, in the seventh year of the king's reign, also involved a widow. She gave the most detailed account of the attack. A man had grabbed her from behind and threatened her into silence with a knife. He put his arm around her throat and touched her in a disgusting manner. He defiled her with an object, she did not know what it was, before he took her, like an animal. She came to report the crime to Raneb with the *swnwt per aa*, Ashayt, who confirmed the details from her examination of the victim. The *swnwt* noted there were black smudges on the woman's dress, both front and back. Again, the woman left Waset several months after the attack and travelled to Men-nefer.

The final scroll was an account of a conversation Raneb had with the second victim. It was in the twelfth year of the king's reign. He had sought her out because another woman had been attacked in a similar manner. But

she had remarried and now had two children. She seemed to have recovered from the attack, and she begged Raneb to never speak of it. Her husband, who was not from Waset, did not know of the attack, and she had put that horrible night behind her. No further mention of her was found in any other scrolls.

What had Qaa uncovered? Was there a rapist also in Waset? Or were they the same person? His head and shoulders ached from being hunched over the scrolls. His throat was as dry as the Red Land. Raneb knew these people well, while Qaa was considered an outsider; how could he ever convince any of them to speak with him? He stood and got his vessel of wine off the dressing table. He removed the top and drank from the vessel, until he drifted off into a wine-induced sleep.

Day 19 in Month 3

Qaa awoke before sunrise. His head pounded from too much wine, too little sleep, and not enough food. He staggered down the corridor and cleansed quickly. He would eat in the temple kitchen before he left for the day. Back in his quarters, he dressed in loincloth, kilt, *wesekh* collar, and the Medjay belt and sash. He picked up the small offering bowl and asked one of the Medjay to carry it. The guards fell into step with him as he stopped by the kitchen; the guards were treated to a sumptuous meal, while Qaa could barely choke down bread and fruit. Having satisfied themselves, the Medjay accompanied Qaa through the mortuary complex toward the Western gate and the goldsmith tents. Qaa spotted the overseer and motioned to him. The man stopped what he was doing and came quickly.

"*Hem netjer*, how may I assist you?" The overseer bowed low to Qaa.

"Overseer, I understand you spoke with Raneb last month about some items found back here by one of the goldsmiths. Is this one of the items?" Qaa motioned with his hand and the Medjay handed the overseer the offering bowl.

"It looks like our work, but it is an inferior item. By weight, I am able to say this is not gold, only gold coated."

"Can you tell me, by the mark, who created this piece?"

The overseer turned the piece over and looked at the flat bottom. "I am astonished. It appears to be Khety's mark. He is a fine craftsman, and would never create a piece of such inferior workmanship. Would you like to speak with him?"

"No, overseer, and I would prefer you not mention my visit to anyone, especially Khety."

"Do you suspect he has done something improper?"

"I am just looking into some information I found in Raneb's quarters at the temple. Many thanks."

The overseer bowed as Qaa turned and headed toward the northern wall of the enclosure and the military barracks. Unas was still hiding something and Qaa had no more patience for him.

"Unas, I did not want to have to come back here to interrogate you further. If you continue to withhold information, I shall lose my temper." Qaa withdrew the leather switch from his belt.

"Medjay, I do not know what you mean?" Trembling and terrified, Unas knelt in front of Qaa. "Ask me anything and I will tell you what you want."

"Tell me about the wine vessel that went missing from Bek, the merchant."

Unas bowed his head. How had Qaa found out? Had Takhat told him? "I will tell you all I know, Medjay, just spare Takhat. She only did what I asked her to do."

"Who did you steal the wine for and why?"

"I do not know why. Khety has been trading replica temple items with Bek and has paid me to keep quiet about it. He told me he needed a special vessel of wine. He grabbed Takhat by the hair and threatened her if I did not do what he wished."

"So you distracted Kiya while Takhat took the wine."

"I gave the vessel to Khety. A few days later, he gave the vessel back to me. He told me to have Takhat trade it in the marketplace with the Phoenician. I wanted to go with Takhat, but Khety went with her, to make sure nothing went wrong."

"Unas, has Khety asked you and Takhat to steal any other items?"

"He saw a dagger he fancied, but it was more than any of us could afford. He shook Takhat and told her to get it for him. She is with child, and I did not want him to hurt her. I told her to do what he asked."

"One more question, how well did Iput know Khety?" Iput could have been helping Khety get into the temple for his thefts.

"Iput? I do not think she ever spoke to him. Why, Medjay?"

"Unas, you know you are in serious trouble. Khety, by having you and Takhat steal for him, has made you an accomplice to his crimes."

"Medjay, I am willing to accept my punishment. But, I beseech you, to have mercy on Takhat. She only did what she was told to do, out of her love for me, and out of my fear of Khety." Unas looked up at Qaa, pleading with him to spare Takhat.

"Her punishment shall be set by the king, but I shall do what I can for her." Still simmering with anger, Qaa could not bring himself to beat Unas. Before his punishment, Qaa would torment Unas further with the fact Khety had coerced him and Takhat to steal the very weapon used to kill Iput. It was beginning to appear Khety was his murderer, as well as a thief, unless Khety was in concert with someone in the temple.

🜨🜨🜨🜨🜨🜨🜨

"*Swnwt*, it is important that I speak with you." Qaa wanted to confirm what he had read the previous evening.

"I need to return to the princess Tentopet. She has delivered her baby, a prince, but it was a difficult delivery. Both mother and child are weak."

"I am afraid, *swnwt*, you shall have to speak with me. Tetisheri is tending to Nebettawy and her father is also with her. We may speak, privately, in my quarters." Qaa lightly took Ashayt by the arm and guided her to the doorway of Nebettawy's room.

"My son, is this really necessary?" Ramesses was not pleased with his tone of voice.

"My king, you have asked me to solve the murder of a young woman and your friend of many years. Your daughter lies near death, due to my negligence, and my inability to get the answers I need. My questions are for the *swnwt*. I shall keep you apprised of my investigation." Qaa bowed to the king and led Ashayt down the corridor, to his quarters.

"*Swnwt*, you may sit at the table, if you wish. I hope to make this brief." Qaa was tired and the heat was compounding his headache from his intemperance.

"Is this about the *hemet netjer* or your investigation?" She sat, trying to avoid eye contact with Qaa.

"It is about both. You have seen similar injuries on the women of Waset in the past, have you not, *swnwt*?"

Ashayt was not easily shaken, but Qaa's question stunned her. "How much do you know, *hem netjer*?" She bowed her head. She had kept this terrible secret for so long, and she prided herself on her discretion.

"Only what I read in Raneb's notes on the three previous cases."

"Three? I attended two women, both widows. One refused to discuss the matter, until she found herself with child. I arranged to have her go to Men-nefer and she gave her child to a barren couple. Unfortunately, the attack and giving up her child were too much for her. She killed herself a short time later."

"I gathered most of that from what I read last evening. I did not know why she had travelled to Men-nefer, but you have confirmed Raneb's notes. And the other woman?"

"She also found herself with child after the attack. She is a remarkable woman, but did not want to raise a child born of violence. She too travelled to Men-nefer and her child was adopted by a couple there. She has since remarried and has two children of her own. I still attend her, but we never speak of the incident."

"In Raneb's notes, I found mention of black smudges on the dress of one woman and the recollection of the smell of smoke. Did you not think that relevant to tell me, *swnwt*, after what happened to Nebettawy?"

"The cases were years apart. How could they be related? But, you said three women. When did the other attack happen?"

"Raneb received a report of an attack, but the woman denied the allegation. With no further evidence, he kept a report of the incident, but did not follow up on it. He did not even record the woman's name. She was referred to as the wife of a priest."

Ashayt went pale. She was just starting her practice in Waset when the attack occurred. The *swnw per aa* handled the case himself.

"*Swnwt*, your face betrays you. Tell me the circumstances of the first case." Qaa's voice softened. He knelt next to Ashayt and took her hand. "If you wish to help the *hemet netjer*, I need to know. From what I have read in Raneb's scrolls, it may be the work of the same man."

"*Hem netjer*, I was only apprentice to the *swnw per aa*. He went out on the case alone."

"Tell me what you know, Ashayt. No detail of those months is insignificant. Who were the priests here at that time?"

"Raneb's wife had already joined Auser. He spent much of his time here at the temple. I had just begun attending Thanuny's wife; she was pregnant with her second child."

"Did she show any signs of injury when you examined her?" He stood and began to pace around his quarters, to help him formulate his thoughts.

"No, *hem netjer*. She was in the middle of her pregnancy. She was a small, fragile woman and required much rest. She was confined to their residence for the remainder of her pregnancy, for fear she would lose the child. Her first delivery had been very difficult, but she still wanted to give Thanuny many children."

"What of the other priests' wives? Did you attend any of them around that time?"

"Harkhuf's wife was still nursing their first child. I was called to the residence for the usual complaints, but nothing out of the ordinary. The child developed a fever and recovered soon afterward, but the wife seemed well."

Qaa considered what he had heard. Anedjib had just recently joined the temple and was too young to have had a wife at the time. Weni's wife had given birth to a daughter, who was now fifteen. And if the attack happened the previous year, could she have been the unnamed priest's wife and become pregnant by her attacker?

"*Swnwt*, what about Weni's wife? What can you tell me about her?"

"She only began seeing me the following year, after the *swnw per aa* joined Auser and I became the *swnwt per aa*. She had delivered her daughter several months previously." She squirmed nervously. She did not care for where the questioning was headed.

"I know Anedjib was not the *hery heb* then. Do you remember the priest who was here?"

"He was an aged widower. I do not believe he had any children. But I did not know him well. Thanuny could tell you more than I."

"Many thanks, *swnwt*. I know I am perceived as an outsider here and I appreciate the delicacy of this matter. I do not wish to cause any more harm than has already been done."

Ashayt breathed a sigh of relief. She had long suspected something; Merti did not resemble her father, as his sons did. She had a wild nature and her mother seemed unable to control her. The woman rarely left her residence and, even when Ashayt visited, did not like to be touched.

"*Swnwt*, I shall allow you to leave to attend the princess Tentopet, in a few moments. As *swnwt per aa*, am I to understand you are a woman of discretion?" Qaa had stopped pacing and stood in front of Ashayt.

"Yes, *hem netjer*, I know how to keep a confidence." She stood and faced Qaa, whose face had turned grave.

"You examined Nebettawy the evening of the attack." Qaa shifted uncomfortably under the *swnwt's* sharp gaze. "I need to know ... Nebettawy and I ... "

Ashayt reached up and placed her hand on Qaa's shoulder. "*Hem netjer*, Nebettawy told me where she had been before the attack. I know she was with you and I know what you did with her. She told me because she was concerned the attack would leave her unable to have children, your children."

"*Swnwt*, it is my fault Nebettawy lies ill. I lost control and I shall never be able to forgive myself." Qaa had turned crimson from embarrassment and could no longer look at the *swnwt*.

"*Hem netjer*, you are a man who has waited many years for the woman he loves. It is not up to me to judge you on your actions, but you may trust I shall keep your secret." She turned to leave his quarters, then remembered what Khamaat had told her. "*Hem netjer*, I thought you said you did not want to be *swnw*."

"I do not understand."

"My apprentice tells me you gave the *hemet netjer* powdered willow bark in honey."

"I did, and I shall continue to give it to her." Qaa straightened up, ready to quell any objections from the swnwt.

"Let us see how she responds to it. If she rallies, I may wish to consult with you in the future." She smiled at him and exited his quarters.

Claudia R. Dillaire

Ramesses was still in his daughter's room when Qaa returned. Nebettawy had not eaten and was refusing the wine her father was offering. Qaa put his hand on the king's shoulder and took the drinking bowl from his hand. He knelt next to the bed and stroked Nebettawy's hair and cheek.

"Sister, it is Qaa. Your father is worried. You do not drink for him and you are not getting better. Will you drink for me?" His voice was calm and soothing.

"Qaa? Will you sit with me?" Her flesh was hot and slick with sweat.

"I shall sit if you eat and drink with me."

"I am so weak. Will you feed me?"

"Yes, Sister." He slid his arm under her shoulders to bring her head up. He brought the bowl to her lips and got her to sip the mandrake steeped wine.

Qaa let her lay down, stood, and crossed to her dressing table. The ornate box was there, next to the jar of honey. He dipped his finger in the box, tapped the side, but increased the amount slightly. He then placed his finger in the honey. He came back to her bed, knelt down, and put his finger to her lips. She tasted the sweetness and let him place his finger in her mouth, as she greedily licked the honey.

"Father, give me something to feed her." Qaa extended his arm to the king. Ramesses handed him a slice of date. Qaa lifted Nebettawy's head and made her eat the fruit. When Qaa extended his hand again, Ramesses handed him a piece of cheese. Qaa managed to get her to eat that, as well. He picked up the drinking bowl and she sipped the wine, before drifting off to sleep.

Ramesses buried his face in his hands. His daughter's condition had worsened; he did not need to be a *swnw* to know that. She refused food and drink from anyone but Qaa. He needed to consult his father, Amun. He would do whatever the god requested of him, if only he would spare his daughter's life, even if it meant blessing a marriage between her and Qaa.

"Father, I have much work to do. I shall return this evening to feed her again. May I get you anything before I retire to my quarters?"

"No, my son. Are you any closer to a suspect?" Ramesses voice was flat, emotionless.

"I shall know more after I read Raneb's scrolls again." Qaa bowed and exited into the corridor.

Qaa stood and lit the lamps in his room. His muscles ached and his stomach rumbled. He had spent the better part of the day reading scrolls and making notes. He would go to the temple kitchen for some refreshment and then to Nebettawy's quarters. The *swnwt* would be coming to examine her and he would need to get her to eat again. After a meal of sliced duck, fruit, cheese, bread, and beer, Qaa was ready to check on Nebettawy. He walked the quiet, dark corridor to her room. The *swnwt* had already examined Nebettawy; by her face, he knew the prognosis was not favourable.

"*Swnwt*, you must save her. I have waited twelve years to make Nebettawy my wife. The amulet she gave me has kept me safe all these years; she said it would bring me back to her. I can not lose her now."

Ramesses was about to enter his daughter's quarters, when he heard Qaa and Ashayt discussing her condition. Though he was not one to interfere, he long suspected Qaa and Nebettawy had been much closer as children. He concealed himself, back against the wall, outside his daughter's room, to listen to Qaa's confession.

"*Hem netjer*, I am doing all I can. She calls for you and says only you can heal her."

"I am not a *swnw*. How can I heal her?" Qaa bowed his head, the weight of his sorrow and guilt crushing him.

"May I see the amulet she gave you?"

Qaa slid the amulet from under his *wesekh* collar. It had been expertly crafted from electrum, a uadjet eye, which was hinged at the bottom. When the eye was opened, there was a lock of hair inside along with a small scrap of papyrus. It was difficult to see the writing, but Ashayt assumed it was a protection spell.

"The night before I left Waset, Nebettawy and I met in the palace gardens. She gave me this amulet to protect me and bring me safely back to her. She said we would then join as husband and wife. And to remember our pledge to each other, we exchanged rings." Qaa raised his right hand. On the smallest finger, he wore a ring of electrum with three stones.

"The blue stone represents me, the black stone represents Nebettawy, and the red stone represents our undying love. She wears the same ring on her hand still."

The *swnwt* raised Nebettawy's right hand and found an exact copy of the ring. Nebettawy stirred and began to thrash about.

"Qaa, come to me. Only you can save me. I need you, Qaa." Nebettawy curled up in pain and began to cry.

"Ashayt, I should not be touching her. But I can not stand by and watch her suffer." Qaa knelt at Nebettawy's bedside, helpless, his massive frame racked by sobs. The *swnwt* placed her hand on his head to comfort him.

"*Hem netjer*, you must do what is best for her. I have done all I can."

Qaa looked at Nebettawy lying on her bed, so pale, her body shaking uncontrollably. All he wanted to do was hold her, touch her, comfort her. He reached out and touched her hand.

"Qaa, heal me." Her voice was barely audible. She clasped his hand and placed it on her chest, over her heart. "Heal me, you have the power to make me well."

As if from distant memory, he placed his other hand on her head. Nebettawy began to moan and thrash about. But he kept his hands on her, willing her back to health. Somewhere, in his mind, he could hear his mother's voice, urging him on; he could almost feel her inside him.

"Help me, Qaa. I ache to join with you. Touch me, Qaa." She was burning with fever and sweating profusely. She was in agony from the infection coursing through her body. Nebettawy moved his hand down to her abdomen, now holding it in both her hands. She pressed it into her abdomen over and over, as if trying to expel whatever was inside her.

"Qaa, something lives inside me. Make it stop. Make me well. Help me. Fill me with your strength to fight." She was delirious, hysterical. Her eyes were staring wildly at him, seeming to accuse him for her current condition. Her body shook, as if taken over by spirits.

Ramesses had moved to the entrance of his daughter's room. He stood transfixed, watching the horrifying scene, his daughter screaming in pain, dying before his very eyes. Qaa held her fast and the *swnwt* kept her shoulders on the bed. She continued to thrash and shake and scream in pain. When she began to choke and gag, Ashayt sat her up and Nebettawy vomited up bile. As the *swnwt* lay her back down, Nebettawy writhed on the bed, trying to expel something from deep inside, as if a woman in the pains of labour.

"Qaa, help me. Do not let me die. Give me your strength. If you love me, Qaa, you shall heal me." Her hands had the power of ten men, holding his hand at her abdomen, trying to push something out. With a loud scream and a final shudder through her body, she finally lay still. But the horror had just begun; the linen sheet was bloody between her legs and the stain was spreading rapidly.

The *swnwt* tore away the sheet to examine Nebettawy. Qaa fell back, into a sitting position on the floor, and sobbing, dropped his head into his hands. His entire body shook with fear, anger, desperation, and helplessness. The *swnwt* took her long tongs and inserted a linen strip, treated with honey, far into Nebettawy's womb. She gently swabbed the womb and, when she removed the linen, it was only lightly stained with blood. Ashayt began to clean the pool of blood from the bed when she recoiled in horror.

"Qaa, you may have saved her life." She beckoned him to look. In the midst of the blood and fluids on the bed was a fragment of something hard. Qaa picked it up and crossed the room to Nebettawy's dressing table. He dropped the item in the bowl of scented water and rubbed it clean. When he withdrew it from the water, it appeared to be a fragment of nicely carved bone. Even in his state of shock, he knew this may have come from the hilt of a dagger.

"*Swnwt*, will she recover?"

"Her chances have greatly improved. It must have been embedded in the wound. Now that it has been expelled, I should be able to draw out the infection. Let me attend to her now. When I have cleaned her, you may return. It is important to try to get her to eat, to build up her strength."

Qaa headed for the doorway and saw Ramesses, pale, trembling, a defeated man. He reached out to comfort the king, but Ramesses turned and stumbled in the direction of the temple sanctuary.

Claudia R. Dillaire

Day 20 in Month 3

Qaa awoke before sunrise. He wanted to feed Nebettawy before he left the temple for the day. He had a few more questions before he could bring in his suspect. He cleansed and dressed, then sought out Thanuny, to assist him with the morning ritual. From there, he headed for the temple kitchen to prepare a serving tray for Nebettawy and Ramesses. He carried the food to her quarters; Ramesses was already at his daughter's bedside and Khamaat was bathing her limbs in scented water.

"*Swnwt*, would you like me to get her to eat?"

"*Hem netjer*, you have been a tremendous help. Many thanks. She has been calling for you and talking incoherently. Try to calm her."

Ashayt appeared at the doorway to check on her patient. Ramesses and Qaa left the room and waited in the corridor while the *swnwt* examined Nebettawy. Ramesses wore the expression of a man consumed with his own thoughts. Qaa, not wanting to further incur his wrath, kept silent. When Ashayt motioned them to return, Ramesses stepped aside to let Qaa enter and stood by the door. Qaa knelt by the bed and placed the cool linen cloth on Nebettawy's forehead. Her flesh was still hot, but she did not appear to be in as much distress.

"Sister, it is Qaa. Will you eat for me?"

"Qaa, you must listen to me." She still had trouble focusing her eyes and her face was troubled. "It is important I speak with you."

"Nebettawy, you are very ill. You need to eat to regain your strength. Whatever you need to tell me can wait until you have recovered." He stroked her cheek to calm her.

"No, my brother." She would not calm down and was quite distraught. "You must find the man who did this; he has done this before."

"Sister, do you know what you are saying?" Did she know of the other attacks? How could she? From what he had read from Raneb's scrolls, no one in Waset wanted to speak of the attacks.

"He wheezes when he speaks. Sadeh told me; it is the same voice I heard." She looked around the room wildly. "You must tell no one. Sadeh is in great danger."

"Sister, I shall check on Sadeh for you. Will that please you?" Qaa took her hand and kissed the palm.

"That will please me." She closed her eyes, as if to sleep. Qaa released her hand, stood, and went to her dressing table. He opened the ornate box, dipped his finger in the powdered herb, and tapped the excess. After sliding his finger into the honey jar, he came back to the bed and knelt beside it. Putting his finger to her lips, he gently rubbed her lower lip and she tasted the sticky sweetness.

"Sister, I need you to open your eyes. I shall feed you and you must eat. You shall not recover if you do not eat."

She licked the honey from her lips and his finger. Qaa extended his arm and Khamaat handed him a small piece of bread. She accepted the bread and chewed contentedly. The *swnwt* next handed him a slice of apricot, then a piece of cheese. Nebettawy took several sips of lotus steeped wine. Qaa then reached for the honey cake he had brought especially for her.

"Sister, I almost got caught stealing it for you this morning. Will you share it with me?" He broke off a small piece. She smiled and accepted the piece of cake. Though still weak, she took his hand and kissed his palm.

"You still remember that honey cakes are my favourite." A tear slid down her cheek.

"Rest now, Sister. I shall return after the noon ritual." He stood, bent over the bed, and kissed her on the forehead.

Ashayt and Ramesses still stood at the doorway. The king appeared to have aged overnight, but Ashayt's face showed signs of hope.

"*Hem netjer*, I had Khamaat stop giving her mandrake steeped wine. Her pain has lessened and she slept better. You have a gift with her. I have not seen many men with the compassion you have."

"Many thanks, *swnwt*. Your majesty, I need to return to the military barracks. If all goes well, I should have a suspect in custody soon." Qaa bowed to Ramesses and strode in the direction of the avenue of the Festival Calendars.

"*Swnwt*, may I speak with you, privately." Ramesses was distressed by what he had seen the previous evening.

"Khamaat, I wish to speak with the king and then I must check on the princess Tentopet. Do you have any further need for me?"

"No, *swnwt*. The *hemet netjer* seems better and Tetisheri shall be arriving presently to relieve me." The apprentice had been sitting with Nebettawy all night.

Ramesses led Ashayt to his temporary quarters next to his daughter's room. He pulled out a chair for her and motioned her to sit. She settled herself in the chair and Ramesses sat on the side of the bed. She had been so preoccupied with his daughters she had not noticed how tired and old the king had become.

"*Swnwt*, I am greatly distressed by the events of the past few days."

"My lord, am I to assume you are distressed by the way Qaa has touched your daughter?"

"She is my daughter, she is sacred. You are a *swnwt*, trained to heal. He is ..." Ramesses's voice trailed off, unable to finish his thought.

"My king, I know you do not approve of Qaa, as a husband for your daughter. But, it is time I speak plainly. If Qaa had not reached into your daughter's womb and removed the clot, she could have died. And last evening, if he had not assisted her in expelling the fragment of bone, she could have died from infection."

"I love my daughter dearly and I am not ungrateful to him, *swnwt*."

"Qaa risks your punishment every time he touches her. He loves her enough to sacrifice his own life to save hers."

"You do not understand my reservations." Ramesses had struggled with the closeness of his daughter and Qaa since they were children.

"I understand more than you know. I know he is patient and gentle with her. He would rather cut off his own arm than cause her pain.

Is it his parentage that concerns you or is it that you fear Qaa shall take your place in your daughter's life?" Ashayt silently hoped she had not overstepped her authority with the king. "I know he is not fully Egyptian, but he loves your daughter, and she loves him."

Ramesses's face was crimson. He was furious that she would say such a thing to him, but he was embarrassed as well. He could not love his daughter, not the way a husband could, but she was his daughter. He had always had a special relationship with her. The *swnwt* made it sound as if he were jealous of Qaa, like a spurned lover.

"*Swnwt*, my love for Nebettawy is as a father only. All I want is what is best for her."

"I meant no disrespect, your majesty. But, is not her happiness what is best for her? You have watched him with her, how she responds only to him. Do you honestly believe he is not the best husband for her? Does she not deserve to be happy?"

Ramesses buried his face in his hands. He prayed he had not angered the gods with his refusal to give her to Qaa. Her mother's mother foretold that she would marry Qaa, but he would not allow his daughter to marry a man who was not Egyptian. It was his fault his daughter was near death.

"My lord, this has been difficult for you to bear. Tetisheri shall sit with her. If there is any change, she shall summon you. Let me give you something, so you may rest." She took some powders from her instrument bag and dissolved them in wine. "Drink this and you should find your sleep undisturbed."

"Overseer, where were you the night of Unas's marriage feast?" Two men associated with Unas spoke with a wheeze, the overseer and Khety. He had not suspected the overseer, due to his injury, which left Khety as his prime suspect.

"I had travelled across the Nile with the party. I was at the marriage feast."

"Did you see Khety at the feast?"

"No, *hem netjer*. He stayed on the West bank. He has a daughter who is not well. He does not like to leave her alone."

"May I speak with Khety?"

"He did not come to work today. I sent a fire tender to his residence, but his daughter said he was not at home."

"Many thanks, overseer. Notify the temple immediately if you should see Khety." Qaa, with his two Medjay guards, headed for the military barracks.

"Unas, I urgently need your help. Did you invite your fellow workers to celebrate your marriage?"

"Yes, Medjay, they were happy for Takhat and me."

"Did they all attend the feast?"

"No, Medjay. Three men did not make the trip across."

"Tell me who did not attend."

"A young fire tender, he has only been working at the temple a few months. One of the goldsmith apprentices, I have known him since childhood. He walks with a stick. He fell ill as a child and has a withered leg. And, Khety." Unas's voice dropped.

"If you were in fear of Khety, why did you invite him to your marriage feast?"

"Takhat told me to. She was afraid he would hurt her if we did not."

Qaa remembered the man who ran from the temple the night of the attack. It could not have been a man with a withered leg, and a young fire tender, new to the temple, would have no reason to attack the *hemet netjer*. All the evidence pointed to Khety, and now he was missing, giving him the appearance of guilt.

"Many thanks, Unas. One more question. Where would Khety go, if he were not at work?"

"He has a daughter who is ill. She has been plagued with evil spirits for many years. He would never leave her alone, so he must be at his home."

Qaa had brought additional Medjay with him. If Khety was at home, he would be taken into custody. If he was not, he would station Medjay there until he returned. It was an unremarkable house, next to other unremarkable houses. Two story, mud-brick, but his was larger than most. Qaa remembered someone told him Khety had five daughters, some still at home. The house, though large, was not suited to accommodate seven people.

"May I enter? I am Qaa, Chief of the Medjay." Qaa stood at the doorway and called in to the dark, cool interior.

"You may enter." The voice was of a young woman.

Qaa entered and took a moment until his eyes adjusted to the darkness. He looked around the main room; it was small, but neat and well kept. A woman, in her twenties, sat in the corner at a loom. The young woman standing in front of him was in her late teens.

"My name is Aahotep, daughter of Khety. What do you need, Medjay?" The young woman bowed in deference to Qaa.

"I am looking for your father. I am investigating the murder of a young woman, and he knew the victim's husband. I was hoping he could assist me." Qaa did not want to frighten Aahotep, nor did he want her to help her father escape.

"He left for work this morning. I have not seen him since."

"Would your sister know where he might be?" Qaa started toward the woman at the loom, but Aahotep cut him off.

"Medjay, do not disturb my sister. She has the mind of a child. She has been like this since our mother left us. She can not help you."

"Aahotep, many thanks. I am anxious to speak with your father. I shall leave Medjay outside your house, should he return."

"Is my father coming home?" The speaker was looking at Qaa, with the eyes of a child, in the body of a lovely woman. "My mother left and never came back."

Qaa, pushing past Aahotep, walked slowly to the woman at the loom. He stopped, knelt down, and admired her weaving. Though she had the mind of a child, she was an exceptionally skilled weaver.

"Child, what is your name?" Qaa's voice was low and soothing.

"My name is Nithotep. What is your name?" She had put down her threads and reached out to take Qaa's hand.

"My name is Qaa. I was admiring your weaving. You do lovely work, Nithotep."

"I do all the weaving for the house." She sat up straight, very proud of her accomplishment. "My mother taught me to weave." Her smile disappeared and she looked as if she were about to cry. "She left us, and never came back."

"May I come back and see you again?" He released her hand and patted her cheek.

Her face brightened. "I would like that very much."

Qaa stood and turned to Aahotep. He knew he would learn no more here. He bowed to the two sisters and exited into the unrelenting sunlight.

"May I enter? I am Qaa, the new Chief of the Medjay." He stood at the entrance to the home of Weni and Sadeh. It was a large, mud-brick two story home, nestled between similar houses, belonging to merchants, priests, and the nobles of Waset. He motioned for the Medjay to remain outside.

"You may enter." The female's voice trembled.

He stepped inside and stood while his eyes adjusted to the darkness. The main room was brightly painted, well kept, and spacious. In the far corner, a small, fragile looking woman, in her forties, sat at a loom.

"You are Sadeh, wife of the *wab*-priest Weni?"

"I am. I understand you are also the new First *hem netjer*. I wish to extend my compliments on your appointment. May I get you refreshment?" She started to rise from her chair.

"No, but many thanks for your offer and kind words. I have come at the behest of the *hemet netjer*."

Sadeh's hands trembled and her face turned ashen. "I spoke with the *hemet netjer* the other day and told her not to worry about me. What has she told you?"

"She told me you are in danger. Your secret shall remain safe with me; I shall be discreet in this matter. But, please allow me to leave Medjay outside your home. The suspect I am seeking has disappeared."

"Your Medjay can not protect me, nor can they make me feel safe. I have lived in fear of this day for fifteen years." She bowed her head, knowing she would have to face the shame and indignity of that night again.

Qaa walked to the woman and looked at her weaving. She would be a wonderful teacher for Khety's daughter.

"Mistress, if I may inquire, there is a young woman who is a skilled weaver, but could learn more from you. Would you consider meeting her, when this ugly business has been resolved? She lost her mother quite some time ago and your guidance could help her."

"*Hem netjer*, are you trying to prepare me for the loss of my own daughter?"

"I can not answer. I am just a Medjay, I follow the clues and gather the evidence. The king and the court shall set her punishment." Qaa wondered how much she knew about her daughter's crimes.

"My own desires clouded my judgment. I should have been grateful to have had four healthy sons. But, I would go to the Temple of Amun and pray for a daughter. Amun has punished me for my selfishness and now the son of Amun shall punish her. It is as it should be." Sadeh looked directly at Qaa, her eyes sad and tired.

"I wish you would reconsider my offer of guards." Qaa would speak with the king. If the king ordered their protection, Weni would not have to know the reason.

"Many thanks, *hem netjer.*" Sadeh had returned to her weaving. Qaa started for the door. "What is your interest in this young weaver?"

Qaa stopped and turned back to Sadeh. "She has the mind of a child and, I suspect, has witnessed some terrible things. The only enjoyment she has in life is her weaving and she is quite skilled."

"When this business is concluded, I shall meet your young weaver. I make no promise of any more than as a teacher."

"Many thanks, Mistress." Qaa turned and exited the house, to return to the temple and Nebettawy.

Qaa assisted Thanuny with the noon ritual before preparing food for Nebettawy. She had seemed better this morning, but he did not want to be too hopeful. She had been through an ordeal and it would be some time before the infection was drawn out of her. The best way to help her recover was to build up her strength. He carried the tray to her room and looked in. Tetisheri was sitting next to the bed, bathing her limbs in scented water, singing to her. But, Ramesses was not present. He entered and set the tray down. He would give her the powdered willow bark first, then feed her.

"Was the king called away?"

"No, *hem netjer.* The *swnwt* gave him an herbal, so he could sleep."

Tetisheri moved to the table so Qaa could kneel beside the bed. He placed his honeyed finger on Nebettawy's lips, and she immediately responded. When she had cleaned his finger of the honey, she opened her eyes and smiled at him.

"My brother, I am so weak. But, I shall recover, now that I see you."

Qaa's heart leapt. This was the first time in days she seemed coherent. "Sister, we are all concerned for you. Let me feed you, so you shall build up your strength."

She struggled to sit up, but was unable. Qaa gently pushed her shoulders down on the bed and patted her. He slid his arm under her shoulders to raise her head. She leaned toward him and laid her head on his chest. Though her face was still flushed, her skin was not as hot to the touch. Her breathing, which had been regular, seemed to quicken slightly. Qaa reached out his hand to Tetisheri and she handed him small slices of meat, cheese, fruit, and bread. He fed her slowly, stopping to give her a sip of wine from time to time. It was the most food she had consumed in days. He could feel her relaxing in his arms and knew she was tiring.

"Sister, let me lay you down. You have done well. Do you wish to share a honey cake with me?"

"I shall gladly share with you, my brother." She closed her eyes and smiled.

He broke off a small piece of honey cake and brought it to her lips. Without opening her eyes, she accepted the cake and ate it. She opened her eyes and reached for Qaa, taking his hand and squeezing it lightly.

"Will you stay with me this afternoon?" Her eyes pleaded with him.

"If that is your wish, I shall stay."

Tetisheri brought Qaa a chair and placed it next to the bed. Without letting go of her hand, Qaa settled himself in the chair. With his back to the doorway, he did not see Ramesses, standing in the corridor, watching Qaa comfort his daughter.

After assisting with the evening ritual, Qaa prepared refreshment for Ramesses and Nebettawy. He brought the tray to her quarters and found it filled with activity. Ashayt had just finished her examination and Khamaat had returned to relieve Tetisheri. He waited in the corridor patiently until Tetisheri had departed. He put the tray on the table and was about to speak with Ashayt when Ramesses took him by the arm.

"Qaa, the *swnwt* shall sit with her so we may speak in private." Ramesses wore the expression of a man carrying a heavy burden.

"My lord, we may speak in my chambers, where we shall not be disturbed. Ashayt, shall you remain until I return?"

"Yes, *hem netjer*. The princess and the young prince are much improved. I am able to spend more time here."

Qaa and Ramesses walked the corridor in silence. Ramesses entered the room and took the seat at the writing table. Qaa, sensing displeasure from his king, chose to stand.

"I have spoken with the *swnwt* about my daughter's condition. Though she shows improvement, she is still quite ill."

Fearing Ramesses found out he had lain with Nebettawy, Qaa fell to his knees in front of the king. "Father, I deserve your punishment for what I have done. I would rather be dead than live without Nebettawy. She is my life."

"Qaa, do not speak of such things."

"Do you not know why I was so brave in battle? Do you not understand why I was never afraid in combat?"

"My son, this has been a strain on us all." Ramesses reached out to put his hand on Qaa's shoulder. Qaa, tired and on the edge of collapse, pushed the king's hand away.

"You call me 'Son', yet you allowed me to be tormented at the hands of the sons of your body. When I was a child in your house, I was pelted with rocks, for being different from my Egyptian brothers. They would spit upon me, kick me, strike me with sticks. My only champion was Nebettawy. She never cared that I was half Egyptian, she never made me feel out of place. She loved me unquestioningly. She was my protector and now, when she needs me the most, I can not protect her."

The shock of such a revelation was evident on Ramesses's face. He knew Qaa had been ridiculed by his sons, but was that not how you toughen your sons? But physical abuse; he understood now why Qaa had never flinched in battle.

"Father, Nebettawy sustains me. It is from her I draw my strength. I have only aspired to one role in my life. I never wanted wealth or power or titles. My greatest treasure, my greatest joy would be to take your daughter as my wife." Qaa tore the *wesekh* collar and Flies of Valour from his neck and threw them on the bed.

"Your love for my daughter is that strong?" Ramesses voice was quiet, unbelieving.

"My love for her is as eternal as the Nile. You do not know the torment I suffer without her. Sleep is my only solace, for she comes to me in my dreams." Qaa could barely contain his emotions. The painful childhood memories tore at him; he had finally reached his breaking point.

"My son, I did not know."

"I shall be direct with you, my king. We briefly spoke of this upon my return to Waset, but you need to hear what I have to say. The reason I have never taken an Egyptian woman as my wife is because only Nebettawy stirs

my passion. I have tried to take foreign women, out of desperation, but I could not release my seed into them. And now, when I am so close to Nebettawy, the gods punish us yet again. Father, I can not live this way any longer. I beg for death. End my suffering. Appease the gods and it may restore Nebettawy. I shall gladly sacrifice my life for hers. Without her, there is no life for me."

Great sobs racked Qaa as he knelt in front of Ramesses. The king loved him like a son of his body. He could not bear to see him in such anguish and despair.

"Qaa, forgive me for causing you such pain. I can not even begin to understand the depth of your love for my daughter. I pray my ignorance has not sealed her fate. The *swnwt* opened my eyes to what I have done to you both. Go to her, my son, take her as your wife, you have my blessing."

Ramesses again reached out and put his hand on Qaa's shoulder to comfort him, and Qaa did not push it away. The king's eyes welled with tears for the young man who struggled with his own inner torment. Ramesses had always prided himself on being fair and compassionate; he could no longer deny his daughter, or the man she loved, happiness.

Ramesses had taken his position by his daughter's bedside when Qaa returned to speak with the *swnwt*. She confirmed to him that Nebettawy's condition had improved slightly, but she was still quite ill. Qaa prepared the dried willow bark for Nebettawy, knelt by her, and lifted her up to take the herbal preparation.

"Sister, will you eat for me?"

Nebettawy smiled at Qaa and nodded her head. She closed her eyes while Qaa broke bread into small pieces and cut slices of fruit, cheese and meat. When he was ready, he again knelt by her bedside. He lifted her up and she rested her head against his shoulder. Ramesses handed Qaa food to feed his daughter. She managed to eat some bread, cheese, fruit, and meat, with sips of lotus steeped wine. When Qaa felt her strength diminishing, he laid her back on the bed.

"Sister, will you share a honey cake with me?"

"Only with you, my brother."

Ramesses handed Qaa the honey cake and Qaa gave her a few small pieces, before letting her drift off to sleep. Qaa held her hand and stroked her hair and cheek. He leaned over the bed and kissed her forehead, stood, and turned to see Queen Iset standing in the doorway with the *swnwt*. Qaa immediately bowed to her. Ramesses, unaware of her presence, turned toward the door. He stood and greeted his wife warmly, with outstretched arms.

"Husband, the *swnwt* tells me my daughter is still quite ill, but her fever has come down, since Qaa began giving her willow."

"She seems to be improved. She is still weak. Only Qaa is able to get her to take nourishment." Ramesses guided his wife to his seat next to the bed.

Qaa shifted uncomfortably under the queen's stern gaze. Iset touched her daughter's forehead for fever and leaned in to listen to her breathing.

"*Swnwt*, the princess Tentopet is much improved and does not require her mother's constant care. May I remain here with my daughter for a short while? I shall not wake her."

"Your majesty, you may remain as long as you wish." Ashayt bowed to the queen and took her leave. Ramesses dismissed Khamaat, asking her to return later. Qaa started for the door on Khamaat's heels, but Ramesses held out his hand and stopped him.

"Qaa, my wife shall want to know how you have been attending to Nebettawy. I have some documents in the next room which require my attention. Stay and converse with the queen." Ramesses placed a chair by the table for Qaa, then departed for his temporary quarters. Qaa sat heavily, expecting to be interrogated by the queen; she had seen him touch her daughter, which was forbidden.

"Qaa, you expect me to be angry with you."

"Your majesty, I know what you saw. You saw me holding your daughter. I expect you shall ask the king to punish me." Qaa had difficulty meeting her gaze. He grew up in her home, but had never been able to call her 'Mother'. He always felt she was judging his every move, especially when he was with Nebettawy.

The queen reached out and put her hand on his shoulder.

"Qaa, I came to see my daughter, and the man who saved her life. The *swnwt* has told me how difficult this has been, not only on my husband, but on you as well. My daughter has no secrets from me."

"Your majesty, I have spoken with your husband about my feelings for Nebettawy." Qaa could feel the colour draining from his face.

"I know how you feel about her, and how she feels about you. My husband has tried to disregard the wishes of the gods, but he can no longer deny what is meant to be."

Claudia R. Dillaire

"What do you mean?"

"My mother was *dwat-netjer* in the Temple of Amun. When you came to our home, she told Ramesses you were to be husband to my daughter Nebettawy. He did his best to keep you away from my daughter. He did not do this out of malice or hatred; he is a kind and beneficient ruler. But, he was blinded by the lineage of your mother."

"Your majesty, I remember little of my mother. I can still see her face, in my dreams, but I do not even know of her parentage. Why is that so important?" Qaa's voice was filled with desperation. He so wanted to know about his mother and it was apparent the queen knew of her.

"There is much you deserve to know, my son. But, first, I must give this to you. It belonged to your mother." Iset withdrew a necklace from her robe, with an amulet hanging on it. When Qaa saw the amulet, he inhaled sharply. He wanted to touch it, but his limbs did not want to move. He felt as if he had turned to stone and he was chilled to the bone.

"How did you come by this?" Qaa could barely get the words out.

"Your mother gave this to me on her deathbed. She made me promise I would give this to you at the appropriate time. She gave me a great many things to give to you. I had her chest of personal items and scrolls in my chambers, at Men-nefer. When my husband told me he had summoned you to Waset, I brought the chest with me. You shall find it at the palace. This amulet I have carried with me always. Now, it is time for you to take it and wear it proudly." She handed him the necklace.

With his hands trembling, Qaa took the amulet. It was a heavy piece, crafted in electrum. He had never seen anything like it before. The amulet was completely round, almost as big as a man's fist, and carved in concentric circles. Powdered lapis lazuli and malachite were inlaid, along with a golden-white sand, in each circle. Set on top of the sand, each circle held a raised circle of metal, one of gold, one of silver, one of a metal he had never seen. It appeared to be copper, but the colour was lighter, more brilliant. In the very center, inlaid in gold, was a square structure, which could have been a palace or a temple. His mother never removed the amulet, but he was very young when she joined Auser, and never saw it again. He could almost feel her energy coming from the amulet.

"Qaa, your mother was a great sorceress and her people possessed tremendous power. Many nations feared them, which is why you know so little of her. Within you lies her gift which you must discover and nurture. You have demonstrated your inner strength, in many ways, but you also possess a great magical ability. You may even have the power to heal, as she did."

Qaa was shocked. Nebettawy, in her delirium, cried out to him that only he could save her, he could heal her, that he had the power. But, how could she know that?

"In many ways, Nebettawy is closer to you than you know. When I gave birth to her, I was quite ill. The *swnw* could do no more for me, so your mother attended to me. You were still being suckled, and she was able to take Nebettawy to her breast as well. You would help your mother with Nebettawy; I never saw a young boy so gentle with a new baby. It was months before I recovered, and I owe my life to your mother. Once I was well enough, I was still unable to suckle my own daughter, so Tetisheri became Nebettawy's wet nurse. When your mother fell ill, I attended to her."

Qaa wanted to know much more, but he could not find the words. He covered his face with his hands and began to sob softly.

"Qaa, you have grown into a fine man. You attained honours and titles for your fearlessness in battle, you have proven yourself as a diplomat in Kush. Your mother would be very proud of you. I have waited patiently, to fulfill my promise to her, to help you find peace in who you really are. Put on the amulet. After you have examined the items in the chest, I shall answer any questions you may have." The queen gently pulled Qaa's hands from his face. She took the amulet from him and placed it around his neck. When the amulet touched the skin of his chest, Qaa felt the breath being sucked out of his lungs. He steadied himself with the table and slowed his breathing until it became regular again.

"My husband tells me you have permission, and his blessing, to take Nebettawy as your wife."

"Yes, your majesty. He has not yet told Nebettawy."

"I am pleased with his decision. Qaa, I do not expect you to call me 'Mother,' but you may call me 'Sister' or 'Mistress' or you may call me by my given name of Iset. I leave the choice to you, my son." She took his hand and squeezed it. Ramesses, standing in the hallway, smiled at the compassion of his favourite wife.

DAY 21 IN MONTH 3

"Qaa, I have serious matters to attend to in Men-nefer. When Tentopet is well enough, we shall be travelling back to the Lower Capital." Ramesses paced like a caged animal in his private quarters, scrolls held tightly in his hand.

"Father, how may I be of assistance?"

"I need you here in Waset. Though two of my sons reside on the East bank, I know I can depend upon you to keep the peace here. Keep my daughter safe and nurse her back to health. When do you expect to have this fiend in custody?"

"I have dispatched soldiers and Medjay to search for him. He has not left the city and I have shut the port temporarily, so he can not escape by water. If he chooses to flee into the Red Land, the jackals are welcome to feast upon him." Qaa wanted only to spit on the bones of Khety.

"In my absence, you are welcome to occupy the palace with my daughter. You only have a room at the temple and it may take time to find a suitable residence. There shall be servants here, as well as some of the harem women. Nebettawy is quite capable of handling the staff here. I shall remain as long as I can, to see this man brought to justice."

"My lord, I have spoken with the mistress Sadeh, wife of the *wab*-priest Weni. Nebettawy is in fear for her and I believe her life may be in danger, though she refuses protection. I do not wish to overstep my authority, as this is a rather delicate matter." Qaa did not want to reveal what he knew. He had promised Sadeh he would keep her confidence.

"I would like to offer all my citizens protection against this man, but if the woman refuses, I shall not disregard her wishes. Am I to understand, by your concern, her safety is related to the case you are investigating?"

"Yes, it is, and I fear she may become his next victim."

"Unless you can offer me an explanation, I shall not disregard her wishes."

"I gave her my word I would keep her confidence."

"Then, my son, we may both regret my decision. If you wish to have Medjay check on her periodically throughout the day that shall be acceptable. But I shall not station guards at her residence if she refuses them."

"I understand, my lord." Qaa was crestfallen. He would check on her personally; he had given his word to Nebettawy he would look in on her.

The Captain of the Medjay rushed into the private chamber. "Your majesty, the Phoenician has been returned to Waset. He is being held at the military barracks." The Medjay bowed to the king and Qaa. "You should know, he came back willingly and did not try to flee. He is anxious to clear his name of any charges."

"My lord, you have more important matters on your mind. I shall interrogate the Phoenician and report back to you." Qaa bowed to Ramesses. The king dismissed the men and turned back to the dispatches he had been reading.

At the entrance to the palace, Qaa turned to the Medjay captain.

"Return to the military barracks. I need to see someone and shall meet you there presently."

The captain scurried off in the direction of the barracks. Qaa, flanked by his escorts, headed for the First Pylon and turned right, headed to the home of Weni and Sadeh.

"May I enter? It is Qaa, Chief of the Medjay."

"You may enter."

Qaa stood inside the cool, dark residence, waiting for his eyes to adjust to the dim light. Sadeh was sitting at her loom, alone.

"You refused my offer of protection. I wanted to come and see if I could change your mind."

"*Hem netjer*, the truth shall be revealed soon enough. My fate is in the hands of the gods." Sadeh's hands were no longer trembling.

"Mistress, this man is dangerous and you have suffered enough at his hands."

"My husband shall be coming from the temple soon. I would prefer he not see you here." Sadeh stood, the look on her face told Qaa he could not dissuade her.

"I shall have Medjay, discreetly, check on your home until this man is in custody." Qaa bowed and exited the residence, the heat of the day almost unbearable, and the sky darkening with the threat of a sand storm. He would have to hurry to the military barracks, or soon he would not see his hand in front of him.

"The Phoenician is in here, my Chief." The Captain of the Medjay led Qaa into a room in the military barracks. The Phoenician was pacing, but did not appear to be distressed by his incarceration.

"That is the Phoenician?" Qaa looked at the man quizzically. He knew many Phoenicians and this man did not resemble them.

"Yes, his name is Ghedi."

Ghedi bowed to Qaa, but when he really looked at the Chief of the Medjay, he recognised that Qaa was certainly not Egyptian. The Phoenician, without a word, knelt in deference.

"I am Qaa, the new Chief of the Medjay. Phoenician, why did you depart Waset?"

"Raneb told me I could depart when my business here was concluded."

"Trader, do not test my patience. Raneb is dead." Qaa wanted to see his reaction, but Ghedi did not flinch at the words. He knew very well what had happened.

"Tell me about the vessel of imported wine." Qaa began pacing around the kneeling man. Ghedi looked up, concern mixed with relief on his face.

"Medjay, I did not kill Raneb. He was my friend. I had no reason to kill him."

"I know you received the wine vessel in trade. And I know Raneb cleared you in the young woman's murder. So I shall ask again, tell me about the wine." Qaa fingered the switch at his waist.

"A young woman came to my tent and wanted to trade. She did not seem the type to possess such an expensive item."

Qaa had stopped pacing and eyed the trader. "What do you mean?"

"I have seen her selling bead jewelry in the marketplace. She barely makes a living."

"Did you think the vessel was stolen?"

"I looked at the bottom, but there was no mark. I had no reason to doubt her and the man with her seemed to be forcing her to trade it with me."

"Can you describe the man?" Qaa was now interested in what the Phoenician had to say and began to pace again.

"I can do better. I trade often with a local merchant, Bek. For some time now, we have been supplied with replica ritual items from a temple goldsmith. His name is Khety. He is the man who coerced the young woman to trade away the wine."

Qaa had all the proof he needed. "Phoenician, I need to know what he said to you."

"He did not say so, but he seemed angry I had been cleared of the murder. He said I should give the wine as a gift to the Chief of the Medjay."

"What did it matter to him? Why would he care?"

"He said I was fortunate, being a foreigner. I should give the wine as a gift to stay on the right side of the Medjay. He intimated the Medjay, including Raneb, were corrupt and not above taking gifts. It was best to give them expensive items if I wished to continue trading in Waset."

Qaa again fingered the switch at his belt, but did not withdraw it. "Tell me what happened at Raneb's home."

"Medjay, you must understand. If I had known the wine was poisoned, I would not have given it to him. I checked the seal myself and saw nothing wrong."

"Tell me what happened." Qaa stopped pacing, stood in front of the Phoenician, and withdrew the switch from his belt. He was tired, concerned about Nebettawy, and wanted to finally put an end to this ugly business.

"I waited outside Raneb's residence. He came from the direction of the temple. I gave him the vessel and we stepped inside."

"He offered you a bowl. Why did you not drink with him, if you did not know the wine was poisoned?"

"Yes, he did offer, Medjay, but I do not take strong drink. He drained one bowl and poured another. He lurched about as if drunk and began sweating, then the convulsions; it was horrible. When he stopped moving, I exited his home and went back to my ship. I was afraid, Medjay, I would be blamed for yet another death."

"Much of your story I have verified through interrogation of other suspects."

Ghedi looked up at Qaa expectantly. "Then, I am free to depart?"

"No, Phoenician, I shall need your testimony. I have discovered Khety was supplying you and Bek with items stolen from the Temple of Amun."

Ghedi's face lost its colour, as he looked for mercy. "Bek assured me they were replicas. Had I known, I would have turned them over to Raneb. My reputation is as an honest trader."

"How well did you know the Chief Medjay that you call him by his given name?" Qaa looked suspiciously at Ghedi.

Ghedi swallowed hard. Raneb was the only person in Waset who knew his secret. He would have to trust Qaa. Did the Chief of the Medjay not recognise him as a fellow countryman?

"Medjay, Raneb knew I was not Phoenician, it is my adopted homeland; I was born and raised there, but my parents were foreigners. Raneb did not care about my lineage. His only concern was to solve the murder."

Qaa considered all the Phoenician had told him. The man was straightforward with his answers and did not appear to be hiding anything. He slid the switch back into his belt.

"I see you wear the amulet of our homeland. If I may speak plainly, Medjay, we are very much alike." Ghedi removed his head covering to reveal a head of long flowing hair the colour of wheat.

"Stand so I may look at you."

The trader stood and met Qaa eye to eye. Qaa had never been face to face with a man who resembled him. It was like looking into polished metal. He was tall and athletic, with pale skin and blue-green eyes, like his own mother's. Though he wore the colourful patterned robe of a Phoenician, Qaa knew he was no more a Phoenician than Ramesses himself. The trader pushed up the right arm of his robe to reveal his tattoos; Qaa gasped at what he saw.

"Do you recognise these, Medjay?"

Without a thought, Qaa reached out and touched the tattoos, to trace them as he used to trace his mother's. The Medjay were stunned to see Qaa collapse to his knees, shaking violently, almost immediately. But for Qaa, it had been more than one instant; what he saw and felt seemed to go on for an eternity.

It was the same sensation he had as a child, when his mother touched him. His senses sharpened, his feelings were more intense. It was like being in a sand storm, only greatly magnified — he could almost taste colour, feel sounds inside himself, see fragrances, touch the clouds.

Unconsciously, he could taste the warm, sweet milk of his mother. The only time in his life when he felt he belonged, was when she, like Auset, held him in her protective embrace and suckled him at her breast. He was like her and she used to tell him how special he was, that he had tremendous power, just like her.

"Medjay, my apologies. I did not know. Your gift is great, but untrained." The guards had pulled Ghedi away from Qaa and held him by the arms.

Qaa was helped to his feet by one of his escorts. He excused himself and stumbled to the door of the barracks. The sand storm had just passed, but it was still difficult to see. Once outside, he scrambled around the building and vomited. When he stood up, his head aching and his mind unclear, he feared he would lose control of his bladder. With hands still numb, he just managed to move his kilt and loincloth aside to urinate on the sand. Having relieved himself, he straightened the loincloth and smoothed down the kilt.

The feeling was starting to return to his hands, so he used the side of the building as leverage to wobble back to the door. His Medjay escort was stepping outside to check on him and came to his aid.

"Many thanks. The air has helped clear my head. I shall recover presently."

The escort helped Qaa back into the barracks, where Ghedi was still being held by two guards.

"Medjay, again, my apologies." Ghedi, though restrained, sank to his knees.

"I wish to speak with this man privately. You may wait outside." Qaa sat heavily on a chair, offered him by the Medjay. The guards released Ghedi and exited the barracks with Qaa's two escorts. When the men were alone, Qaa could not seem to formulate the proper questions to ask, his mind did not seem to comprehend what had happened.

Claudia R. Dillaire

"You wish to know where you came from, or rather, where your mother came from." Ghedi looked deep into Qaa's eyes, almost into his soul.

Qaa was dumbfounded. Could this man read his mind? What kind of people was his mother descended from?

"If I may inquire, Medjay, what were the names of your parents?"

"Why is that important?" Qaa ran his hand over his face. He had not spoken his mother's name since her death, over twenty years previous.

"If they were still alive, you would already have your answers." Ghedi stood and approached Qaa, but kept a respectful distance.

"My father was Pentaweret, an Egyptian. I do not know of my mother's family; she joined Auser when I was very young." Qaa's voice had dropped to a whisper. "Her name was Omreah."

Ghedi looked at Qaa with wonder and amazement. Could this really be the son of the man who had saved them from certain death?

"You are the son of the diplomat and the sorceress?"

"My father was Chief of the Royal Chariotry, in service to the king. You are the second person who has referred to my father as a diplomat. Tell me what you know of my father."

"We live because of your father. Though we are scattered far and wide and our race will die out, our legends will survive. We owe our very existence to the diplomacy of your father." Ghedi knelt again before Qaa and prostrated himself on the earthen floor.

"Phoenician, you may rise. I am only the Chief of the Medjay. I ask only respect for the office I represent."

Ghedi stood and faced Qaa. "No, my lord, you possess great power, the power of generations. All our people know of you; it was through the actions of your father we were saved from annihilation. He risked much to save us, disregarding even the orders of his king. Your mother was the greatest sorceress in all the land."

"I do not understand any of what you say." Qaa was Egyptian, raised by his father and Ramesses to be a soldier. He believed in their gods, in their magic; but, he was no magician.

"Medjay, you recognised my tattoos. Your mother bore the tattoos of her station. When you touched me, you felt my power, and mine pales in comparison to yours."

"Phoenician, I am a soldier by profession, *hem netjer nt Amun*, and I serve my king and country. My only concern is in bringing a murderer to justice. I wish for you to remain here. I shall arrange for accommodations until the magistrates have heard your testimony." Qaa did not wish to hear any more. He stood and turned to leave.

"Medjay, you shall never find peace until you make peace with who you are."

After the evening ritual, Qaa hurried to Nebettawy's chamber in the temple. He had asked Thanuny to prepare a tray for him, so he could feed her. He wanted to speak with the *swnwt* before she departed. She was in with Nebettawy, so he waited in the corridor, until she motioned him into the room. Nebettawy still looked fragile and deathly white; would she ever have her lively spirit back?

"*Swnwt*, is she well enough to be moved to the palace?"

"I suppose I could have a litter dispatched from the palace for her. I shall require help lifting her into it."

"No, *swnwt*. I do not wish to call attention to our actions. I am able to carry her, but I do not want to cause her any pain." Qaa had carried heavy men from the battlefield, though he had carried them over his shoulder.

"*Hem netjer*, are you sure you can travel that distance?"

"To me, she would be light as a feather. Cover of darkness shall afford privacy and she shall not be overcome by the heat of the day."

"She would have servants to attend her, as well as Tetisheri. Her chambers at the palace are light and airy, much larger than this small room, and it may speed her recovery."

"If she does not experience pain when we move her, could I take her into the palace gardens in the evenings? The change of air and the smell of growth may lift her spirits."

"That would be acceptable. Let me go to the palace and have her chambers prepared. I shall notify the king and return when all is in readiness."

Ashayt exited with her Medjay escorts. Thanuny brought the tray minutes later and placed it on the writing table. Qaa motioned him to remain, while he went to the dressing table and prepared the dried willow bark. He crossed to the bed, knelt beside it, and lifted Nebettawy's head.

"Sister, it is Qaa." He placed his honeyed finger on her lips and she licked it clean.

"Have you come to feed me?" She reached up to touch his cheek.

"Yes, Sister, Thanuny is going to assist me."

Nebettawy rested her head against Qaa's shoulder. Each time Qaa reached out his hand, Thanuny placed a slice of food in it, cheese, sliced gazelle, melon, plum, and bread. Qaa also managed to get her to drink some pomegranate wine, before she began to tire. He laid her back on the bed and motioned for the honey cake. He broke it and put a piece to her lips.

"Nebettawy, share with me." He lifted her head gently off the headrest.

"Yes, Qaa, I shall share with you." She took the honey cake and closed her eyes.

Thanuny remained with Qaa, both refreshing themselves, until the *swnwt* returned. All the preparations had been made. The two Medjay had escorted her back and the four Medjay guarding Nebettawy's room would come with them to the palace. Qaa's guards could remain at the temple and he would receive an escort back. The *swnwt* wrapped Nebattwy in a warm linen robe and a linen sheet to make carrying her easier. Qaa bent down, picked up Nebettawy, and held her close. He could not comprehend how little she weighed in his arms. The guards surrounded Qaa and the *swnwt* and escorted them to the palace.

Ramesses awaited them at the entrance. He conducted them down the hallway to Nebettawy's private chambers. Qaa placed her on her bed and moved away for the *swnwt* to settle her. He looked around the room and was in awe of the luxury. It was a large, whitewashed room, with scenes of gardens and ponds painted on the walls. The windows, and there were many, were high up in the wall, to afford light and breezes, but to afford privacy and security. There were four fans, one at each corner, which could be manned at any time by royal fan bearers.

Her bed was carved ebony, inlaid with gold, silver, and precious gems, and large enough for three people. She had a writing table in the middle of the room, two dressing tables covered with oils, unguents, makeup, perfumes, and small chests, and several large clothing chests rested against the far wall. The shelves on the far wall contained scrolls and jars of herbs and potions. Opposite the bed, the room opened onto other rooms, possibly a dressing room or private bath and waste facility, but it was too dark to see, even though lamps had been lit throughout the room. The other doorway led out to the palace gardens.

Once Ashayt had removed the robe and settled her under a light linen sheet, Ramesses placed two chairs next to the bed. Nebettawy was awake and smiling. Ramesses sat in one of the chairs and motioned to Qaa to join him. He lowered himself into the chair and relaxed, now that she was safe.

"Brother, I pray you did not have too much of a burden carrying me." She reached out and took Qaa's hand and kissed his palm, before releasing it.

"Sister, it was a pleasure to have you in my arms." Feeling Ramesses's gaze, Qaa blushed crimson.

"I fear I shall see less of you. Father, can a room be prepared for Qaa, here in the palace, so he may be close to me?"

Ramesses shifted nervously. He wanted to speak to Nebettawy in private about his decision to give her his blessing to take Qaa as her husband. Qaa, sensing the king's discomfort, came to his aid.

"Sister, I still have much to attend to in my investigation. Speak with your father tomorrow, when you are feeling better; I may have completed my investigation by then. I shall return after sunset and we may spend time in the gardens, if you wish." Qaa took her hand and kissed her palm, then placed it on the bed.

"I wish to spend my life with you, Qaa," she whispered, exhausted from the move. She looked at Qaa with tears in her eyes.

"And I with you, my sister." Qaa leaned in and whispered in her ear.

DAY 22 IN MONTH 3

After the morning ritual, Qaa and his Medjay guards headed for the palace. He would check on Nebettawy, before going to the military barracks. Soldiers and Medjay would be dispatched to search house by house, if necessary, to find Khety this day. The *swnwt* examined Nebettawy and found her improved. Qaa, alone, entered the private chamber. She was awake, but physically depleted; her fever finally abated during the night.

"Qaa, come sit beside me." Her eyes had regained their light and her smile was no longer forced. For the first time since the attack, she was not deathly pale.

"Sister, you look much improved this day." Qaa felt as if he could breathe again, as he sat and took her hand.

"I am still so very tired and my limbs feel like lead. But my head has cleared, and I am no longer burning with fever."

"Sister, if you are able, I must ask you about something that troubles me. In the course of my investigation I have heard men make reference to a Bes tattoo. I did not wish to appear unknowledgeable about such matters, so I said nothing. Can you tell me what it is?"

Her laugh was music to his ears. "Qaa, do you know so little about Egyptian women? *Shemayets* often have the god Bes tattooed on their upper thigh, as it adds to their sensuality. How did you hear of this?"

"From what I have learned, Merti is quite proud of her tattoo." Qaa looked down, blushing.

"Brother, did she show it to you?" Nebettawy was quite amused at Qaa's distress.

"No, beloved, but I may be one of the only men in Waset who has not seen it."

After Qaa left the palace, Ramesses entered his daughter's private chambers. He needed to speak with her, as a father, about his decision and he had little time. Tentopet would be well enough to travel by the end of the month. If he wanted to celebrate his daughter's marriage before returning to Men-nefer, he could wait no longer.

"Daughter, are you well enough to enjoy the company of your father?"

Nebettawy looked up at him and smiled. He looked so tired and worn, as if he had aged a century. She reached out and took his hand.

"Yes, Father, sit with me."

Ramesses sat next to the bed and held his daughter's hand. This was the first time since her attack that she seemed pleased to see him. She only wanted Qaa when she was ill and delirious; she did not need her father any longer and it saddened him.

"Nebettawy, I have seen terrible things, things no father should ever see." Ramesses's eyes filled with tears and his hands trembled.

"Father, I have only myself to blame. I should not have left the safety of the temple."

"No, Daughter, I am to blame. I defied Amun, out of my own ignorance and my desire to protect you. I do not deserve your forgiveness for bringing this illness upon you." Ramesses finally broke down and sobbed.

"I love you, my father, and always shall." Nebettawy released her father's hand and stroked his cheeks with both hands. "You have my forgiveness, if that shall soothe your troubled heart."

Ramesses took time to compose himself. He had always kept his emotions in check, but this unpleasantness had almost destroyed him.

"Nebettawy, I do not know how much you remember. You need to know, if it were not for Qaa, you may have joined Auser." His voice was soft and quiet. "He risked my punishment for his actions, but thought only of you. He would prefer to die, than to live without you."

Nebettawy tried to remember what had happened when she was ill. The fever clouded her mind, but she knew Qaa was there. She saw his face often, a mask of concern, but his voice was only calm and soothing.

"I have spoken with my father, Amun, and I know what must be done. After consulting your mother, I met privately with Qaa and have given him my permission to take you as his wife."

Nebettawy wanted to leap from her bed and hug her father, but she was too weak. Her smile and the light in her eyes told Ramesses all he needed to know. She took his hand and kissed the palm, tears filling her dark eyes.

"You have given me the greatest gift, my beloved father. My heart has belonged to Qaa since the first moment I saw him, but you always have a special place in my heart. Nothing shall ever change how I feel for you."

Qaa and his escorts turned the corner toward the residence of Khety. When he saw the guards lying on the sand at the doorway, he broke into a run. He knelt beside one man and saw he was breathing, but unconscious. The other man was in the same condition. Without asking permission, Qaa entered the residence. Aahotep tried to block his entrance, but he pushed her aside. Nithotep, sitting at her loom, looked frightened by the commotion.

"Aahotep, where is your father?" Qaa grabbed her by the arm.

"I will not help you, Medjay." Aahotep spat on the ground at Qaa's feet.

"What happened to my men?"

"I gave them lotus flower and wine. Father told me to take care of them, so he could leave unseen."

"Where was he going?"

"I know." Nithotep had moved from her loom to stand next to her sister.

"Say nothing, Sister." Aahotep, stroking her sister's cheek, pushed her in the direction of her loom.

"Medjay, take Aahotep outside." Qaa released his grip on Aahotep and the Medjay took her by the arms and escorted her out of the residence.

"Nithotep, do you remember me?" Qaa knelt down and spoke to the young woman in quiet, soothing tones.

"Yes, your name is Qaa."

"Will you help me, child? You have done nothing wrong and I promise you shall not be punished for speaking with me." He took her hand and squeezed it gently.

"I like you, Qaa, so I will help you."

"Do you know where your father has gone?"

"Is my father coming back? My father made my mother leave." Nithotep's face changed in an instant, from smiling warmly to consternation.

"What do you mean, child, he made her leave?"

"I was supposed to be asleep on the roof, but I wanted to see Father when he came home."

"What happened when he came home?"

"My mother came home before he did. She put clothes in a chest, like we were going on a journey. When Father came home, he was very angry."

"Can you tell me what you saw the night your mother left, Nithotep?"

"Father and Mother raised their voices. I could not hear what they said. Then Father tore open Mother's linen dress." She started to cry.

"Did he hurt your mother?"

"He dragged her by the hair to the table in the main room. He bent her over the table and kept bumping into her, from behind. I could hear Mother crying and screaming. I was afraid, so I stayed very still on the stairs. Father let go of Mother and she turned around and slapped him in the face. Father's face got very red; he put his hands around her throat and shook her for a long time."

"What happened after he shook her?" Qaa realised she had witnessed her mother's death and no matter what Khety had done to his daughter, he could not erase that memory.

"When he took his hands from her throat, she fell to the floor and did not move. I started to cry and that's when Father saw me. He was very angry with me. The last thing I remember, Father came toward me and struck me across the cheek. When I woke up, Mother was gone, and I was in the big bed with Father." Nithotep reached up and rubbed the side of her head, remembering how her head hurt the following morning.

"Nithotep, your father has been hiding here, has he not?"

"Yes, Aahotep made sure the guards did not see him."

"But, he wanted to leave the house today. What did he ask Aahotep to do?"

"He asked Aahotep to make the guards go away. He said if she did not make them go away, he would. He was very angry and he scared me." She began to tremble at the thought of her father's anger.

"Did he tell you or your sister where he was going?"

"He said he had to see the only person who ever accepted his gift."

"Many thanks, Nithotep. You have been a great help."

She smiled at Qaa, turned, and returned to her loom. Qaa went to the doorway; he knew where Khety was going.

"Medjay, I want one of you to remain here and keep watch over the two women. The guards have been given lotus steeped wine and hopefully shall recover. The other of you shall go to the barracks and send Medjay here and to the house of the *wab*-priest Weni."

"Chief, I can not allow you to go alone."

"Do as I say. I shall not be alone long and I can handle Khety."

Qaa stopped in front of the residence of Weni and Sadeh long enough to catch his breath. The unrelenting sun and the waves of heat reflecting off the sand made it difficult to run. He would need as much strength as he could summon to overpower Khety, if necessary. He cupped his hands over his eyes to block out the sun, while he listened at the doorway. He wanted to know who was inside and where they were.

He could hear Weni begging for Khety to stop what he was doing. From the sound of his voice, Weni was close to the doorway. The other voices came from further inside the residence. Sadeh was sobbing, pleading for forgiveness from Amun. The sound that disturbed him the most was coming from Khety. He could hear the man grunting and squealing like a pig, and the words he spoke, interspersed with the grunts, were the most foul he had ever heard uttered. As he closed his eyes to slits, so they would adjust to the darkness quickly, he heard Khety bellowing in pleasure, while Sadeh cried and screamed. Qaa could wait no longer for Medjay to arrive; he entered the residence alone.

"Khety, do not hurt her further." Qaa could not believe the scene before him. Weni, bloodied and badly beaten, was tied and seated to the left of the doorway on the tile floor, struggling to free himself. In front of him, Khety, his loincloth lying in a heap at his feet, had Sadeh, naked, trembling, and obviously in pain, bent over a table and was in the act of raping her.

"Stay back, Medjay. I will kill her." Khety held his bronze dagger to the throat of the terrified woman. His other arm held her tightly around the waist.

"Your daughter, Nithotep, sent me. She fears for you."

"Aahotep will look after her."

"Aahotep has been taken into custody for killing my Medjay. Nithotep shall be all alone. She can not care for herself." Qaa wanted Khety to believe the guards had been poisoned, rather than only rendered unconscious. It would make it easier to negotiate if Khety thought he could save Aahotep from punishment and Nithotep from an uncertain future.

"I am at fault for my daughter's illness. She will be better without me."

"Khety, what about the princess Nebettawy? She asks for you often. She sent me to find you. I have been instructed by the king himself to bring you to the palace. The princess is anxious to meet you; she awaits you now."

"She is a beautiful woman, Medjay. I have never seen a woman more desireable." Khety was remembering the evening of the attack and it had distracted him. He released his grip on Sadeh and was backing away from her.

Qaa saw his chance to rush Khety, as he dropped the weapon to his side. His long legs closed the gap between them almost before Khety could react. The goldsmith was able to raise his dagger to slash at Qaa, getting in one deep cut across his left shoulder. The Medjay Chief struck him a sound blow to the face, knocking Khety to the tile floor. Qaa placed one sandaled foot on Khety's hand, making him release the dagger, before moving it to Khety's neck.

Medjay arrived within minutes and took Khety into custody. Qaa untied Weni and helped him into a chair. He asked a Medjay to find Sadeh a robe, as Qaa put his arms around the hysterical woman and pulled her close to cover her nakedness.

"Medjay, summon the *swnwt* and have her brought here immediately. Mistress, he can not hurt you any longer. I shall stay with you until the *swnwt* arrives." Qaa stroked her hair and tried to calm her.

"*Hem netjer*, many thanks." Sadeh shook violently in Qaa's embrace, but rested her head on his chest, while he comforted her.

"Let me attend to my wife." Weni took the robe from the Medjay and covered his wife. Qaa released Sadeh and she put her arms around her husband's neck and cried.

"My Chief, your arm. The wound is quite deep."

Qaa tore off part of his kilt to tie around his arm to slow the bleeding until it could be attended to.

Qaa returned to the palace after assisting Thanuny with the evening ritual. His arm throbbed, his stomach rumbled, and his legs ached from exertion. He would make his report to Ramesses, so the magistrates could be summoned in the morning. He was conducted into the king's private chamber.

"Son, I understand the wound is rather deep. Have you eaten yet?"

"No, my father. I finished interrogating Khety and had to hurry to the temple for the evening ritual." Qaa felt light headed and put his right hand on the writing table to steady himself.

"My apologies, Qaa, sit down and rest. I shall have refreshment brought to us in here. Then, you may wish to visit my daughter." Ramesses summoned a servant, requesting refreshment, before retrieving two drinking bowls from a shelf on the far wall. He put them on the table and crossed the room to a large chest. He came back with a vessel of wine.

"Qaa, you look like you need this. It is the mandrake wine the *swnwt* gave me." Ramesses poured wine for them both and returned to his seat.

"Many thanks, my father." Qaa wanted to drain the bowl, but was afraid he would black out. He took a sip, waited a few moments, and took another, before collapsing into the chair. The lack of food sped the effect of the herbal wine and he felt the tension finally leave his muscles.

"Qaa, you have done well. The Captain of the Medjay told me only that Khety, the goldsmith, was in custody. Based upon his words, I have already sent messengers to the magistrates. The court shall convene in the morning, after the sunrise ritual."

"I shall write my report when I return to the temple. Ask me what you wish to know." Qaa could barely keep his eyes open. The strain of the investigation, the attack on Nebettawy, the heat of the day, and the wine were all having their effect upon him.

Before the king could respond, the servant returned with a tray of refreshment, which he placed on the table and exited the chamber.

"Qaa, all I want is for you to eat and then rest. I shall hear all I need to hear during the proceedings tomorrow. You may give me your written report when you have recovered sufficiently."

Ramesses and Qaa ate a light meal of sliced duck, prepared liver, grapes, melons, lentils flavoured with garlic, cucumber, cheese, and bread. The wine had lessened the pain in his arm and the food had cleared his head. Qaa felt renewed; he would feel even better when he saw Nebettawy.

"Qaa, I took the liberty of speaking with the vizier. My daughter is not yet well enough to see him and you have been far too busy. I asked him to register your marriage to Nebettawy. I do not wish to keep you from her any longer. Though she is unable to fulfill her duties to you as a wife, I am sure she would welcome sharing her bed with you."

Qaa stared at Ramesses in disbelief. The wine must have made him delirious; he thought the king was allowing him to share Nebettawy's bed this evening.

"Before I depart for Men-nefer, I shall host your marriage festivities, to make the official announcement. But I see nothing improper with you spending the night with my daughter. She is your wife now. She awaits you in the gardens." Ramesses nodded and smiled at his new son.

Qaa was unable to speak. He slid out of the chair and fell to his knees in front of the king. Ramesses put his hand on Qaa's shoulder and squeezed it gently.

"Go to her, my son. You have proven yourself to be a worthy husband for my daughter."

Qaa kissed the top of the king's hand, stood with a bit of difficulty, and exited the private chamber. In the corridor, he could not contain himself any longer and ran to the gardens, and the embrace of his new wife.

Ramesses and Qaa arose before sunrise to go to the temple. After the morning ritual, Ramesses remained in the sanctuary, alone, to consult with his father, the Great Amun. On the walk back to the palace, Qaa and Ramesses talked about the proceedings. When they arrived at the palace, Ramesses told Qaa he would find the proper clothing for court laid out in Nebettawy's private chamber, turned, and hurried down the corridor to prepare himself.

Qaa entered the chamber, quietly, so as not to disturb Nebettawy. He found a new loincloth, as well as a new kilt and shawl of the finest royal linen, with threads of silver and gold woven into them. His Flies of Valour had been laid out, his *wesekh* collar, the Medjay belt and sash, and leather switch. But the one item which took his breath away, was the true symbol of his station as First *hem netjer.* It was the most magnificent leopard skin he had ever seen. When he entered the private bath to cleanse, a steward was waiting, to assist and clothe him.

The royal scribe began writing down the court proceedings against Khety.

In year 17, month 3 of the Peret season, day 23:

King Usermaatre-meryamun, Ramesses III, may he live, prosper, and be healthy (l.p.h.), convened the magistrates, in the main reception chamber of the palace, to hear of the abominations of Khety, a temple goldsmith in the Temple of Amun. The evil doer was brought before the magistrates to answer for his crimes. The magistrate, Qaa, Chief of the Medjay and First *hem netjer* in the Temple of Amun, interrogated Khety in the presence of:

Djehuty — Vizier of Waset; Ankhtify — Lord of the Treasury; Intef — Royal Scribe; Hemon — Royal Scribe; Nebka — Royal Cupbearer; Kheperkare — Nobleman and Merchant; Djeserkare — Chief of the Royal Chariotry; Siptah — Doorkeeper of the Palace; Sobekhotep — Overseer of the Temple Goldsmiths; Amenhirkopshef II — *wab*-priest of Mut on the East bank of Waset, son of King Usermaatre-meryamun, Ramesses III, (l.p.h.); Usermaatre — Great Commander of the Army, son of King Usermaatre-meryamun, Ramesses III, (l.p.h.); and King Usermaatre-meryamun, Ramesses III, (l.p.h.).

The magistrates sat in chairs, along the left side of the chamber, and Ramesses sat on his throne, in the center of the raised platform used to receive diplomats. Qaa, to be able to present the evidence, chose to stand, rather than sit in the chair provided for him next to the king.

"Goldsmith, the charges against you are serious. What do you have to say for yourself?"

Khety, with hands and feet bound, was carried forward by Medjay to kneel in front of King Usermaatre-meryamun, Ramesses III, (l.p.h.), and the assembled magistrates. The Oath of the Lord was given to the accused to not speak falsely. He was interrogated by the magistrate, Qaa, Chief of the Medjay, to speak plainly of the crimes he had been charged with.

"Medjay, I have confessed to you my crimes."

"You must now attest to your crimes, in front of the magistrates, and your words shall be recorded by the royal scribes. I shall read each charge against you, witnesses shall be called to give testimony for and against you, and then you shall explain yourself to the magistrates. Do you understand goldsmith?"

"Yes, Medjay, ask your questions."

"The first crime you are charged with is the murder of your wife, Sitkamose, in year one of the reign of the king, (l.p.h.). Your daughter, Nithotep, shall give testimony against you. Medjay, bring the young woman forward."

Claudia R. Dillaire

Nithotep, accompanied by Medjay, was brought before the magistrates. When she saw her father, she ran to him, threw her arms around his neck and kissed his cheek. The Medjay pulled her away and took her to stand in front of Qaa.

"Nithotep, do you remember me?" His voice was calm and gentle.

"Yes, you are Qaa. You came to my home, looking for my father."

"Child, will you tell me again, what happened to your mother?"

"My mother left us and never came back."

"The night your mother left, tell us what you heard and saw."

"I was on the roof, it was cool up there. I was supposed to be asleep, but I wanted to see my father. I heard him and my mother. I crept down the stairs. I saw my father with his hands on my mother's neck, shaking her."

"Tell us what happened when your father saw you."

"He was very angry. He released my mother and she fell to the floor. He came at me and I screamed. I remember he hit me, hard, across the face. I awoke the next morning, and my mother was gone."

"Many thanks, Nithotep. You may go now."

The young woman was led out by the Medjay.

"Magistrates, I did not administer the Oath of the Lord to the witness. She has been examined by Ashayt, *swnwt per aa*, and she has a healed depression on the side of her head. Since the night her mother left, she has been like a child. It is my contention that Khety, in striking his daughter to silence her, caused the damage to her skull, from which she never recovered. Though a grown woman, she is still a child, and could not speak falsely to this court. Khety, how do you answer to this charge?"

Khety was not without feeling for his daughter. He had caused her injury, though by accident, and he had to admit his fault.

"My wife had followed me and saw me with another woman. We argued and, in a fit of rage, I choked her. When I saw my daughter, I just wanted to quiet her. I did not mean to hurt her, but I hit her too hard. She has the mind of a child, and it is my doing."

"What did you do with your wife's body?"

Khety bowed his head. His wife was blameless and deserved a proper burial, which he denied her. "I carried her body into the Red Land and left her there for the jackals."

"Is it true you killed your wife to cover another crime you had committed, which she had witnessed?" Qaa's left arm had begun to throb. The wound was deep and continued to ooze blood, even though the *swnwt* had treated and wrapped it.

"Yes, Medjay, I took a woman of higher status against her will."

"Why would you commit such an abomination?"

"I can not control myself. I would see the woman going to the temple each evening. I would hear her praying to Amun to bless her with a daughter. I had five daughters. I could provide her with what her husband could not. I tried to fight my urges, but she was a beautiful woman. I waited for her, beside the temple wall. I took her from behind, like an animal, so she would not see my face."

"The woman you defiled is waiting to testify against you. But, when your present crimes were discovered, you feared she would come forward and reveal your previous crime. So you entered her home, assaulted her husband, and threatened her. You made her husband watch as you defiled her again. I would prefer not to put her through this ordeal if you shall admit to the abomination you committed sixteen years ago and the attack on her and her husband on day 22 of this month."

"I am not without feeling, Medjay. I will admit that I defiled the woman sixteen years ago. I assaulted her husband, tied him up, and forced him to watch as I defiled her again. She has suffered enough, because I could not control myself."

"These crimes have only now come to light because you have continued to commit abominations. The next charge against you is theft of ritual items from the Temple of Amun for your personal gain. How long have you been stealing from the temple?"

"I began taking items from the temple in year 14. My daughter, Nithotep, was ill. I had to provide a suitable dowry for my daughter, Inhapi. She was marrying a man of higher status, a merchant in Waset. But this does not excuse my actions."

"You took ritual items and statues from the temple and replaced them with replicas. I have three such items here as evidence."

His left arm felt weak, so Qaa picked up the offering bowl first, then the statue, and presented them to the magistrates. Lastly, he handed them the ritual cup. The magistrates, comparing the items, could tell the difference in weight between the replicas and the solid gold cup.

Claudia R. Dillaire

"The ritual items you traded in the marketplace with local and foreign merchants. Two of the merchants are here to give testimony against you. Medjay, bring forward the Phoenician, Ghedi."

Ghedi, accompanied by two Medjay, was escorted to Qaa. He stood in front of the magistrates, bowed in deference to the king and Qaa, and willingly took the Oath of the Lord to not speak falsely.

"Have you received items in trade from the goldsmith, Khety?" Qaa motioned to the accused.

"Yes, Medjay. He told me he was a goldsmith in the Temple of Amun. In his spare time he created replica items from scrap metal. All the pieces he traded with me were represented as being copies, not true ritual items used in the temple. I have a number of wealthy customers in Mycenae and the Near East who are interested in Egyptian arts and crafts. I was more than happy to trade with him."

"Did you ever suspect the items were not replicas?"

"Most of the trading I do in Waset is with Bek, the merchant. He looked over the items and we both felt they were replicas. Bek believed, as I did, we were dealing with an honest man."

"As a foreigner, you are not bound by the Oath of the Lord. Why did you allow me to administer it to you?"

"I am a trader. I do a great deal of business in Waset. I wish to be allowed to continue to trade here. If I am not an honest trader, how shall I make my living? And as a foreigner, my reputation must be beyond reproach."

"Many thanks, Ghedi."

The Phoenician left the chamber and Bek was brought forward by the Medjay to give his testimony. After bowing in deference, Qaa administered the Oath of the Lord to not speak falsely.

"Merchant, you have been trading with Khety, the goldsmith, for three years. Have you ever doubted the goods he was trading with you were not replicas?"

"No, Medjay, the pieces were well made and of fine quality. I had no reason to doubt him."

"What would you have done if you had known the items were from the temple?"

"I would have notified Raneb, who was the Chief of the Medjay when I began trading with Khety. I was questioned by Raneb, before his death, and he was satisfied I was blameless. When you questioned me about the items, I gave you the one item I still had. You were far too generous with payment for the item, or so I thought at the time. Now that I know the item was not a replica, I am ashamed to have taken the items in the beginning."

"Many thanks, Bek."

Bek was escorted from the reception chamber.

"Magistrates, the next witness has direct knowledge that Khety was creating replica ritual items. Medjay, bring forward Unas, the goldsmith apprentice." Unas was brought in, bound at the hands and feet. He knelt before Qaa and was administered the Oath of the Lord to not speak falsely. Knowing Unas did not always speak the truth, Qaa slid his leather switch from his belt.

"Unas, do not make me use the switch on you. You were apprentice to Khety, temple goldsmith. Were you aware of his thefts?"

"I knew Khety was making replica items. He told me he was trading them in the marketplace."

"Did you know the items he traded were not replicas?" Qaa clenched and flexed his left hand, which was losing feeling.

"Not in the beginning. Shortly before my wife, Iput, moved out of our residence, she told me she had seen Khety coming from the temple. Iput went to the temple often to consult the *hemet netjer*. I asked Khety why he had been at the temple. He grabbed me by the throat and told me to keep my mouth shut and to tell Iput to do the same."

"Did there come a time when Khety enlisted your aid in the theft of goods?"

"Khety told me he was having trouble with someone. He wanted me to steal a dagger for him. I told him he had a perfectly good bronze dagger. He told me if I did not help him, he would hurt Takhat, the woman who is carrying my child. I created a disturbance in the marketplace, while Takhat took the dagger. It was a Near East dagger, nicer than any of us could afford. I gave the dagger to Khety."

"Is this the dagger?" Qaa put down the switch to pick up the blood-stained dagger from the table.

"It looks like the one Takhat stole." Unas recoiled in horror from the bloody dagger, with the realization that the blood was his wife's.

"That was not the last time Khety enlisted your aid. Did he ask you to steal again for him?" Qaa replaced the dagger on the table.

"Yes, Medjay. The day after Iput's death, Khety told me he needed an expensive vessel of wine, as a special gift. He grabbed Takhat by the hair. He ran his hand over her belly and asked me how much I wanted the child. Takhat and I did what he asked."

"What happened to the wine vessel?"

"A few days later, he told me he wanted Takhat to trade the vessel with the Phoenician. I wanted to go with Takhat, but Khety said he would. He did not want anything to go wrong. When I asked Takhat what had happened, she said Khety pushed her away from the stall after the transaction. She did not hear what Khety said to the Phoenician."

"Is this the vessel?" Qaa picked up the broken clay vessel from the table.

"It looks like the vessel, Medjay."

"Is this the knife you were carrying when you were taken in for questioning?" Qaa put down the vessel and picked up the nearly pristine bone and bronze dagger.

"Yes, Medjay, that is my knife."

"Unas, many thanks for not making me use the switch. You may go." Qaa replaced the switch in his belt.

Unas was led out by the Medjay. Takhat was the next to testify, to confirm what Unas had said. When Takhat saw Unas, she fell to her knees, crying hysterically. The Medjay lifted her off the tile floor and brought her forward.

"Takhat, if you hope to influence the punishment to be imposed upon Unas, you shall answer the questions of this court." Qaa did not want to appear lenient, though she was with child. Takhat composed herself, bowed in deference, and allowed Qaa to administer the Oath of the Lord to not speak falsely.

"Did Khety ask you to steal for him?"

"Yes, Medjay. The first item was a fancy dagger. Unas said Khety would hurt me if I did not help him. I stole the dagger from Bek's tent. A few days later, Khety grabbed me by the hair. He put his hands on me. I was afraid for my baby. I stole the vessel of wine, again from Bek. Khety dragged me with him to trade the wine with the Phoenician. After the trade, Khety spoke to the foreigner, but I could not hear what he said."

Qaa picked up the bloody dagger, then the broken wine vessel, replacing each on the table. "Takhat, are these the items Khety forced you to steal?"

Takhat swallowed hard to keep from retching. "They appear to be the items, Medjay."

"Why did you steal for Khety?"

"I did not like him, but Unas was apprentice to him. He threatened Unas and me, we were afraid of him, so we did what he asked."

"Is this the knife that Unas carries?" Qaa picked up Unas's dagger.

"Yes, Medjay. I wanted him to have a proper knife. I saved for months to purchase it for him. I gave it to him about a month ago."

"Many thanks, Takhat. You may go." When Qaa placed the dagger on the table and turned, his head was swimming. It felt unusually warm in the reception chamber and his throat was dry.

The Medjay led her out.

"Khety, what do you have to say for yourself, against these witnesses?"

"They speak the truth, Medjay." Khety bowed his head, knowing his punishment was a foregone conclusion.

"Khety, the next charge against you is the murder of the wick-maker, Iput, wife of Unas. And to throw suspicion upon the foreigner, Ghedi, you enlisted Unas and Takhat to steal a dagger like his. How do you answer to this charge?"

"I had to silence her. She caught me stealing from the temple."

"How did you silence her?"

"I saw her coming from the temple and I waited at the end of the enclosure. I grabbed her from behind, but I could not control my urges. I knew she would be too ashamed to tell anyone what had happened."

"Are you telling the magistrates you took Iput against her will, prior to killing her?"

"I took her like an animal, from behind. She did not see my face. I told her to forget what she had seen at the temple. She had allowed her husband to beat her; what kind of woman would do that? I told her, with her reputation, no one would believe her if she reported the attack."

"When did this occur?"

"In the month of Paopi, last year."

"Then, why did you subsequently kill her?"

"She came to me the first day of this month. She told me she was with child and it was mine. I told her no one would believe that. She told me the *hemet netjer* would believe her. I told her if she opened her mouth, she would be sorry. I began watching her. She went to the temple every evening. I forced Unas to steal a dagger for me and I waited for her. Before she could enter the temple, I killed her. After she was dead, I made it look as if she had been attacked by a wild animal."

Qaa again picked up the bloodied dagger. "Is this the weapon you used on her?" He put the item back on the table.

"Yes, Medjay. I left it next to the body, hoping the Phoenician would be charged with the crime."

"How could you be sure she had not told the *hemet netjer*?"

"I was not sure. And, when the Chief of the Medjay, Raneb, started asking questions, I had to do something, to cover my crimes. He had cleared the Phoenician. That is when I had Unas steal the vessel of wine."

"Khety, you are further charged with the poisoning of Raneb, the Chief of the Medjay in Waset and First *hem netjer* in the Temple of Amun on day 8 of this month. The Phoenician shall give testimony regarding the vessel of wine."

Ghedi was returned to the main reception chamber. Qaa reminded him he had been given the Oath of the Lord. He nodded his acceptance, bowed to the king, and stood before the magistrates.

"You received a vessel of fine imported wine, in trade, on day 8 of this month. The accused was with the young woman who traded it, is that true?"

"Yes, Medjay, he was with her."

"Is this the vessel of wine that was traded to you?" Qaa motioned to the broken vessel.

"Yes, Medjay, it is the vessel I took in trade, and gave to Raneb."

"What did Khety say to you, about the wine?"

"He said he heard the Chief of the Medjay had cleared me in the murder of the wick-maker. The vessel of wine would make him a fine gift, to show my appreciation."

"What did you do with the vessel?"

"Medjay, had I known the wine was poisoned, I would not have brought it to Raneb. He was my friend, I had no reason to harm him."

"Tell the magistrates what happened."

"I waited at Raneb's residence. I was sailing at first light for Phoenicia, so I wanted to bring him the gift. He was coming from the temple. He asked me to join him for a drink, but I do not take strong drink. He drank a bowl of wine and told me I could stay and keep him company. He had started on a second bowl, when he began to choke and shake violently. He died within minutes. I was terrified I would be accused of yet another death, so I went to my ship, and at first light, I set sail for Phoenicia."

"You were intercepted at a port down the Nile. Did you return willingly?"

"Yes, Medjay, I wanted to clear my name. You interrogated me at the military barracks and I told you all I knew."

"Many thanks, Ghedi. You may go."

After Ghedi had exited the room, Qaa turned to Khety. He steadied himself with the table, as the room tilted.

"What do you have to say for yourself, Khety?"

"I was afraid the Chief of the Medjay had discovered my crimes. He questioned me about the temple thefts and Iput. I poisoned the wine with lotus flower, mandrake, and monkshood. I knew he would die quickly. I watched from the shadows for the Phoenician to leave. I searched the residence for his report on the investigation, but I did not find any fresh scrolls. His palette was on the table, so I felt safe, until you started asking questions, Medjay."

"Khety, you are charged with committing an abomination upon the princess Nebettawy, daughter of the king, (l.p.h.), *hemet netjer* and *dwat-netjer* in the Temple of Amun. The princess is too ill to appear before the magistrates."

"I wish to face the man who touched me in such a disgusting manner."

Qaa looked startled to see Nebettawy, on a litter, being carried into the chamber by four servants and accompanied by the *swnwt per aa*. Rather than stand before the magistrates, she requested to be placed next to her father. The king knelt next to his daughter and tried to dissuade her from speaking before the court. Qaa could not hear the exchange, but saw Nebettawy shake her head at her father's request. The *swnwt* spoke to the king and, reluctantly, he returned to his throne.

"Medjay, please administer the Oath of the Lord, so I may give testimony in this matter." Nebettawy's voice was quiet, but firm.

With some difficulty, Qaa knelt next to the litter. Nebettawy was pale and trembling. She was holding a scroll of papyrus in her hands. He looked at the *swnwt*; her expression told him there was no talking Nebettawy out of confronting Khety. He leaned in so the magistrates would not hear.

"Sister, you do not have to do this. You are too ill to be here."

Claudia R. Dillaire

"Beloved, I need to hear his voice. He haunts my dreams. Until I know, I shall not feel safe."

Qaa asked the litter bearers for assistance to stand. Resigned, he administered the Oath of the Lord to Nebettawy to not speak falsely. He had to tread carefully with his questioning. If her whereabouts before the attack were revealed, in front of the magistrates, the king would be forced to punish them both. Qaa held his breath and began his questioning.

"On the evening of day 14 in this month, you had gone to the Sacred Lake. Is that true?"

"Yes, Medjay. I often go there at night. The water is cool and the temple enclosure is quiet."

"Were you alone at the Sacred Lake?"

"Yes, Medjay. When I started back to the temple, I saw Anedjib, the *hery heb*, in the First Court."

Qaa could breathe again. "Princess, tell the magistrates what happened when you arrived at the entrance to the First Court."

"I felt a strong hand grab my left arm and the point of a knife at my throat. I did not recognise the voice of the man who spoke to me. I have written down his words, to the best of my recollection." She handed the scroll to Qaa. "If this is the man who attacked me at the temple, I shall recognise him by his voice and these words."

Nebettawy had never told Qaa what the man said to her that night. He looked at the scroll and thought he would retch. He handed the scroll to the king, who read the words; his face flushed with anger.

"I could kill you myself, with my bare hands." Ramesses came half out of his seat. Qaa did his best to restrain the king. It was then Ramesses noticed Qaa's face was the colour of unpolished silver. Khety recoiled from both men, expecting to be severely beaten.

"His grip on me was firm. He took the knife away and wrapped his arm around my throat. When he felt me going weak in the knees, he released his grip on my arm, and ran his hand over my breasts and down my body. He forced his knee in between my legs, and forcefully inserted an object into me. When I cried out from the pain, he withdrew the object, released his grip, and ran from the temple."

The words hung in the room, shocking those in attendance. Ramesses had buried his face in his hands. She was his favourite and he had not protected her from this abomination. Qaa flushed crimson, ashamed of what had been done to Nebettawy, guilty of his assignation with her that very evening, and angry he had not been with her, to protect her from this monster. The magistrates, all fine men, many of noble families, could not fathom the indignity perpetrated upon the princess.

"Medjay, if you would ask the accused to recite those words, I may be able to identify him as the man who attacked me." Her voice was soft and filled with trepidation. The last words she ever wanted to hear were the words he had spoken that awful night.

Qaa approached Khety with measured, unsteady steps. "Are you able to read, goldsmith?"

"I am able to read some signs, Medjay." Khety's voice was quiet and scared.

In one swift movement, Qaa withdrew his switch and struck the goldsmith, hard across the left cheek. "Read this, or I shall read it into the record for you."

"I do not need to read the words, Medjay. I told the princess to forget what Iput had told her or she would regret it. When I was holding her against me, I could not control myself. I asked her if she had ever been with a man. I knew she had not, she was sacred, but she was so beautiful. I knew I had to take her. I told her I would show her what it was like to have a real man."

"I have heard enough of his voice. He called me 'Princess' and it is his voice that I heard the night of the attack."

"Many thanks, Princess. You are free to leave the proceedings." Qaa felt the sweat trickling down his back and left arm. When he touched his arm, he noticed it was blood. The leopard skin would cover it for the present.

The king stood, knelt by the litter, and kissed his daughter on the forehead. He spoke briefly with the *swnwt* and motioned for the litter bearers to take his daughter back to her quarters. When the *swnwt* and litter had left the chamber, Qaa turned to the accused.

"What do you have to say about your actions?"

"I have no excuse, Medjay. My urges control me. The princess was in my arms, soft, fragrant. It was not my intention to take her against her will, but I was erect. I knew I would have to open her up first, she was a virgin, so I used the handle of my knife. If she had not cried out, I would have taken her like an animal, to satisfy my desires, and then I would have killed her, to keep her quiet."

Khety was squirming in front of Qaa. Relating the events of the night had excited Khety, and he was attempting to relieve himself by rubbing his erection against his loincloth. Qaa could not control his fury any longer; he began beating the goldsmith about the back. When Khety tried to fend off the blows, he fell backward. Now Qaa could really teach the man a lesson. The loincloth would cushion the blows slightly, but Qaa wanted to take out his anger on Khety and his erection. He struck the man soundly a dozen blows, until his hand was stayed. Qaa was in a blind rage and turned to see who had stopped his hand; he looked into the face of his king. With his anger and strength draining away, Qaa nearly collapsed into Ramesses's arms.

"My son, you have conducted yourself well to this point. Let us conclude the questioning, so punishment may be set." The king spoke in calm, measured tones. "The *swnwt* is standing by, to attend you."

Qaa composed himself and put away the switch. Turning to face the magistrates, Qaa held up his pieces of evidence, one by one from the attack on the *hemet netjer*.

"This is the dress the princess was wearing the night of the attack. You shall note the black soot smudges on the front and back of the dress, as well as the blood." Qaa held it up and turned it, front and back, for the magistrates to see. Some of the men were too horrified to look. The pain in his left arm was now a searing heat, traveling all the way down to his hand and into his chest.

"This is the bone and bronze dagger Khety was carrying when he was taken into custody. Note the blood on the hilt and the missing piece of bone." Qaa picked up the dagger and handed it to the magistrates to examine.

"And, finally, this is the piece of bone which was imbedded in the wound, inflicted by Khety, and which caused the princess to fall ill. You shall note that it fits the hilt of the dagger perfectly." Qaa handed the fragment of bone to the magistrates, none of whom really wanted to touch it.

"Khety, the final charge against you is defiling the Temple of Amun, by the actions of your thefts, by the murder of Iput at the pylon gate, and for the abomination you committed against the princess Nebettawy, daughter of the king, (l.p.h.), *hemet netjer* and *dwat-netjer* in the Temple of Amun. What do you have to say for yourself?" It took all Qaa's attention to utter these words.

"I have nothing to say, Medjay. I have committed all the crimes I am charged with and I deserve my punishment."

The Medjay bent down and picked up Khety to return him to the military barracks to await his fate. Ramesses stood so the magistrates could exit the reception room. As he turned to Qaa, the Medjay Chief had sunk to his knees. Seeing the commotion, the royal scribe dropped his scroll and palette, rushed forward, and reached Qaa, preventing his head from striking the tile floor.

"Medjay, have Qaa brought to the antechamber and summon the *swnwt*." Ramesses knelt next to his son; his skin was warm and slick with sweat.

"*Hem netjer*, there is only one way for me to stop the bleeding."

"*Swnwt*, do what you must. I must appear before the magistrates after midday." Qaa reclined on a bench in the antechamber. "Captain, summon Medjay. They shall need to restrain me for the *swnwt*."

Ashayt began her preparations. She first mixed up a paste of honey, natron, and resins of acacia and myrrh, to apply to the wound once it was sealed. She searched her instrument box for the wooden handled blade; she placed it next to the oil lamp and then located the strongest wine she possessed. She poured Qaa a bowl of straight Cyprus wine, which was steeped with poppies. She only used it for traumatic wounds and injuries requiring the heated-knife treatment.

"*Hem netjer*, let me cleanse the wound." She handed him the bowl of Cyprus wine. "Drink this, it should lessen the pain."

She had Ramesses hold the knife in the flame of the oil lamp while she cleansed the oozing, gaping wound as best she could. Three Medjay had returned with the Captain and stood ready. On Ramesses command, the men held Qaa's shoulders and legs, while Ramesses handed the glowing knife to the *swnwt*. Ashayt applied the knife to one side of the wound, holding it for several moments, to make sure the wound was sealed. Qaa screamed in agony, the Cyprus wine having little effect.

Ashayt handed the knife to Ramesses, who reinserted the knife into the flame. The *swnwt* took the honey paste and lightly coated the burnt flesh. She would apply more after she had treated the other side of the wound. Ramesses lifted Qaa's head to drink another bowl of Cyprus wine, but Qaa shook his head. Ashayt reached for the knife and the men held Qaa firm for her. She applied the glowing metal to the other side of the gaping wound and, once more, Qaa shrieked in pain.

Now that the bleeding had stopped, Ashayt coated both sides of the wound with the honey paste. It might be necessary in a day or two to draw the wound together with thorns and string, but she would wait to see how well it was healing. She wrapped linen around his arm to cover the coated wound and picked up the drinking bowl. Ramesses lifted Qaa's head for the *swnwt.*

"*Hem netjer,* please drink." She put the bowl to his lips and he sipped the wine. The first bowl had started to take effect, making him feel like he was no longer in his body.

"Many thanks, *swnwt.*" Qaa struggled to sit up, but his head felt like it was filled with water from the Nile.

"Rest for now. When the magistrates have returned, I shall speak with them and request we continue tomorrow." Ramesses knew Qaa would not be able to stand before the magistrates for the remainder of the day.

"Father, if I may be allowed to sit, the charges against the other conspirators do not require me to present evidence. Then we may put this awful incident behind us." Qaa could feel nothing in his arm, nor anywhere else in his body. If he could keep his thoughts clear, he would be able to preside over the proceedings.

When the magistrates began to arrive at the palace, Ramesses instructed the Medjay to carry Qaa into the main reception chamber. His chair had been moved closer to Ramesses's throne, so the king could assist Qaa if he became ill. The wine had deadened the pain, but had also affected his thoughts. He needed to focus on his scrolls to read the charges and remind him of what information he wished to elicit from the accused. Once the magistrates had returned to their seats in the chamber, the charges against the remaining perpetrators could be read.

The royal scribe began writing down the court proceedings against the conspirators of Khety.

In year 17, month 3 of the Peret season, day 23:

"Merti, daughter of Sadeh and Weni the *wab*-priest, *shemayet* in the Temple of Amun, stand before the magistrates and confess to your crimes." Qaa sat with the scrolls on his lap, thankful Ramesses had allowed him to continue.

Merti, hands tied in front of her, was escorted into the main reception chamber by two Medjay. She glared at both Qaa and Ramesses and refused to bow to them. The Medjay forced her to her knees in front of the king and Qaa administered the Oath of the Lord to not speak falsely.

"Young woman, the charges against you are serious and still you are insolent to your king. What do you have to say for yourself?"

"Medjay, you know what my crimes are. I shall not speak. You may present your evidence, bring forward your witnesses. Do whatever you wish with me." Merti was still defiant and refused to answer to the charges.

"The man you assisted was brought before the magistrates this morning and he conducted himself with respect to this court. You shall answer the charges brought against you, *shemayet*." Ramesses, who rarely spoke during proceedings, was not amused with the attitude of the young woman before him.

"The first crime you are charged with is defiling the Temple of Amun, by allowing men to have relations with you on temple grounds. Two men, a temple scribe and a temple goldsmith apprentice, are here to bear witness against you."

"Save your words and witnesses, Medjay. I took many men behind the sanctuary, some of them are in this room sitting in judgment of me." She looked at the magistrates, a few of them blushing at the thought she might reveal their crimes.

"Do you wish to call these magistrates as witnesses?" Qaa would gladly question the men she named; it would only serve to strengthen his case against her.

"No, Medjay, I do not deny the charges. And I shall not name the magistrates who took their pleasure with me on temple property. But, they are just as guilty as I."

"Merti, you allowed men, of lower status, to take you like an animal. How could you defile the temple in such a manner?"

"Given the chance, Medjay, I might have even lured you behind the sanctuary." She looked Qaa in the eyes, smiling and moving her hips seductively.

"Since you do not deny the charges and you have demonstrated the charges are true, I shall spare the witnesses the further indignity of appearing before the magistrates. The next crime you are charged with is speaking falsely. You attempted to blame a crime on the temple goldsmith apprentice, Unas, and when you were questioned about the crime by the Chief of the Medjay and Usermaatre-meryamun, Ramesses III, (l.p.h.), you spoke falsehoods to cover for the true criminal. How do you answer to these charges?"

"I was told not to trust you, Medjay, and the man who spoke those words did not lie to me. I do not trust you. You are not Egyptian, and you have clouded the king's mind. I shall tell you nothing."

"Merti, had you been truthful with me, you would not be in the trouble you are in and would not be facing punishment. You believed an evil man who tried to kill the *hemet netjer*, a woman who loves you like a sister." Qaa wanted to find some way to be merciful, but Merti wanted none of it. She spat at Qaa's feet. Under normal circumstances, he would have struck her with his switch; all he wanted now was an end to this unfortunate incident.

"The final charge against you is aiding and protecting the criminal, Khety, by giving him information to commit his crimes against Iput, the wick-maker, and the princess Nebettawy, daughter of Usermaatre-meryamun, Ramesses III (l.p.h.), *dwat-netjer* and *hemet netjer* in the Temple of Amun. How do you answer to this charge?"

"Medjay, you determined I was guilty and so I am guilty. I do not care what punishment you pronounce upon me."

"Medjay, you may take the accused out."

The Medjay lifted the young woman from the floor and carried her out of the chamber.

"Bring forward the accused Unas, the temple goldsmith apprentice, and Takhat, the widow." Qaa was pleased the proceedings were moving along quickly. Judgment could be pronounced this day, and the sentences carried out tomorrow.

The Medjay had untied Unas's feet, so he and Takhat could walk into the chamber under escort. Takhat, because she was with child, was not restrained. Qaa reminded both accused they had been administered the Oath of the Lord earlier. Both acknowledged they understood, and would give true statements to the magistrates.

"Unas, goldsmith apprentice in the Temple of Amun, you are charged with assisting Khety in his crimes, by stealing a dagger and a vessel of wine. How do you answer to this charge?"

"Medjay, I am guilty. I did not know Khety wanted the dagger to kill my wife, Iput." Unas, though he was glad to be rid of his wife, certainly was appalled by what Khety had done to her.

"The former Chief of the Medjay was a good man. I did not know why Khety wanted the wine vessel." He hung his head, ashamed of his role in the death of Raneb.

"Unas, many thanks for speaking truthfully. I am confident your sincerity shall be taken into consideration when fixing punishment." Qaa had already made his recommendation for punishment to

Ramesses. The proceedings were only a formality, in the presence of magistrates, to have a written record of the charges.

"Takhat, wife of Unas, you are also charged with assisting Khety in his crimes, by stealing a dagger and a vessel of wine. How do you answer to this charge?"

"Medjay, I was afraid of Khety. He threatened me and the child I carry. He told me he would hurt Unas. I did what he asked. I stole the dagger and the wine." Takhat began to cry softly, as she ran her hand over her stomach. Her pregnancy was noticeable to the magistrates.

"Medjay, you may remove the accused."

Takhat and Unas were led out of the main reception chamber. Qaa leaned back in his chair, trying to maintain his composure. The wine had taken hold of him and he could barely focus. His head nodded and his hands shook. But, the proceedings were almost at an end.

"Medjay, bring forward the accused, Aahotep."

Aahotep was escorted into the chamber by the same men she had drugged. She knelt before the king and Qaa, fearing not for herself, but for her sister, Nithotep. Qaa administered the Oath of the Lord to not speak falsely and proceeded to question her.

"Aahotep, you love your sister, Nithotep, very much, do you not?"

"Yes, Medjay, she has been my responsibility for many years."

"And, you love your father. You were willing to hide him from the Medjay and you refused to help me in my investigation."

"Yes, Medjay. My father was a good man, once. I would do almost anything for him. He asked me to kill your Medjay, so he could make his escape. But, I could not do it. I prepared lotus wine for them, to drug them into unconsciousness. I told my father I would take care of them for him and he knew he could trust me."

"You have been charged with aiding your father by hiding him and by interfering in an investigation, by drugging my Medjay. These are serious charges."

"I understand what I have done, Medjay. But, I had to protect my sister. She is ill and can not care for herself. If my father was taken from us, I am the only one she would have. I had to protect her, no matter what the consequences."

"Medjay, you may escort the accused from the chamber."

Once the Medjay and Aahotep had left the chamber, the magistrates could consult with Ramesses and fix punishment. Qaa did not rise from his chair for the deliberations. He had made his recommendations to Ramesses when they went to the temple that morning. Ramesses had then consulted with his father, the Great Amun, for enlightenment and mercy for those who deserved his kindness. Qaa closed his eyes and his head fell forward onto his chest. He was so tired. A steward came to his side and refreshed him with a bowl of pomegranate wine. The steward, upon seeing Qaa, directed two royal fan bearers to come forward and cool the Medjay.

Ramesses stood in front of his throne. He had consulted with the magistrates and was ready to pronounce judgment upon the accused. Qaa could only sit and watch. Whether or not Ramesses had been moved by his eloquence, he would have to wait for his pronouncements.

"Bring forward the accused, Khety."

Khety, still tied at the hands and feet, was carried in and placed on his knees in front of the king.

"Khety, goldsmith in the Temple of Amun, having been brought before his majesty, Usermaatre-meryamun, Ramesses III, (l.p.h.), your punishment has been fixed. For the crime of the murder of your wife, Sitkamose, for the murder of Iput, wife of Unas, and for the killing of Raneb, Chief of the Medjay and First *hem netjer nt Amun*, your punishment is death."

Qaa was not surprised by the punishment. There was no other punishment which could be pronounced.

"Khety, having been brought before his majesty, Usermaatre-meryamun, Ramesses III, (l.p.h.), your punishment has been fixed. For the crime of defiling the princess Nebettawy, for the defiling of the Temple of Amun, and for the defiling of a noblewoman, your punishment is death."

Khety bowed his head.

"For your crimes, on day 24 you shall be taken behind the temple mortuary complex, into the Red Land. You shall be given on top of the stake, a stake of cedarwood, until you are dead. Your body shall be hacked to pieces and scattered in the Red Land as a feast for the jackals, vultures, and other prey animals. Your *ka* shall be doomed to eternal darkness and endless torment."

The Medjay bent, picked up Khety, and carried him out of the chamber and back to the military barracks. His punishment would be exacted after sunrise, the following day.

"Bring forward the accused, Merti."

The Medjay had tied Merti's ankles and carried her before the king, placing her on her knees at his feet. She still looked defiantly at Ramesses.

"Merti, *shemayet* in the Temple of Amun, having been brought before his majesty, Usermaatre-meryamun, Ramesses III, (l.p.h.), your punishment has been fixed. For the crimes of defiling the temple, speaking falsely to the king and the Chief of the Medjay, and aiding the criminal, Khety, your punishment is death."

Merti, still believing as a daughter of a priest she would not face execution, began to sob, the enormity of the offense finally setting in.

"For your crimes, as befitting your status, you shall be allowed to do the honourable thing. The princess Nebettawy and your mother, the mistress Sadeh, having spoken passionately on your behalf, were unable to sway my pronouncement. Your hands and feet shall be bound and your organs shall remain intact. Natron shall be sprinkled over your body, then you shall be wrapped in a sheepskin and placed in a plain, white wooden coffin. No protective spells shall adorn the coffin, no grave goods shall accompany you. Your crimes have stripped you of a proper burial. You shall be condemned for all eternity to smell the earth."

The Medjay bent and picked up the wailing young woman. She was carried out of the chamber to the military barracks; she would be allowed to commit suicide within the next twenty-four hours. Again, Qaa was not surprised. He had recommended a harsh punishment, considering the severity of the offense against Nebettawy.

"Medjay, bring forward the following individuals: Unas, the goldsmith apprentice; Takhat, wife of Unas; Bek, the merchant; Ghedi, the Phoenician."

A buzz ran through the magistrates. This was highly unusual. Punishment was always pronounced upon one individual at a time. Qaa, sensing he was about to see something momentous, sat up in his chair. Would the king follow his recommendation? It would be out of the ordinary, but it would leave a legacy of being fair and merciful in dispensing punishment.

The Medjay brought forth the individuals, as requested by the king.

"Unas, goldsmith apprentice in the Temple of Amun, having been brought before his majesty, Usermaatre-meryamun, Ramesses III, (l.p.h.), your punishment has been fixed."

Unas bowed his head, ready to hear his punishment.

"For the crime of theft, it is customary to sentence lashes and restitution. The Chief of the Medjay has spoken persuasively upon your behalf. The sentence shall be written into the record, and it shall stand, if you do not change your behaviour. You are sentenced to 50 lashes. The Chief of the Medjay shall administer 10 lashes to you. If you raise a hand to your wife, Takhat, or to her children, or to any other woman in Waset, the Chief of the Medjay shall be free to administer the remaining 40 lashes."

A gasp went up among the magistrates. There was murmuring and questioning looks. The king put up his hand for silence. Unas raised his head in amazement.

"You shall further be required to work an additional two hours per day, for the next three months, receiving no compensation, to make restitution to the temple, for aiding Khety in his theft of temple items. Sobekhotep, the Overseer of the Temple Goldsmiths, who sits in judgment of you, shall carry out your sentence."

Unas, staring in disbelief at the king, bent forward and kissed the king's feet.

"Your majesty, many thanks, for myself and my wife."

"Unas, do not thank me. The Chief of the Medjay made a convincing argument why I should spare you further punishment. But, your wife is free to lodge a complaint against you, should you hurt her, as you did your wife Iput. So tread lightly, apprentice. The Chief of the Medjay shall not be merciful a second time."

Unas, tears streaming down his face, looked up at Qaa. Qaa nodded to the apprentice, thankful that Ramesses had taken pity on the man.

"Takhat, wife of Unas, having been brought before his majesty, Usermaatremeryamun, Ramesses III, (l.p.h.), your punishment has been fixed."

Unas was picked up and moved behind his wife. Takhat was brought forward to kneel before the king.

"For the crime of theft, I was prepared to fix your punishment as amputation of your right ear, to be carried out after the birth of your child. Again, the Chief of the Medjay, as well as the princess Nebettawy, spoke eloquently on your behalf, reminding me you only committed these crimes out of fear for yourself and your unborn child. I am therefore setting punishment according to his recommendation."

Qaa could hardly believe his ears.

"Restitution shall be made to the Phoencian, Ghedi, by working for him for a period of ten days, with no compensation. Restitution shall be made to the merchant Bek, by working for him for a period of twenty days, with no compensation. The items stolen were expensive and the amount of time seems adequate to the amount of the items."

Takhat fell prostrate in front of the king and kissed his feet.

"Young woman, you are fortunate and you have the Chief of the Medjay to thank."

"Many thanks, Medjay." Takhat, still kneeling, had straightened up and was looking at Qaa, who nodded to her.

"Bek, merchant, step forward." Ramesses was not yet finished.

Bek stepped forward and bowed to the king. The Medjay led Takhat to stand next to her husband.

"It is my understanding the Chief of the Medjay has spoken to you about this punishment for the widow. Are you satisfied by the terms of the punishment?"

"Yes, your majesty, I am quite satisfied."

"Having listened to the testimony given here and the words of the Chief of the Medjay, I do not believe you were aware the goods you received from the goldsmith were stolen. You might wish to make a donation to the temple, in offering to the Great Amun."

"I would be honoured to make an offering, my lord." Bek bowed to the king.

"Ghedi, the Phoenician, step forward."

Ghedi came forward to stand where Bek had been, as Bek stepped backward from the raised platform. Ghedi bowed to the king and to Qaa.

"The Chief of the Medjay has spoken to you about this punishment. You are satisfied with the recommendation?"

"Yes, your majesty, the Chief of the Medjay is a fair and compassionate man."

"I have read the report Raneb made before his death, as well as the report of the new Chief of the Medjay. Both felt you were blameless in receiving stolen goods. You went on the word of Bek, an honest trader, with an unassailable reputation and accepted his assessment of the goldsmith."

"Bek has always dealt fairly with me. I had a great deal of respect for Raneb. I would have turned over any items I believed were stolen. The present Chief of the Medjay is a wise man."

Claudia R. Dillaire

"Phoenician, you are welcome in Waset, to continue trading. You are not required to, as a foreigner, but if you wish to make a donation to the Temple of Amun, it would be greatly appreciated."

Ghedi bowed to the king. "It shall be my pleasure to present a donation."

With a wave of his hand, the four individuals were dismissed. The Medjay led them all out of the main reception chamber, with Unas returning to the military barracks to await his lashes.

"Bring forward the accused, Aahotep."

Aahotep was not bound and bowed deeply to the king, before kneeling at his feet.

"Aahotep, having been brought before his majesty, Usermaatre-meryamun, Ramesses III, (l.p.h.), your punishment has been fixed."

Again, Qaa hoped the king had accepted his recommendation. He had worked hard to get an agreement.

"For the crime of aiding a criminal, I have a number of ways to set your punishment. I have consulted with my father, the Great Amun, and the Chief of the Medjay. You drugged two of his men, in order to help you father escape justice. I have been swayed by his argument on your behalf. You shall be banished from Waset for a period of one year, upon which time, you may return, if that is your desire. You shall be conducted to a ship leaving for the quarry town of Ibhet, as suggested by the Chief of the Medjay."

Aahotep bent and kissed the king's feet.

"Many thanks, your majesty." The young woman was led out of the chamber, under escort of the Medjay.

Ramesses turned to the magistrates and dismissed them with his thanks. Qaa, with assistance from Medjay guards, struggled to his feet. He had one more person to attend to and then he could rest.

"Aahotep, do you have all you wish to take from this house?" Qaa, with the help of his Medjay, sat in a chair in the main room of Khety's residence. To make restitution, Khety's residence and its contents would be seized and distributed to the temple.

"Yes, Medjay, I do. I have also packed up Nithotep's things. They are in the large chest by the door. Will she be able to take her loom with her?" Aahotep wanted to know her sister would be well taken care of.

"We shall carry her loom to her new home." Qaa had two servants pick up Nithotep's chest and carry it outside. "Call her, now, so I may speak with her."

Aahotep went up the stairs to get Nithotep, who was sitting on the roof, catching the cool, evening breeze. When she saw Qaa, she smiled and ran to him. She put her arms around his neck, then looked at the man seated next to him.

"Qaa, who is he? He looks like our king."

"You are a very bright child, Nithotep. This is our king. He has come to see you; I have told him so much about you, he wanted to meet you. We have come to ask if you would like to go on an adventure. Your sister, Aahotep, must leave Waset for some time, and your father shall not be returning. I have a new home for you, where you can weave all day. Would you like that?" Qaa hoped Nithotep would not cry.

"Will Aahotep come back?" Nithotep's lower lip began to tremble.

"She shall, but it shall be a long time. She is going to Ibhet for one year. But, she would like to come back and see you then."

"Are you going away, too?"

"No, child, I am going to make my home in Waset."

Nithotep's face brightened. She nuzzled into Qaa's neck. "Will you come and see me, at my new home?"

"I would be honoured to come and visit with you." Qaa stroked Nithotep's cheek.

"Would you bring the king with you?" She looked at Ramesses and smiled mischievously.

"Would that please you, my child?" Ramesses spoke quietly to Nithotep, so as not to frighten her.

"That would please me. Do you really live in the palace? I have never seen the palace."

"I shall have Qaa bring you to the palace. The princess Nebettawy has heard much about you and would like to meet you." Ramesses found Nithotep just as enchanting as Qaa had.

"Many thanks." Nithotep giggled at Ramesses.

"Say goodbye to your sister. The king and I shall accompany you to your new home." Qaa blinked back tears. He remembered when his

father took him to live in Ramesses's home. His mother was dead and his father was a soldier, with no time for a small boy. Ramesses placed his hand on Qaa's shoulder.

"She is a lovely young woman. Does the *swnwt* think she may improve?"

"In a different home, with people to nurture her, she may progress. The *swnwt* can not tell how much damage has been done."

The servants had picked up Nithotep's loom and carried it outside. Two Medjay had removed Aahotep's chest, and would carry it for her, as she was escorted to the docks.

"Nithotep, do you have everything?" Aahotep choked back tears. She loved her sister, but she would be better off in a new home.

"My doll is on the roof. I want my doll."

"I will go and get her." Aahotep raced up the stairs. Qaa stood with difficulty and waited for Aahotep at the foot of the stairs, to speak with her privately. Ramesses, slow to rise, walked gingerly to Nithotep and held her hand, just as he had with his own children.

Aahotep descended the stairs of her home for the last time. Qaa held out his hand to the young woman. She handed him Nithotep's doll and tried not to cry.

"Medjay, many thanks. How did you choose Ibhet for my banishment?"

"I spoke with your father. I understand you wish to marry a young stone cutter, but you are entrusted with the care of your sister. Khety told me the stone cutter was sailing for Ibhet, where there is work in the granite quarries. Marry your young man and start a life with him. When your banishment is completed, you may return to Waset to see your sister." Qaa handed her a scroll, with the seal of the king. "This shall provide you safe passage back to Waset."

Aahotep had no words to express her gratitude. She threw her arms around Qaa's neck and kissed him on the cheek.

"May we enter? It is his majesty, King Ramesses."

Sadeh appeared at the doorway and bowed to the king. She saw Qaa holding onto a young woman's hand.

"Is this the young woman you spoke to me about, *hem netjer*?"

"It is, Mistress. This is Nithotep. She is anxious to show you her weaving."

"Come in and refresh yourselves." Sadeh stepped aside to let the king enter, followed by Qaa and Nithotep. Weni came forward to help the servants and the Medjay with Nithotep's chest and the loom. Ramesses and Qaa both took seats. Sadeh poured them wine and offered wine to the Medjay and servants. Nithotep, still standing in the middle of the main room, was looking around in wonder. She had never seen so fine a house.

"Nithotep, would you like some wine?" Sadeh had come to stand next to the young woman.

"I have never had wine. My father gives me beer, when Aahotep brews it."

"I asked my husband to place your loom next to mine. We may pass many pleasant hours weaving together. Would that please you?" Sadeh handed Nithotep a drinking bowl of wine and stroked the young woman's cheek.

"I like to weave. My mother taught me." Nithotep took a sip of the wine and giggled.

"Child, would you like to remain here? Weni is a *wab*-priest in the Temple of Amun. Sadeh, his wife, would like to have someone who can help her run her home." Qaa put out his hand to Nithotep and she came to him and knelt next to his chair. She took his hand and held it tightly.

"Will I be a servant here?" Nithotep did not understand what her duties would be.

Sadeh walked to Nithotep slowly and held out her arms to her. "No, my child, you shall not be a servant here. We would like you to make your home here, with us. I have prepared a room for you, on the second floor."

"Do you mean I will have my own room?" Nithotep always shared a room with someone.

"Yes, child, the room is yours. If you would like, we can paint it with colourful scenes. There are clothes in the chests upstairs. If you find something you would like to wear, they are yours as well."

Nithotep looked at Weni. "Will I be sharing my bed with you?"

All in the room were shocked by the question. The full extent of Khety's depravity was finally being revealed.

"No, child, I share my bed with my wife." Weni was visibly shaken.

Nithotep smiled and squeezed Qaa's hand. She stood up and let Sadeh embrace her. Sadeh led Nithotep upstairs to see her new room. Weni, still shaken, poured wine for himself, the king, and Qaa.

Claudia R. Dillaire

"Weni, I do not know how to express my gratitude. It may take her some time to adjust, but the *swnwt* shall check in on her."

"Having the young woman in the house may help my wife. It has been a long time since Sadeh had a reason to smile. And Nithotep seems like a lovely young woman."

"The *swnwt* thinks she may progress, with your help. She has endured so much, just as your wife has. This may help them both." Qaa hoped it would ease the pain of Sadeh losing her daughter, but more than that, it might give Nithotep a chance at a real life.

Nithotep ran down the stairs, laughing and happy. She had an armful of clothes and toys and jewelry. She sat on the floor, at Qaa's feet, and wanted to show him all that she had found. Qaa bent down and stroked her hair.

"Nithotep, are you happy to be here?" Qaa tried to hide the tears in his eyes. She was still a child, but he knew Sadeh and Weni would take care of her.

"Oh, yes, Qaa. Will you stay here with me?"

"This is your home now. I have a home, with my wife. But, I shall come and visit often, if that is your wish?" Qaa wiped back the tears. He had found his home, in Waset, with the only woman he had ever loved. And he knew she was waiting for him now, in the palace gardens, to hold him in her arms and chase away his own tormented childhood.

Ramesses and Qaa walked back to the palace in silence. When they entered the palace doorway, Qaa bowed quickly to Ramesses, turned, and with his remaining strength, sprinted out to the gardens. There he found Nebettawy, seated on a stone bench, waiting for Qaa to return. He ran to her, fell to his knees, and dropped his head in her lap. He could not hold back any longer. This case had awakened the feelings he had about his own troubled childhood, and he wept.

His sorrow came from the depths of his very soul. His tears were for Nithotep and Aahotep; Aahotep for being forced from the sister she loved, and Nithotep for her loss of innocence, her loss of childhood, her loss of an identity. For Sadeh and the other women, whose lives had been touched by Khety's evil. For Merti, for letting herself be seduced by Khety's evil and her own desires. For Nebettawy and the pain she had to endure; they had angered the gods and Nebettawy had paid the price. And, finally, he wept for his mother. He had never been able to grieve for her, his father told him to be a man and a soldier. Since the day she had died, he had never mourned her, and he missed her so much; he missed her as only a child can miss his mother. She was his home.

Nebettawy stroked his head and back, afraid for her husband. His sobs tore at her heart, his grief seemed unending. When he had no more tears, he did not lift his head. His throat was raw, his body ached, and he had no strength. This incident had ripped at the very fabric of his being. As he nuzzled into Nebettawy, he croaked the only words he had left in him.

"Mother, I miss you so."

Ramesses, standing a discret distance with two Medjay, saw his daughter motion to him. He came to her with the Medjay, to help Qaa to bed. He was near collapse and could not stand, from the strain of the trial, the wound to his arm, and the emotional toll upon him. One Medjay slid his arms under Qaa's, the other grabbed his legs, and they carried him into Nebettawy's private chambers. Ramesses helped his daughter to her feet, put his arm around her waist, and led her into the palace. The Medjay sat Qaa on the bed, stripped him down to his loincloth, and settled him.

Nebettawy sat next to Qaa and had her father get her a vessel of water and bowl from her private bath. She bathed Qaa's face and head, soothing him, quieting him. Ramesses poured him a bowl of wine, which Nebettawy put to his lips. He came around sufficiently to sip the wine. Ramesses patted his shoulder and took his leave. Nebettawy leaned in to Qaa and whispered to him.

"Qaa, I am your home now." She looked into his eyes and kissed him gently on the lips.

Qaa smiled at his wife, and squeezed her hand. He had found his home. The burden he carried would be so much easier with Nebettawy by his side. He closed his eyes and slept, soundly, undisturbed, for the first time in years.

ABOUT THE AUTHOR

Claudia R. Dillaire is a passionate researcher of ancient civilisations, with her primary expertise being ancient Egypt. Her love of Egyptian religious practises has led to the publication of three books on Egyptian magic: Egyptian Love Spells and Rituals (Foulsham, 2005), Egyptian Revenge Spells (Ten Speed Press, 2009), and Egyptian Prosperity Magic (Llewellyn Worldwide, 2011).

When not researching and writing, Ms. Dillaire is a freelance copyeditor and proof reader. She maintains a website for her freelancing (www.ewitchfreelancing.com) and a Facebook page, in addition to a blog for writers, (http://claudiardillaire.blogspot.com). She is currently working on a fourth book on Egyptian magic and the second novel in her Egyptian mystery series. She lives in Arizona.

Another great book available through
www.PendraigPublishing.com
by S. P. Hendrick

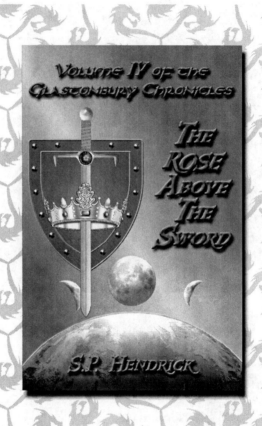

It's been three generations since the Sacred King last poured out his blood to heal the planet Brittania. In the interim, the usurping "Common" government has driven the Old Ways to ground with its pseudo-science. The Windsor line has been hunted to extinction, records of the Old Faith and Sacred King destroyed, all religious practice forbidden, and the people are starving physically and spiritually. But the Sacred King awakens to find that the Gods will always find a way..."

Print Edition	$12.95	ISBN: 978-0-9827263-2-7
Kindle Edition	$4.99	AISN: B00669WCZK
Nook Edition	$4.99	BN ID: 2940013593091

CPSIA information can be obtained at www.ICGtesting.com
Printed in the USA
BVOW05s0853250214

345946BV00006B/177/P